SHATTERING DAWN

TITLES BY JAYNE ANN KRENTZ

THE LOST NIGHT FILES TRILOGY

Shattering Dawn
The Night Island
Sleep No More

THE FOGG LAKE TRILOGY

Lightning in a Mirror
All the Colors of Night
The Vanishing

Untouchable
Promise Not to Tell
When All the Girls Have Gone
Secret Sisters
Trust No One
River Road
Dream Eyes
Copper Beach
In Too Deep
Fired Up
Running Hot
Sizzle and Burn
White Lies
All Night Long
Falling Awake
Truth or Dare
Light in Shadow
Summer in Eclipse Bay
Together in Eclipse Bay

Smoke in Mirrors
Lost & Found
Dawn in Eclipse Bay
Soft Focus
Eclipse Bay
Eye of the Beholder
Flash
Sharp Edges
Deep Waters
Absolutely, Positively
Trust Me
Grand Passion
Hidden Talents
Wildest Hearts
Family Man
Perfect Partners
Sweet Fortune
Silver Linings
The Golden Chance

TITLES BY JAYNE ANN KRENTZ WRITING AS AMANDA QUICK

The Bride Wore White
When She Dreams
The Lady Has a Past
Close Up
Tightrope
The Other Lady Vanishes
The Girl Who Knew Too Much
'Til Death Do Us Part
Garden of Lies
Otherwise Engaged
The Mystery Woman

Crystal Gardens
Quicksilver
Burning Lamp
The Perfect Poison
The Third Circle
The River Knows
Second Sight
Lie by Moonlight
The Paid Companion
Wait Until Midnight
Late for the Wedding

Don't Look Back
Slightly Shady
Wicked Widow
I Thee Wed
With This Ring
Affair
Mischief
Mystique
Mistress

Deception
Desire
Dangerous
Reckless
Ravished
Rendezvous
Scandal
Surrender
Seduction

TITLES BY JAYNE ANN KRENTZ WRITING AS JAYNE CASTLE

People in Glass Houses
Sweetwater and the Witch
Guild Boss
Illusion Town
Siren's Call
The Hot Zone
Deception Cove
The Lost Night
Canyons of Night
Midnight Crystal

Obsidian Prey
Dark Light
Silver Master
Ghost Hunter
After Glow
Harmony
After Dark
Amaryllis
Zinnia
Orchid

THE GUINEVERE JONES SERIES

Desperate and Deceptive
THE GUINEVERE JONES COLLECTION, VOLUME I
    The Desperate Game
    The Chilling Deception

Sinister and Fatal
THE GUINEVERE JONES COLLECTION, VOLUME 2
    The Sinister Touch
    The Fatal Fortune

SPECIALS

The Scargill Cove Case Files
Bridal Jitters
(WRITING AS JAYNE CASTLE)

ANTHOLOGIES

Charmed
(WITH JULIE BEARD, LORI FOSTER, AND EILEEN WILKS)

TITLES BY JAYNE ANN KRENTZ AND JAYNE CASTLE

No Going Back

JAYNE ANN KRENTZ

SHATTERING DAWN

BERKLEY

New York

BERKLEY
An imprint of Penguin Random House LLC
penguinrandomhouse.com

Copyright © 2025 by Jayne Ann Krentz
Penguin Random House values and supports copyright. Copyright fuels
creativity, encourages diverse voices, promotes free speech, and creates a
vibrant culture. Thank you for buying an authorized edition of this book and
for complying with copyright laws by not reproducing, scanning, or distributing
any part of it in any form without permission. You are supporting writers and
allowing Penguin Random House to continue to publish books for every reader.
Please note that no part of this book may be used or reproduced in any manner
for the purpose of training artificial intelligence technologies or systems.

BERKLEY and the BERKLEY & B colophon are registered trademarks of
Penguin Random House LLC.

Library of Congress Cataloging-in-Publication Data

Names: Krentz, Jayne Ann, author.
Title: Shattering dawn / Jayne Ann Krentz.
Description: New York: Berkley, 2025. | Series: The Lost Night Files ; 3
Identifiers: LCCN 2024010419 (print) | LCCN 2024010420 (ebook) |
ISBN 9780593639917 (hardcover) | ISBN 9780593639931 (ebook)
Subjects: LCGFT: Detective and mystery fiction. | Novels.
Classification: LCC PS3561.R44 S47 2025 (print) |
LCC PS3561.R44 (ebook) | DDC 813/.54—dc23/eng/20240314
LC record available at https://lccn.loc.gov/2024010419
LC ebook record available at https://lccn.loc.gov/2024010420

Printed in the United States of America
1st Printing

As always, to Frank, with love

SHATTERING DAWN

CHAPTER ONE

MAYBE THE STALKER would not return tonight.

Maybe she had imagined the ghostly figure in the hoodie and running sweats. Maybe no one was watching her. Maybe she was falling into a vortex of delusions and hallucinations.

No. She might be losing it but she was not that far gone—not yet, at any rate. She was not hallucinating. She was a rational, logical woman descended from a family tree that had produced a lot of highly successful individuals in fields ranging from psychiatry to engineering.

Okay, so she wasn't one of the overachievers, and yes, there was the occasional self-declared psychic like Aunt Cybil dangling from a branch or two. The point was, none of them had wound up in an asylum. As her mother said, every family had a few eccentrics.

Amelia Rivers hovered in the shadows of her second-floor apartment balcony and struggled to suppress the stirring tentacles of panic. The balmy San Diego night seemed to close in around her.

Dr. Pike was right. She was developing a full-blown phobia, complete with anxiety attacks and excuses. At the rate she was losing ground she would soon become a total recluse after sundown. Pike had warned that the fear would eventually creep into the daylight hours. She probably should not have canceled the last two appointments with him. He meant well. She did not doubt his concern for her mental health. But she no longer had any real hope that he could help her deal with the visions.

She checked her watch. It was almost one o'clock. She clutched the old-school film camera in one hand and waited. The stalker would either show up or not. She no longer knew which outcome she wanted. Both were equally scary. If the watcher was real, she was in danger. If she had hallucinated him, she should probably check herself into a psychiatric hospital.

From where she stood, she had a view of the lushly planted courtyard and the glowing blue pool in the center. The four wings of the two-story apartment complex surrounded the gardens on all sides. There were four entrances. Each was guarded by a high wrought iron security gate and there were cameras, but it was easy enough to slip onto the grounds if you waited for an opportunity to follow a resident inside.

There was no roving guard or drive-by security service. Amenities on that level were only available at the more expensive properties. She was on a budget. It was tough to make a living as a photographer.

Last night the stalker had arrived from the service lane gate, which was veiled by a couple of palm trees and a bunch of strategically planted bushes. No one wanted to look at the massive garbage and recycle bins.

The walls of night seemed to move in on her. She would not be able to stay outside much longer.

Stupid phobia.

She was coming to the grim conclusion that she had imagined

the stalker when she glimpsed a slight movement in the shadows near the service lane gate. She almost stopped breathing.

The figure in the hoodie emerged from behind the mass of greenery that shielded the entrance on the far side of the courtyard. The vintage Nikon camera that she had purchased from an online collector shook a little in her fingers. She was already tense but the fresh dose of fear-driven adrenaline sent shivers through her.

The stalker went swiftly along the path that led to the pool and disappeared behind the equipment shed. Something about the smooth, efficient—one could even say *predatory*—way he moved was as disturbing as the silent shriek of her intuition warning her that she was the stranger's target. Dr. Pike could blame her nerves as much as he liked. She no longer gave a damn. She knew this creepy sensation all too well. This was not the first time she had been hunted.

Down below, the stalker reappeared from behind the pool house. She held her breath, raised the camera, and focused through the viewfinder. She could not use a flash. The bright burst of hot light would interfere with her other vision. But she was not out here on the balcony, braving the oppressive weight of the night, because she hoped to grab a photo of the stalker's face. She was after some very different images, the kind that could only be captured with an old-fashioned single-lens reflex camera and black-and-white film. A digital camera would not work for what she had in mind.

The hooded figure glided toward the courtyard stairs that served her wing of the complex. Sure, he might be a new tenant who happened to live on her floor, but what were the odds?

She waited as long as she dared, letting the stalker get close, and took the picture. The snap of the shutter sounded loud to her ears, but down in the courtyard the figure in the hoodie did not appear to hear it. He continued to head toward the stairs of her building.

A rush of panic hit her. She took another shot, this time with the flash. The bright burst of light grabbed the stalker's attention. He stopped abruptly and looked up. The hood of his sweatshirt still shielded his face.

"You down there in the gardens," she called, going for an irritated but unsuspecting tone. "Would you mind getting out of the way? I'm trying to practice my night photography."

The figure did not move. She got the feeling he was trying to decide how to handle the situation.

"Feel free to stay in the scene," she said. "But I'll be publishing these pics online, so if you value your privacy—"

The stalker made his decision. He whirled and ran, heading back toward the service lane gate.

The balcony door of the apartment two doors down on the right opened. Irene Morgan appeared. She was dressed in a slinky satin bathrobe and a pair of sexy, stylish mules. Her mane of blond hair hung in deep waves around her lovely face. No matter what she wore she managed to project a vibe of Old Hollywood glamour.

"Amelia?" she said in a loud whisper that enhanced her husky voice. "What's going on? Are you okay?"

"Yes, fine," Amelia said. "Sorry to wake you. I was trying to get some night shots."

"Shut up out there," the jerk in the apartment between Amelia's and Irene's yelled through an open window. "I've got an early-morning meeting."

"Right, sorry," Amelia said.

The window slammed shut.

"Jerk," Irene murmured.

"Jerk," Amelia echoed in low tones. She raised her voice. "It's all good, Irene. Don't worry."

"Okay." Irene yawned and went back inside.

Amelia darted into her apartment, closed and locked the balcony door, turned on the lights, and took a few deep breaths. Now came the hard part. She wasn't finished. She had to go downstairs into the gardens to get the other photos.

When her nerves steadied, she went to the table next to the front door of the apartment, picked up the Taser and the key fob, steeled herself, and opened the door.

She went quickly along the open-air walkway that ran the length of the second floor and rushed down the stairs to the courtyard. The panic monster crouched at the edges of her awareness, threatening to pounce. In an effort to hold the anxiety at bay she chanted the signature sign-off of the podcast she and her friends, Pallas and Talia, produced. *We're in this together until we get answers.*

Unfortunately there was no *we* involved tonight. She was on her own.

Cold sweat was trickling between her breasts and dampening the front of her T-shirt by the time she reached the courtyard path. She went into her other vision and reminded herself to focus on what she had come out here to see. *Do not get distracted by the fog,* she told herself.

Technically speaking, there was no fog. She had finally come to understand that what she was viewing was an ankle-deep river of luminous paranormal radiation flowing the length of the garden path. The mist was the result of the many layers of energy prints that had been laid down over time by people who had walked along the sidewalk.

In the past few months she had struggled to adapt to her strange new talent, but the learning curve was steep, not to mention unnerving. The one thing she had concluded was that the splashes of energy laid down by individuals were as unique as their fingerprints.

She had also figured out that the energy in the prints faded with time as others walked the same path and left their own tracks.

Fortunately the stalker's footprints were only minutes old. They seethed with strange, erratic currents that sent icy frissons across her senses. Her intuition was screaming at her again but she did not know if it was reacting to the stalker's prints or the claustrophobia generated by the night. She managed to focus through the view-finder and snap off a couple of shots.

That was it; all she could handle. Taser in one hand, camera in the other, she fled back toward the stairs. She was breathing hard and trembling by the time she was safely inside her apartment.

Stupid, stupid phobia. This was getting ridiculous.

She slammed home the three locks on the door; set the camera, key fob, and Taser on the small hall table; and went around the corner into the kitchen. She opened a cupboard, took down the bottle of pricey cognac that Irene had given her for her birthday, and poured a healthy shot into a water glass.

She carried the glass around the end of the wide island that divided the kitchen from the living room and began to pace, sipping methodically, until she had her nerves back under control.

When she was satisfied that she was no longer a complete wreck she set the unfinished cognac aside. She had work to do. She went back around the corner into the front hall, picked up the camera, and kept going. She passed the laundry room and continued on to the walk-in closet she had converted into a darkroom.

In the morning she would take the stalker problem to the one private investigation agency in the San Diego area that might treat her case with the seriousness it required. She had found only minimal information about the firm online. The website consisted of a single page.

Sweetwater Investigations.

Private clients only. No corporate or business
accounts.

Fees negotiable. Call for appointment.

The number had dumped her into voicemail, where she had been
instructed to leave her name, a brief explanation of her problem, and
her contact information. The lack of a proper receptionist had been
worrisome but half an hour later a man identifying himself as Gideon
Sweetwater had returned her call. He had asked her a few cursory
questions about the case and then provided her with the address of
his office. The appointment was for nine o'clock in the morning.

She'd had two takeaways from the brief conversation. The first
was that she liked Sweetwater's voice. She liked it a lot. It was dark
and compelling and it sent unfamiliar but very pleasant little thrills
across her senses.

The second impression was that she was pretty sure he had made
the decision to take her case before he returned her call.

CHAPTER TWO

GIDEON SWEETWATER LOOKED up from the photos scattered across his desk. "What do you expect me to do with these pictures, Ms. Rivers?"

"As I told you on the phone, I have a stalker," Amelia said. "I want you to identify the individual in those photos."

"You said you are a professional photographer."

"That's right."

"No offense, but these images are not helpful. All I can see is a lot of foggy glare around the figure in the hoodie, and the spots on the sidewalk look like splashes of phosphorescent paint."

Amelia tried to suppress her disappointment. She told herself not to give up. It wasn't like she had a lot of alternatives. But the interview with Gideon Sweetwater was not going well.

The address of Sweetwater Investigations had been her first clue that Sweetwater might not be the private investigator she had been hoping to hire. Instead of the parking lot of a commercial building, she had found herself in the driveway of a lushly landscaped Spanish

Colonial bungalow. The house was in an exclusive, gated community perched on the bluffs above the Pacific. It was the sort of neighborhood that had not only a guard at the front gate but actual, roving security.

It had immediately become evident that Sweetwater Investigations was a one-man agency. There was no sign of any staff.

She had told herself that Gideon Sweetwater had to be very good at his work if he could afford such a high-end residence. Her next thought was that she hoped he was serious about his "negotiable" fees. That morning Bridget Hampstead, one of her real estate clients, had left a message explaining that the can't-miss deal on the McCall listing had fallen apart and that the payment for the property photo shoot would be delayed. Again.

The upscale address of Sweetwater Investigations had given her an uneasy feeling but the real shock had been Gideon Sweetwater himself. He looked like he had recently survived a serious accident. He was not in a neck brace or a cast, but he was not in good shape. He had answered the door leaning on a cane. When he led her down a hallway lined with creepy, depressing, dystopian landscapes, he limped. When he sat down in the chair behind his desk he had winced and gingerly touched his ribs.

He had not offered any explanations for his injuries and she told herself it would be rude to ask about them, so she was pretending not to notice his beat-up condition. She knew she was probably in denial. She couldn't help it. She was a desperate woman.

He considered her in silence for a long, unnerving moment, as if he had never before encountered a client like her. Fair enough. She had never met anyone like him.

She was not sure how professional private investigators dressed, but she had not expected one wearing a button-down oxford cloth shirt, chinos, and wing tips. It was all very ordinary.

The man, himself, however, was anything but ordinary.

Her photographer's eye was intrigued by his watchful, hazel eyes and fiercely etched profile. The whisper of energy in the atmosphere around him tugged at her senses. She could not see his aura or his energy prints, because her new vision only worked at night or in deep darkness. Nevertheless, she had been sensitive to the energy of other people for most of her life. That ability told her that Sweetwater radiated the centered strength of a man who had mastered himself. He would make a very good friend or a very bad enemy.

A very interesting—make that fascinating—man, but probably not her type. The fact that the thought even crossed her mind was alarming. The closest thing she'd had to a dating relationship in the past seven months was the therapy sessions with Dr. Pike. She wasn't looking for a type. She needed a qualified investigator. *Focus, woman.*

Gideon's office was as unexpected as the man himself. It was more of a private library. There were a lot of floor-to-ceiling bookcases. Many of the books on the shelves were old and worn. A few were bound in leather. There was an assortment of nonfiction, memoirs, fiction, and poetry. Judging by the titles she could make out from her position in front of the desk there was a disturbing theme to the collection. All of the volumes she could see appeared to deal with the subjects of dreams and visions.

There were several more of the end-of-the-world landscapes on the walls. Like the paintings in the hallway, the bleak scenes raised the fine hair on the back of her neck.

There were no helpful placards to provide details but she was pretty sure *Visions of Nightmares* would be an accurate title for the collection.

"I was hoping you would find the photos useful," she said.

Gideon glanced again at one of the black-and-white pictures and shook his head. "I don't see how I can use these to identify anyone. Perhaps the lighting was bad? Nighttime photography is complicated, especially when you're using film instead of a digital camera. Even the experts have difficulty getting good images after dark."

She gave him her most polished smile. "I *am* an expert, Mr. Sweetwater."

"Right. Well, these pictures might qualify as art, Ms. Rivers, but I don't see how I can use them to identify anyone."

"They aren't examples of art photography," she said. "I assumed you would recognize the pictures as aura and energy prints."

"I'm aware that sort of fake photography was popular in the late nineteenth and early twentieth centuries but I didn't know people were still claiming to be able to take pictures of that kind of thing."

Crap. Now he was watching her as if he was wondering if she might be delusional or, possibly, a con artist. The situation was deteriorating rapidly. So much for her intuition.

She had not plucked his name off a search engine at random. She had selected him because she had every reason to believe he possessed some genuine psychic talent. If that was true she did not expect him to advertise his ability. It was only to be expected that he would try to keep a low profile. Everyone she knew on the *Lost Night Files* podcast crew had a sixth sense, and they were all careful to maintain a veneer of normalcy.

And if, like her and the others involved on the podcast, Sweetwater had experienced a night lost to amnesia and awakened with enhanced abilities, he had every reason to be wary of her.

She had to convince him to take her seriously. There wasn't time to find another private investigator. She was certain that whoever was hunting her would act soon.

She would have to take the chance of showing a few of her own cards first.

"Yes, Mr. Sweetwater, I see auras and energy prints, but only after dark," she said, doing her best to sound crisp and self-assured.

"Interesting," Gideon said, his tone unnervingly polite. "And you believe that you can photograph that kind of energy?"

She plunged ahead because it was too late to bail.

"Yes, but only with a traditional film camera, one that uses old-school prism-and-mirror technology. Digital cameras don't work for me. Even if they did, I would prefer not to use one, because it would leave a digital trail. I see energy fields in color, but unfortunately color film isn't technologically capable of capturing the various shades of aura light, because they come from beyond the normal, visible end of the spectrum. You know, like ultraviolet light."

Was she flailing? Talking too much? Did she sound delusional? She could not be sure, because Gideon's reaction was unreadable.

"I understand you believe you can see someone's aura and perceive energy prints," Gideon said. "But how can you get them on film?"

"I'm not sure," she admitted. "Aunt Cybil thinks it probably has something to do with the way I manipulate the camera's prism and mirror with my own energy field. I just know that if I get the focus right I can use gray scale to capture some of the bands of energy."

Gideon contemplated her in silence for a long moment. "Who is Cybil and what does she know about auras and energy?"

Amelia winced. "Aunt Cybil is what my mother likes to call the family eccentric. I seem to be following in her footsteps. But that's not important. Can we focus on my case?"

"Yes. After you tell me a bit more about your aunt."

It was clear Gideon was not going to move forward unless she met his demand.

"All right, I come from a long line of overachievers," she said briskly. "Academics, researchers, doctors, and writers. But occasionally the DNA gets screwed up and someone like Cybil or me appears on the family tree. We get stuck with a psychic vibe. Mostly we fail at a lot of things until we figure out what to do with our other vision. To be honest, there aren't a lot of practical uses for the ability to see auras and prints."

Gideon looked fascinated now, and not in a good way, she decided. He was watching her as if she had just dropped in from outer space.

"Out of curiosity, what does your aunt do with her other vision?" he asked.

Amelia raised her chin and narrowed her eyes, prepared to defend Cybil to the end. "My aunt makes a very good living as a psychic. She gives demonstrations on cruise ships. She is very popular and is always booked out for months. At the moment she is on a round-the-world cruise."

"I see," Gideon said. He picked up one of the photos and tapped it gently on the desk. "Are you considering a similar career in show business?"

"I would rather not go in that direction," she said. She gave it a beat and then added, "Not that my career plans are any of your business. Do you mind if we get back to the subject at hand?"

"Right," he said finally. "Do you think you might have attracted a stalker because of that podcast you and those other two women produce? *The Lost Night Files?*"

Excitement sparked through her. She smiled. "I can't tell you how relieved I am to know that you follow the *Lost Night Files* podcast. That's wonderful news. It makes things so much easier. Relax. It's okay. You don't have to pretend that you don't believe in the paranormal. Not with me. As we say at the end of every episode, we're in this together until we get answers."

Gideon did not move. "To be clear, Ms. Rivers, I did not say I was a fan. I didn't know your podcast existed until I ran a background check on you after you called for an appointment."

"Oh." Her spirits dropped like a rock. "I see."

"I listened to some of the episodes. They are quite . . . imaginative. Murders committed by psychic means. Rumors of illegal experiments disguised as legitimate drug trials. Convenient episodes of amnesia. Reminded me of old-fashioned radio dramas."

Fury surged through her. She had been willing to work with an investigator who was afraid of revealing his own talent. She had been prepared to deal with skepticism and questions. But damned if she would tolerate outright insults.

"This isn't going well, is it?" she said in her iciest tones. "My fault. I assumed you would understand, or at least hear me out."

Gideon's expression didn't change but she could have sworn his eyes got a little hot.

"Don't give up on me, Ms. Rivers," he said. "You are here in my office because your case interests me."

The energy in the atmosphere became more intense. Somewhat

belatedly she realized that she was alone in a house with a man she did not know. Yes, given his physical condition she could outrun him, maybe even topple him with a well-placed kick to his injured leg. Still. If he pulled out a knife or a gun she was in an extremely vulnerable position.

Cold perspiration trickled down her sides. She finally remembered that her voluminous tote was on the floor beside the chair, her Taser inside. She leaned down and picked up the bag with what she hoped was a casual motion. She rested her hand on top. The tote was open. The weapon was tucked into a side pocket.

She smiled again, cool and composed this time—a client preparing to terminate an interview and walk out the door.

"It's obvious I'm wasting your time and mine, Mr. Sweetwater," she said. "My apologies. If you'll give me my photos, I'll be on my way."

She gripped the handles of the tote and got to her feet.

"Please sit down," Gideon said, his dark voice very soft. "I like unusual cases, and yours qualifies. I will take it."

Be careful what you wish for, she thought. But she was short on options. She sank back down onto the chair, careful to keep her hand on the tote.

"Tell me the truth," she said. "Do you think I'm delusional?"

"No, Ms. Rivers, I don't think you're delusional. But when it comes to clients there are other categories."

"Such as con artist? Conspiracy buff? Or maybe you think I'm one of those gullible, naive people who get sucked into cults?"

To her surprise, something dangerous shifted in Gideon's eyes. She knew she had struck a nerve.

"It's interesting that you mention cults," he said.

"Why? There is a long history of people joining cults because they are convinced the leaders have some sort of psychic powers." She paused a beat and gave him another cold smile. "You know, like the ability to see auras."

"I am well aware of that," Gideon said. His jaw tensed as he appeared to consider whether or not to pursue the topic of cults. "Let's focus on your case."

"I thought that's what I was doing until you made it obvious you don't believe I can see auras or prints."

"Let's just say I'm keeping an open mind."

"Really? I hadn't noticed."

He watched her closely. "What made you think I wouldn't question your claim to be able to view auras and such?"

She hesitated and then decided she did not have a lot left to lose. Time to play another card and see how he responded. "I found your name on a certain list."

"A list of search engine results?"

"No, a list of people who participated in a certain psychological research study several years ago. I'm on that list, and so are my friends on the podcast crew. The study consisted of a lengthy questionnaire and some odd tests. We were told the results would help provide us with career guidance but now we're convinced the study was a cover for the real purpose."

"Which was?"

She got ready to take the next big leap. Gideon's reaction would tell her everything she needed to know.

"We believe that the study was designed to identify individuals who possess some natural level of paranormal talent. We all took the test and forgot about it. No one told us we had landed on a list of people who were identified as having psychic abilities."

"After all these years, why are you so concerned about that list now?"

"Because someone is hunting the people on that list," she said. "People like you and me and the members of the *Lost Night Files* podcast team."

CHAPTER THREE

I T DIDN'T TAKE any psychic talent to see that she had blindsided Gideon. Excellent. She had his full attention now. Amelia's spirits lifted.

"Huh," he said finally. Evidently concluding that response did not sound suitably professional, he tried again. "I did not have time to listen to every episode of *The Lost Night Files* and I skipped around a lot because I wanted to get a feel for the content. But I don't recall any mention of a list of people with psychic talents."

"That's because we only recently discovered it," she said. "We haven't done any episodes about it because we've decided to keep the information quiet in order to protect the privacy of the people on it."

"Good plan," Gideon admitted. "If word got out that there was a list of people believed to be genuine psychics you would be flooded with cranks demanding details."

Once again she could not tell if he was being sincere or trying to humor her.

"Exactly," she said.

He started to lean back in his chair but stopped abruptly, wincing a little. He shifted forward and folded his arms on the desktop instead. "What makes you think you and your friends are being hunted because you are on this list, Ms. Rivers?"

She had given up enough information. It was his turn.

"Before I go any further I need to know if you remember participating in that old research study I just told you about," she said.

Gideon hesitated. For a moment she thought he would deny everything.

"I seem to recall participating in *a* study that was focused on career counseling," he said eventually. "There's no way to know if it's the same one you're talking about. Career guidance is a very common service."

She allowed herself another little flash of relief. Evidently he had not lost a night to amnesia, but at least he remembered that he had been involved in a study. It had to be the same one that she and the others had participated in, because his name was on the damned list.

It was entirely possible that he possessed only a minimal amount of talent—very strong intuition, perhaps—a sixth sense he took for granted and did not label paranormal. That would account for his skepticism.

"Did you receive any serious career guidance after you participated in the study?" she asked.

"I may have but I can't recall it." Amusement flickered briefly, *very* briefly, in his eyes. "I'm pretty sure no one advised me to pursue a career as a private investigator."

She made a sweeping gesture that included the library, the expensive house, and the upscale neighborhood. "You seem to have done very well in the business."

"I've had some luck with my investments," he said. "That gives me the freedom to focus only on the cases that interest me."

"I see."

She struggled to quash another wave of disappointment. Perhaps an intuitive ability to play the markets was his real psychic talent. Apparently the private investigation work was more of a hobby. That did not bode well. She did not need investment advice. She didn't have any extra cash to invest. She needed a skilled investigator who could track down a stalker.

Gideon seemed to be unaware that she was having second thoughts about hiring him.

"Why are you convinced someone is hunting you and your friends?" he asked.

"We aren't delusional, Mr. Sweetwater. We're not imagining that the people on the list are being hunted, we *know* it, because they have already found some of us—my friends and me, for example."

He stilled. "What do you mean?"

"Everyone on the podcast team has experienced a kidnapping followed by a bout of amnesia at some point within the past year." She paused. "I take it you have not?"

"There are a few nights I would prefer to forget, but no, I haven't lost any to amnesia."

She sighed. "I suppose that explains why you're having a hard time believing me. The thing is, something happened to us during those missing hours. We were used as unwitting research subjects in an off-the-books drug trial."

He did not move but she sensed that once again she had startled him.

"Designed to test, what?" he asked cautiously.

"A drug that can enhance an individual's psychic senses." She paused for emphasis. "Or kill you. Or drive you insane. Not everyone can tolerate the formula."

"I see." Gideon moved deeper into his place of intense watchfulness. "Do you think you were kidnapped by aliens?"

"No, Mr. Sweetwater." She fought to conceal her anger, reminding herself yet again that she did not have a lot of options when it came to investigators. "The people who abducted us and ran their experiments on us are human. Very dangerous humans. I suggest you listen to a few more episodes of the podcast. They are factual reports, not works of fiction."

"Did you, personally, experience any aftereffects from the experiments?"

"Yes, I did."

"A new vision that allows you to see auras and prints?"

"I have always had an ability to sense energy in people and the rooms and buildings they have inhabited. But since my lost night I have begun to perceive human auras and energy prints in great detail."

He assumed an air of polite interest. "Can you see my aura?"

"No, not now during the daytime. I have some sense of your energy field, but nothing specific. My ability works best at night or in deep darkness."

"That does not sound like a convenient talent."

"You're telling me."

He raised his brows at that but he didn't pursue the subject. "How did you come across this list you're concerned about?"

"That's a long story. If you decide to take my case, I'll be happy to give you some of the details."

"Why so secretive?"

"That list is worth a fortune to certain people. You just told me you are an investor. You might decide you could make money selling the list."

"You don't trust me," he said. He did not seem to know what to do with that news.

"Nope." She smiled an icy smile. "Just as you don't trust me. Perfectly understandable. We don't know each other very well, do we?"

"No," he said, "we don't. All right, tell me about the stalker."

"It's about time." She leaned forward a little. "Three days ago I got that feeling you get when you sense that you're being watched."

"A feeling," he repeated without inflection.

She ignored the interruption. "The first few times I turned around I didn't see anyone, at least no one who looked suspicious. But yesterday afternoon when I came out of the grocery store I saw a man in a white delivery van in the parking lot. He was wearing dark glasses and I wasn't close enough to get a good look, but I knew he was watching me."

"Because you had a feeling."

"Yes, Mr. Sweetwater. Because I had a feeling."

"Go on."

"I could not shake the sensation. Two nights ago I saw someone dressed for running access the gardens of my apartment complex and study the layout. I think the stalker was trying to identify my apartment and figure out the best way to get to me unnoticed."

"Did he do anything threatening?"

"No. Probably because the jerk next door was having a party so there was a lot of activity on my floor. But last night I had a feeling the stalker would return. I turned out the lights in my apartment and went out onto the balcony to grab that aura shot. Then I realized he was crossing the gardens and headed toward the stairs that lead to my apartment on the second floor. I wanted to scare him off so I called down to him."

Gideon's brows rose. "You spoke to the stalker?"

"Yes. I warned him I was taking photos and he was in the scene. That stopped him cold. Then my friend Irene heard me and came out onto her balcony to see what was going on. Next thing I know, the jerk next door started yelling at Irene and me, telling us to be quiet. The stalker left in a hurry."

"How did he leave?"

"He went out through the same gate he had used to access the gardens. The service lane entrance."

Gideon was quiet for a moment. "A lot of stalkers are exes."

"Not this one," she said. "I haven't been involved in a serious relationship for seven months."

"That doesn't mean some obsessive type from the past hasn't fixated on you."

"I think someone has fixated on me but not because of a past relationship. I've narrowed it down to the three most likely possibilities."

Gideon looked surprised. "That's very helpful." He reached for the notepad and the pen on his desk. "I'm listening."

Taking notes was a good sign, she told herself. They were getting somewhere at last.

"One possibility is that the stalker is a crank podcast fan," she said. "Someone who has become obsessed with me and has managed to track me down here in San Diego. Unfortunately, we do attract a number of weirdos because of the paranormal slant we take on the various cases. We try to be careful when it comes to our personal information but you know how it is these days. They say you can find anyone if you look hard enough."

"That's what they say," Gideon agreed. "Please continue."

"The second possibility is that the stalker is connected to the people or organization responsible for the lost nights that my associates and I experienced. Frankly, as scary as that would be, it would also be the best outcome."

Gideon looked up at that. "Why?"

"Because the *Lost Night Files* podcast team is desperately in need of a fresh lead."

"I see."

Great. Now he was questioning her mental stability again.

"And the third possibility?" Gideon asked.

"I told you I don't have any exes," she said. "And that's true when it comes to my social life. But I do have an ex-therapist."

The pen stilled in Gideon's hand.

"Can I ask why you were seeing a therapist?" he asked quietly.

"I have sleep issues." There was no need to mention her little phobia about night. "Some sort of PTSD associated with the kidnapping. I thought Dr. Pike might be able to help me. But things got . . . messy. Complicated."

"In what way?"

"Pike took what I thought was an unprofessionally intense interest in my problem. He kept pushing for details that I didn't want to give him. Then he started insisting that we have our therapy sessions at night. I got a bad feeling about the whole situation."

"No kidding," Gideon said.

Belatedly she realized what he was thinking. She flushed. "It wasn't like that," she said. She paused, mentally rerunning the last couple of conversations with Norris Pike. "At least, I don't think so. I never got the sense that he was attracted to me in a personal way. To be fair, there were legitimate clinical reasons for meeting at night. My issues were sleep-related, after all."

"Did he suggest spending a night in a sleep clinic?"

"No. He said he wanted to take another approach."

"What was it?" Gideon asked.

"I never found out. I started canceling the appointments."

"How did Pike take that?"

"Not well. He was frustrated by my failure to cooperate. He made it clear he thinks I'm making a huge mistake."

Gideon glanced at the pictures on his desk. "You must have seen Pike's aura on several occasions."

"As I told you, my vision—"

"Only works at night. Right. So you don't know if Pike might have been the runner you saw in the apartment gardens?"

"No. I'll give you his card." She reached into her tote, extracted her wallet and plucked out Pike's business card. She put it down on the desk. "It's got his contact information."

"That will be helpful." Gideon gathered up the energy prints and the aura photo. "You can have these. I won't be needing them."

"Are you sure?"

Gideon's mouth crooked in a faint curve that might have been a smile. "Unfortunately, they are meaningless to me."

Amelia hesitated. "But you're taking my case?"

"Yes. It sounds interesting."

She should be glad, she thought. Relieved. And she was. But . . .

There was no getting around it. Something about Gideon Sweetwater made her uneasy. Maybe it was the ominous paintings. Her intuition told her that he was the artist.

"Well, that's good," she said. *I think*, she added silently. "Thank you. What should I do next?"

"Go home. Keep the doors and windows locked. Make sure there are always people around you whenever you are outside. I'll start making inquiries. Tonight I'll stake out your apartment complex and see if your stalker puts in another appearance."

"How will you recognize him if you can't see his energy field?"

"I'm pretty good at picking out people who are in places where they shouldn't be."

She suddenly felt optimistic again. "So you have very good intuition?"

"Sometimes."

She started to dive into her tote. "You'll want a retainer."

"We'll talk about my fees later, after I've had a chance to evaluate the scope of your case."

"Well, okay, but just so you know, I'm on a budget."

"My fees are negotiable."

CHAPTER FOUR

GIDEON STOOD IN the doorway, braced on his cane, and watched the little blue compact pull out of the front drive and disappear around a curve. She had no way of knowing it, but Amelia Rivers had just thrown his life into chaos.

And to think that only yesterday he had been coping with acute boredom. *Be careful what you wish for, Sweetwater.*

He shut the door and made his way back down the hall lined with scenes from his nightmares and went into the library. He sat down behind the desk, trying to ignore the dull ache in his right leg. Some days were better than others. This was not one of the good days.

It was his own fault. He had tried not to lean too heavily on the cane in front of the client. Tried not to limp. The result was that he had pushed certain muscles to the limit.

The damage done by the bullet had healed, according to the doctors. Yes, he knew he had been lucky. Yes, he was alive, so obviously things could have been worse. But he was beginning to realize he might have to live with the nagging on-again, off-again pain for a long time, maybe indefinitely. He probably ought to shift some of his investment cash into a couple of distilleries that made good whiskey.

He propped his elbows on the arms of the chair and put his fingertips together. For a time he sat quietly and considered his new client. He did not think he had made a good impression. The cane and the sore ribs did not project an inspiring professional image. He had not intended to take any new clients until he was more fit and had also resolved a certain personal problem. So much for that plan.

Amelia Rivers would have been an intriguing distraction under any circumstances—everything about her sharpened his senses. It had started with the sound of her voice on the phone. Smart, warm, and engaging, it had hit his senses like a double shot of a highly caffeinated energy drink. He had suddenly felt more alert, more focused, and very, very curious to find out more about her.

The quick background check he had conducted should have dampened his interest. The whole podcast thing was a real red flag. He should not be getting involved with a client who had been sucked into the murky world of paranormal conspiracy theories and amateur sleuths. He had enough problems.

Still, against his better judgment and compelled by boredom he had made the appointment with Amelia. In hindsight it occurred to him that loneliness also might have been a factor. Virginia had ended what he had considered their very comfortable arrangement shortly before the Colony case. He understood. He *always* understood. They had both known the affair was going nowhere. His affairs never did. He had an unblemished track record of romantic relationships that ended with polite goodbyes, an agreement to remain friends, and the suggestion that he see a therapist about his commitment issues.

He was used to sleeping alone. He liked to think that he had come to terms with the realization that he would be doing so for the rest of his life. He enjoyed the company of interesting, successful, single women. Virginia was a professor of marine biology. She had the athletic, outdoorsy, high-energy vibe of someone who was passionate about the ocean. Her career whisked her away on a research vessel for days, sometimes weeks, at a time, and that had worked out well for both of them. The lengthy separations meant it had taken her longer than usual to grow bored and frustrated with him.

Before Virginia he had dated Dora, an ambitious, sophisticated financial adviser who catered to the high-net-worth individual market. They had shared an interest in the arcane mysteries of finance. The demands of her job had ensured that she spent a lot of time on private jets bound for New York, San Francisco, Aspen, and Jackson Hole. The constant travel had helped keep the relationship going for nearly four months, but eventually Dora had informed him that it was time for both of them to move on.

Amelia Rivers was now a client. He should not be contemplating her from the perspective of a man looking for a date. It was a reckless, dumbass thing to do, but that's exactly what he had started doing when he heard her voice on the phone.

The situation had intensified when he watched her climb out of the blue compact and walk briskly up the path to his front door. When she got close he was deeply aware of the compelling vibe in the atmosphere. *Your pheromones and hormones at work, Sweetwater.*

She was fascinating but in unexpected ways. You had to study her for a while to understand the appeal. There was feminine strength and determination in her profile and insightful intelligence in her sea-green eyes. Her shoulder-length hair was a warm tawny brown, not the familiar Southern California gold. Her jeans and gray pullover hinted at a sleek, feminine body that had not been enhanced by implants.

When she entered his office and sat down across from him it was as if he had plugged in a new lamp. The room seemed to brighten in response to her energy. His paintings looked a bit less ominous—not a lot less ominous; nightmares were nightmares, after all. There wasn't much you could do about them except put some distance between them and the waking mind. Still, while she was in the room the scenes on the walls had looked more like abstract art than snapshots of chaos.

He really needed to get a grip on his imagination.

So many questions, so few answers. Was Amelia Rivers delusional? He didn't think so but he could not be absolutely positive. As he had told her, he had pretty good intuition, but he was not a psychiatrist.

Was she a fraud? The so-called aura and energy print pictures could easily have been faked. There was a long history of fraudulent aura photography. But if she was running a con, why come to him? Was she working a complicated scheme to sell the list to him? Maybe he was her target.

That question led to another possibility. Con artists were bound to accumulate a few enemies in the course of their careers. It was entirely possible that a seriously annoyed mark had found her and was now stalking her for the sake of revenge. It made sense that she would hire a private investigator to identify the individual who was making her uneasy.

But she was more than uneasy. On the surface she appeared cool, calm, and determined, but he was an expert on hidden fears. Amelia Rivers was scared. She might be delusional or she might be a con, but he did not doubt that she believed her stalker was real.

Maybe he was overthinking things. It wouldn't be the first time. There was a possibility that everything she had told him was the truth. If so, she had just opened one hell of a Pandora's box.

He took out his phone and called a number on his list of family contacts. His uncle answered immediately. Shelton Sweetwater greeted him with his usual enthusiasm. Shelton was fond of all his nieces and nephews, but he had always claimed that Gideon was the one who had inherited the biggest dose of what he called the most dangerous of the Sweetwater family traits—curiosity. He also understood that Gideon used curiosity the way other people used fast cars. It was a way to channel the dark side of a very dark talent.

"Gideon," Shelton said. "Good to hear from you. How's the leg?"

"The leg is fine," Gideon lied. Absently he rubbed his aching thigh. "I've got another problem. It's connected to a new case."

"Yeah?" Interest sparked in Shelton's voice. "You know I like to talk about your work."

"My new client selected me because she found my name on a certain list."

"I thought you mostly worked by referral."

"I do. I try to stay off lists. But I know for a fact that I'm on the one my client has, because you're the one who put me there."

CHAPTER FIVE

DON'T UNDERSTAND—" Shelton broke off. "Wait, are you talking about that list of people I developed during the career guidance research study I ran years ago?"

"Yes, Uncle Shelton. That list."

"Well, shit."

"My sentiments exactly."

"The study went nowhere because it couldn't be replicated," Shelton said. "At least, not without me and my device."

"A machine only you can operate."

"What can I say? Crystals are complicated. I was trying to come up with some standard testing and calibration methods that others could use when the agency that commissioned the study pulled the plug on the funding. The project was shelved. A short time later the agency itself disappeared. After years of dropping millions into paranormal research, all of a sudden no one in government wanted to be associated with that kind of work."

"But you managed to develop a list of people who demonstrated some measurable talent."

"That's right." Shelton paused. "Huh. Wonder how your client found it."

"We'll deal with that question later. There is an escalating stalker involved in this case, so I've got to set priorities. Did you keep track of the test subjects?"

"No, of course not. That would have been impossible. Hundreds of people volunteered to participate in the study. I worked with several colleges and a couple of military bases up and down the West Coast."

"What about the people who ended up on your list?"

"I planned to keep an eye on a few of them from a distance, but I got busy with other projects," Shelton said. "I have no idea where any of those people are now. You say your client is on the list?"

"That's what she told me. Amelia Rivers. Does the name ring a bell?"

"No, but it's been several years since the study was shut down. I can dig up my notes if that will help."

"Thanks," Gideon said. "They might be useful."

"You said there's a stalker involved in this case?"

"Amelia thinks so."

"Nasty lot, stalkers. Old boyfriend?"

"Amelia is convinced the stalker is hunting her because her name is on that list. What's more, she claims she and her friends were kidnapped, drugged, and used in experiments designed to enhance their natural abilities."

"What the hell?" Shelton snorted. "That's ridiculous. Did she mention UFOs by any chance?"

"No extraterrestrials were involved. I'm pretty sure she's not delusional."

"You can't always tell, Gideon. If she's on that list it means she does have some talent. But one thing I learned in the course of that study was that people who possess some serious psychic ability don't always have the mental stability required to handle the additional sensory input. A powerful sixth sense can cause an individual to become confused and disoriented. The dream energy overwhelms the normal senses in the waking state."

"I know."

"And don't get me started on what could go wrong if the subject has a criminal mind. When I closed down that research project I couldn't help wondering how many of the people I had tested were headed for an asylum, a life on the streets, or prison."

"Did you try to identify the unstable subjects?"

"I made a few notes about the ones who worried me the most. But there was nothing more I could do. Did your client give you anything else to go on besides a story about being kidnapped?"

"She had some photographs," Gideon said.

"That should help."

"They won't do me any good. Just some fuzzy, glary splashes on a sidewalk and what she claims is a photo of the stalker's aura."

"Really?" Excitement lit Shelton's voice. "She figured out how to take pictures of aura and energy prints? That's amazing. Did she say what kind of camera she used?"

"A film camera, the old-fashioned kind that uses a mirror and prism. She shot with black-and-white film. Trust me, the results are useless."

"Fascinating."

"Speaking of cameras, let's try to stay focused here," Gideon said. "I'd appreciate it if you would get those notes for me."

"Sure, sure. It'll take me a while, though. The file is in my storage locker. I'll drive over there today and see what I can find. Meanwhile, be careful, Gideon. I wasn't joking when I said that there are some potentially dangerous people on that list."

"Understood," Gideon said. "I'm going to hang up now."

"Wait, before you go. Your mother is putting pressure on me again. She's afraid that marine biologist you were seeing broke your heart."

Gideon groaned. "Virginia did not break my heart. Remind Mom that I haven't been in great shape for dating recently."

"She worries about you, Gideon. She's not the only one. Most Sweetwaters are married and firing up a family by your age."

"I'll get right on that," Gideon said.

He ended the call and dropped the phone into his pocket. For a time he sat quietly, studying the nearest painting. He had started it during the course of the Colony case and finished it in the days after Ian Luxford had been arrested.

He had no illusions about his artistic ability. He was an amateur and that was all he would ever be. Fortunately, he wasn't trying to make a living as an artist.

No one responded well to his paintings. His own relatives told him his pictures were creepy. He usually took the unframed canvases down before he interviewed a client because they had a disturbing effect on people who were already anxious about meeting with a private investigator. But, acting on impulse or intuition—he wasn't sure which—he had opted to leave them up today.

Amelia had done a very good job of concealing her reaction, but he had caught a glimpse of something disturbing in her response. He was almost certain she had realized that his muse was his own dreamscape.

CHAPTER SIX

AMELIA BROUGHT THE car to a stop in her assigned parking space, collected her tote, and slipped out from behind the wheel. She did not know if she had made the right move by hiring Gideon Sweetwater, but at least she had acted. She no longer felt quite so trapped. Progress. Maybe.

She tried to look on the bright side. No, Gideon was not the PI she had expected to encounter when she made the appointment, but maybe that was a good thing. True, he either didn't believe in the paranormal or was in denial about his own talent, whatever that was, but he appeared to be serious about trying to identify the stalker. That was what mattered most right now.

She headed for the security gate that serviced her wing of the apartment complex, readying her key chain fob.

"Amelia, you're back. Want to get coffee?"

Amelia looked up and saw Irene Morgan leaning over the railing of the second-floor walkway. She raised a hand in greeting and told herself that now was as good a time as any. She needed to have a

serious talk with her friend. She did not want to take the risk of ruining their relationship but she had put off the conversation long
enough. If she didn't speak up and something bad happened she
would never forgive herself.

"Sure," she said.

"I'll be right down."

THEY WALKED ACROSS the street to Harry's Soon To Be Famous Cof-
feehouse The late-fall day was mild and sunny, so they opted for an
outdoor table shaded by a large umbrella. It would be easier to say
what she had to say outside rather than inside, Amelia thought. Less
chance of being overheard. She ordered her usual Americano. Irene
went for a cappuccino.

Irene looked effortlessly glamorous, as usual, in Katharine Hep-
burn trousers, a white silk shirt, and designer sunglasses. An ambitious, up-and-coming marketing firm consultant, she spent a lot of
time meeting with high-profile clients. She had explained to Amelia
on several occasions that she planned to open her own business
sometime in the next couple of years. Amelia did not doubt that she
would be successful. Irene was a driven woman. A classic over-
achiever. It was a species Amelia was very familiar with, having
grown up in a family of overachievers.

The bond between the two of them had been established quickly
because they were both in the process of trying to reinvent their
badly shattered lives. Irene had been raised with money—a lot of it.
And it had all vanished overnight a few years ago when her father, a
high-flying hedge fund manager, had been arrested for fraud. He had
taken his own life while awaiting trial.

"He always thought he was the smartest one in the room," Irene had explained one night over a second glass of wine. "And he was. Right up until he wasn't."

Her mother having died years earlier, Irene had found herself alone in the world and broke. But she'd had a plan, a strategy, and she was in the process of executing it. *Unlike, say, me,* Amelia thought.

She was barely scraping by as a photographer. She knew she was competent but she also knew that unless she found the right niche she was never going to make a comfortable living with a camera. There just wasn't enough money in real estate shoots, pet portraits, and CEO headshots.

She valued her friendship with Irene so she had taken care not to destroy it by claiming a psychic talent. Few things could screw up a relationship of any kind faster than telling a normal, intelligent person that you took the paranormal thing seriously. As far as Irene was concerned, the *Lost Night Files* podcast was *entertainment.* Fiction. A side hustle that Amelia and the others were producing with the hope of hitting it big in the potentially lucrative podcast world.

Irene sipped some of her cappuccino and lowered the cup. "Any luck attracting a new sponsor?"

Irene was all about the podcast's efforts to increase revenues.

"No, unfortunately," Amelia said, sliding easily into her *of-course-I-don't-take-the-possibility-of-murder-by-psychic-means-seriously* persona. "Lots of competition out there. We're trying to up our game with better production values."

That much was true. Phoebe Hatch, the new producer, was very big on production values.

Irene shook her head. "You and your friends need to get more aggressive with your marketing strategy. Like I tell my clients, you can have cutting-edge tech and a brilliant concept, but if you want to make money you've got to generate sales, and that requires—"

"Marketing. I know. But I've told you a million times we can't afford a lot of high-end advertising."

"You need to think of marketing as an investment."

"Trust me, we know that," Amelia said. "None of us has quit our day jobs. Speaking of which, I need to hustle up some more corporate headshots and real estate work. The problem is that these days anyone with a cell phone and a photo-enhancing program thinks they can do good photography. And they are right."

"Not true," Irene said. "You, my friend, are an artist. You always manage to capture something unique and individual about your subjects—human, pet, or real estate. Just look what you did with your portraits of Daisy and Dahlia."

"I hate to tell you this, Irene, but your goldfish look like a million other goldfish. I could have wandered into any pet store in town and photographed two other goldfish for that portrait. You would never have known the difference."

"I disagree. You brought out Daisy's glamourous side and Dahlia's shy nature."

"Uh-huh."

"Okay, I'm teasing you. My point is, like everything else in life, success in marketing is ninety percent attitude. You need to develop some in order to sell yourself and the podcast."

"Thanks, I appreciate the support and advice." Amelia drank some coffee to give herself time to come up with a nonthreatening way to ease into what promised to be a difficult conversation. When she was ready she lowered the cup. "So, got another date lined up with Mr. Amazing-In-Bed?"

Irene smiled a very feline smile. "Falcon? Yes, as a matter of fact.

Tomorrow night. He insists on wasting time with cocktails and dinner at some new trattoria he's discovered but after that we're going to check in to a hotel for the main course."

Amelia cleared her throat. "Think things might be getting serious for the two of you?"

"Never in a million years. Falcon has a lot going for him in the bedroom but, trust me, aside from the sex we don't have a thing in common. Sooner or later he'll move on or I will."

"How much do you know about him, Irene?"

Irene frowned more in surprise than concern. "Why all the questions about Falcon? Do you have a problem with me dating him?"

Amelia struggled to find a way to explain what she thought she had seen in the splashes of hot energy on the sidewalk at the foot of the stairs three nights earlier. She had been up late, as usual, working in her darkroom, when she heard Falcon leave Irene's apartment.

She had glimpsed his tough-looking SUV in the parking lot a few times when he had arrived to pick up Irene or drop her off, but thanks to the vehicle's heavily tinted windows she had not gotten a look at his face or his aura. To the best of her knowledge he had never visited Irene in her apartment—until three nights ago.

She had waited until Falcon was pulling out of the parking lot before she gathered her nerve, left her apartment, and hurried down the stairs. The disturbing energy that seethed in his still-hot prints sent her intuition into the red zone.

"You always call him Falcon," she said. "I assume he's got a first name?"

"Yes, of course he does. He prefers to be called Falcon, and I think it suits him. What's your problem with him?"

Amelia took a deep breath. "He just looks sort of . . . dangerous. That's all."

Irene was in the process of swallowing some more of her cappuccino. Her eyes widened, and she sputtered with laughter and set the cup down very quickly. She grabbed one of the little napkins and blotted her subtly plumped lips.

"Sorry," she said. "But that is just hilarious. Wait until I tell Falcon. No, on second thought, I'd better not. He might get pissed."

Amelia felt the heat rush to her face. "I know this is none of my business. I've never even met the man. But something about him worries me."

Irene chuckled. "Probably the leather jacket and the mirrored sunglasses and the boots."

"Is that what he wears?"

"Yep, and what's more, he makes the outfit look good." Irene glanced around to make sure no one was within earshot and leaned forward. She lowered her voice. "I appreciate your concern, but you can relax. You were right about one thing—Falcon is dangerous. Frankly, it's one of his best features. All that leather and muscle is sexy as hell."

"Okay, I get that," Amelia said. Falcon didn't sound like her type, but she wasn't the one dating him. "What did you mean when you said I was right about him being dangerous?"

"Falcon is an undercover cop. Vice."

"Oh." Startled, Amelia sat back in her chair and absorbed that information. "Oh, I see."

"He looks dangerous because he works in a dangerous world," Irene continued. "His job and his life depend on him being able to blend in to that world. And now that I've told you the truth you have to promise me you will not breathe a word of what I just said to any-one. He would not be happy to find out that I blabbed."

"I understand." Amelia paused and then leaned forward again. "If he's undercover, why did he tell you the truth about himself?"

"Turns out even undercover cops need to talk to someone once in a while. I gather that, while the job is an adrenaline rush, it's also a very lonely life."

CHAPTER SEVEN

H E DETESTED STAKEOUTS. The boredom factor was off the charts. Gideon absently massaged his aching leg. He was sitting on a small folding stool in the shadows of the rear door of a pizza shop. The restaurant had closed two hours ago. His position gave him a clear view of the service entrance of Amelia's apartment complex.

When he had arrived earlier he had been pushing a rusty shopping cart filled with the accoutrements of the cover he had chosen to use for the night's work—some empty fast-food take-out cartons, a well-worn backpack, and a grungy sleeping roll. Just another homeless person trying to get through the night. Anyone who happened to pass by would look the other way.

Not that he expected a lot of foot traffic, not at one o'clock in the morning. It was unlikely that any innocents would wander into the poorly lit service lane at that hour. It would be the equivalent of taking a stroll down a dark alley. The flip side of that logic meant that if someone did show up it was a good bet the individual would not be an innocent.

He hadn't set out to become a private investigator. Growing up, he and everyone else in the tightly knit Sweetwater clan had assumed he would join the family business, Sweetwater Security. But no, he'd just had to strike out on his own. The problem he had encountered—and that everyone else in the family had warned him about—was that his talent severely limited his career options.

Most of his work involved predictions, but not of the psychic variety. Criminals, like everyone else, were creatures of habit. They planned and carried out their crimes according to the old adage *If it ain't broke, don't fix it*. Amelia's stalker had only had two nights to establish a pattern, but that was enough.

He was wondering if Amelia was still awake when a figure appeared at the far end of the service lane and moved quickly toward the gate. There was no hoodie tonight. Instead, the newcomer wore the uniform of a private security guard company, the cap pulled low over his eyes. He got points for upgrading the disguise, but the rest of his actions fit the pattern. As was the case with so many criminals, he had failed to do his research. Amelia's apartment complex did not employ a security service.

The fake guard stopped in front of the security gate and prepared to open it with a key fob.

Here we go, Gideon thought.

He grabbed his cane and levered himself up off the seat. Pain shot down his right leg. He had been sitting too long. Fortunately adrenaline was kicking in, allowing him to keep moving.

He made it across the service lane just as the fake guard started to open the gate.

"You and I need to have a chat," Gideon said. "I've got a few questions."

The guard glanced at him and immediately lost interest.

"Get lost," he growled.

"That's not how this works."

The guard rounded on him, his eyes hot. "You stupid fuck. You only get one warning."

The bone-chilling jolt of energy struck with the force of an electric shock. Gideon staggered back a couple of steps and nearly went down. He managed to save himself with his cane. But before he could recover, the fake guard delivered another invisible blow.

The second psychic blast sent him to the ground and threatened to freeze his heart. Stunned, he tried to get to his feet.

The guard loomed over him. "Who do you think you are, you crazy fucker?"

The assailant readied himself for a kick to the head. Gideon rolled to the side. The boot caught him on the shoulder. He went with the force of the blow and wound up on his back.

"You're a dead man." The assailant's eyes glittered with a feverish light.

So much for engaging in a conversation that might have provided some useful information. Gideon pulled hard on his talent, got the fix, and channeled a current of energy. He aimed it at the fragile barrier that separated the assailant's dreamstate from his waking state. The delicate border shattered like a wall of glass hit by a meteor. The nightmares roared forth.

Unable to cope with the sea of horrors, paralyzed by the inability to separate dreams from reality, the assailant reeled, lost his balance, and came up hard against the wrought iron fence. He lost consciousness and collapsed. There was an unpleasant thud when he hit his head on the pavement.

Gideon considered the jolt of lethal energy the guard had unleashed. *Some psychic you are, Sweetwater. Did not see that coming.*

When he was back in control, he steadied himself with the cane, got to his feet, and leaned over to search the fallen man. The pat-down produced nothing except the key fob, which had no doubt been stolen. No ID. No forgotten credit card receipts. No phone. No communication devices of any kind.

That was not good news. It meant the fake guard was not a run-of-the-mill obsessed stalker, assuming there was such an entity. He was a professional, one who had been trained to leave all traces of identification behind before going operational. And he had a lethal psychic talent.

Amelia had a serious problem.

Fortunately the stalker was still alive. Between the damage to his head and his trip into Nightmare World, he might not wake up. But if he did there would be a chance to question him. In the meantime, he had to be stashed somewhere. Unconscious people lying out in the open tended to draw attention.

Gideon took a beat to consider his options.

His leg and ribs protested mightily when he leaned down to grasp the fake guard's wrist, but he managed to get a grip. He was preparing to drag his burden across the pavement and into the shadows of an empty doorway when he heard the sound of an accelerating vehicle. He glanced around and saw a delivery van, lights off, rushing toward him.

The pro had brought backup—or maybe this was a cleanup team.

He dropped the unconscious man, gripped his cane, limped across the lane, and used the fob Amelia had given him to open the gate. He stumbled inside the grounds of the apartment complex, closed the gate, and took cover behind a massive trash bin.

He listened as the van braked to a sharp halt. Doors slammed open.

"Hurnley is down," a man said.

"Get him," another man ordered.

The driver, Gideon decided.

"What about the homeless guy?" a third man asked.

"Forget him," the driver snapped. "We can't risk chasing him down. Too many cameras in there. He isn't important. Just some loser trying to grab a little cash for drugs."

"How the fuck did he take down Hurnley?" the first man said. He sounded incredulous.

"Hurnley got careless," the driver said. "Move. We need to get out of here."

There was some commotion out in the alley, a few grunts, and then the van doors slammed shut. The vehicle drove off.

Gideon waited for a moment and then, stifling a groan, he pushed himself away from the side of the bin, took out his phone, and texted his new client.

New developments. I'll be at your door in a
couple of minutes. Don't panic.

He dropped the phone into the pocket of the ancient coat he had picked up at a thrift shop. Had he been too cryptic? Telling someone not to panic was a surefire way to encourage them to do just that. But it was too late now. The message had been delivered.

He made his way through the gardens, heading toward Amelia's wing. This was going to be embarrassing. A lesson in how not to impress a client.

He passed the glowing swimming pool, found the stairs, and climbed what felt like Everest to get to the second floor.

He went down the outside walkway to apartment two-fifteen and knocked softly. The peephole darkened briefly. He heard the muffled sound of three locks being unlocked.

The door opened a couple of inches. Amelia peered out.

"Mr. Sweetwater." She stared at him, appalled. "What happened? Did you fall down the stairs?"

"That's the first thing that pops into your head? Really? I fell down a flight of stairs? Never mind. Are you going to invite me in?"

"What? Sorry, yes, of course." Amelia stepped back. "Sit down. Should I call nine-one-one?"

"No, don't call nine-one-one." He moved past her and turned to watch her lock the three locks. "We don't have time for me to spend the rest of the night in an emergency room. The good news is, you don't have a stalker."

Amelia spun around to face him. "I don't?"

"No, Amelia. Someone is watching you, but what I interrupted tonight was an attempted kidnapping."

CHAPTER EIGHT

AMELIA PLACED A glass of white wine on the table next to the recliner. "At least you no longer think I'm delusional or that I'm a con artist."

"Nope," Gideon said. He was stretched out on the recliner, plastic baggies filled with ice nestled against his ribs and his right leg. He picked up the glass. "Is this all you've got? White wine?"

"What were you expecting?"

"I was hoping for something stronger. Whiskey, for example."

"I see. Well, I do have some cognac that my friend Irene gave me."

"Thanks, I'll take it."

She thought about informing him that the cognac, a birthday gift, was very expensive and then decided that trying to talk him out of drinking some as a painkiller would be heartless—not to mention rude, under the circumstances. After all, she was the reason he had been beaten up tonight.

"Right," she said.

She picked up the wineglass, went back around the island that separated the kitchen from the living room, and took down the bottle of cognac. She poured a small amount into a glass, hesitated, briefly considering her obligations as an employer, and added two more splashes. She picked up the cognac and the white wine and carried both into the living room.

She handed the cognac to Gideon and watched him take a healthy swallow. "Are you sure I shouldn't call nine-one-one or drive you to the nearest emergency room?"

"Positive."

She decided she could use a drink, too. She sipped the white wine and sank down onto the sofa. "All right, what happened?"

Gideon used his free hand to adjust one of the makeshift ice packs. "Best guess? You have stumbled into someone's off-the-books business operation and attracted the attention of some very bad people."

"It's all those trips to Lucent Springs. Someone has realized that I'm closing in on answers."

She drank some more wine and considered the fact that her worst nightmare had become a reality. She was being hunted. Again. But at least this time she was aware of the danger. She started to draw up a list of actions that needed to be taken.

"I've got to warn the others," she said. "That might not be easy. Last I heard, Talia and Luke are following up a lead in the San Juan Islands. Limited cell phone service. Ambrose and Pallas are looking for someone on the list who lives off the grid in the Arizona mountains. I'll ask our producer, Phoebe, to try to track them down. She's a whiz with tech. After I do that I need to hire a bodyguard and head back to Lucent Springs. That's where the answers are, I'm sure of it."

"Amelia, did you hear a word I just said?" Gideon asked.

"What?" She blinked and yanked her thoughts out of planning mode. "Oh. Sorry. I was trying to develop a strategy for moving forward. I didn't expect you to close my case so quickly or—" She broke off and waved a hand in a gesture meant to indicate his physical condition. "Or quite so dramatically."

He narrowed his eyes. "I haven't closed your case. I'm just getting started."

"I hired you to get answers. I wanted to know if I was dealing with a random stalker or the people responsible for kidnapping my friends and me. You confirmed my suspicions. Send me the bill. I'm a little short on cash right now but I promise you'll get paid."

"Are you by any chance trying to fire me?"

"Not exactly. You've done your job. You're through."

"You can't fire me and I'm not quitting. You and I are sticking together until we find the people who tried to grab you tonight."

"I appreciate your professional commitment, but we have to be realistic. You are in over your head."

"I'm aware I don't look my best at the moment, but you should see the other guy."

She managed a weak smile to acknowledge the weak joke. "Thank you for scaring him off."

"You have no idea how much I scared him."

"I'm very grateful but I really do need to find someone else to work with going forward."

"Because of my physical condition?"

"It's not just that. There's the problem of trust."

"You don't trust me?"

He sounded surprised and possibly offended.

"I trust you, but you don't trust me," she said. "You didn't believe me when I told you that I could see auras and photograph energy prints, for example."

"To be fair, I'm in a business that requires some degree of skepticism."

She sighed. "I understand. But I'm involved in a dangerous and complicated situation. I can't afford to waste time with an investigator who is going to question everything I say."

"Amelia—"

"Look, I get that you have doubts. I hoped you would take me seriously because your name was on that old research list. I assumed that meant you had some talent yourself."

"Amelia—"

"I don't know how or why you wound up on that list of people. Maybe the researchers made a mistake when they added your name to it. What I'm trying to say—"

"Amelia, the researcher who designed that damned test did not make a mistake. I'm on the list for a reason."

That stopped her cold. "What?"

"One of my uncles, Shelton Sweetwater, designed and administered that study. A small, clandestine government agency commissioned the research. The goal was to find a reliable method of identifying and measuring psychic sensitivity. Shelton told me he tested a few hundred subjects on the West Coast."

A thrill of discovery sent a shock wave through Amelia. *Progress at last.* "Your uncle was responsible for the test?" In the next breath excitement metamorphosed into outrage. "Why didn't you tell me that when I hired you this morning?"

"Because I wasn't sure who you were or what you were after. The results of that test were classified, after all, and in the end, the project was shelved."

"Why?"

"According to Shelton, the study could not be replicated. None of the standard scientific testing methods or tools proved reliable. The reason my uncle was able to come up with a list of people who demonstrated a genuine psychic vibe was because of a device he invented that only he can operate."

"Hmm." She sat quietly and drank some more wine while she processed the new information. "This is important. I need to update my friends."

"So much for 'classified.'"

She ignored that. "We should contact the agency that commissioned the research and tell them someone is running dangerous experiments on the people on that list."

"Good luck with that. According to Shelton, the agency that commissioned the original research has long since disappeared into the graveyard of shuttered government projects devoted to paranormal research. He has no idea how to contact anyone who might know what to do about our problem."

She paused her glass halfway to her mouth. "So it's *our* problem now?"

"Oh, yeah."

"Well, there have to be records. Who's in charge of them?"

"I don't know, and neither does Shelton. It was a tiny government agency running a clandestine survey, Amelia. Trust me, no one is going to come forward now and take responsibility."

She shot to her feet, wineglass in hand, and started pacing the room. "We've got to follow up on these new leads while they are hot."

"I agree." Gideon shifted a little in an apparent attempt to get more comfortable and watched her stride back and forth in front of the recliner. "I've been thinking about that. You and your podcast friends are evidently the uncontrolled variable in the equation. Your experience in Lucent Springs did not go according to someone's plan and your actions afterward have further destabilized the system. I need to look at the origin point."

She came to an abrupt halt. "What are you talking about?"

"Sorry. I was thinking out loud. You were right when you said we need to go to Lucent Springs."

"I said *I* need to go back to Lucent Springs."

He paid no attention to the small correction.

"I want to take a look at that old hotel," he said. "Lucent Springs is out in the desert, about a two-hour drive." He checked his watch. "I'll spend the rest of the night here. We'll stop by my place in the morning so that I can change my clothes and pick up a few things, and then we'll head out."

Amelia came to a halt in front of the recliner. "How much do you know about Lucent Springs?"

"I listened to a few more of the podcasts this afternoon."

"I see. Well, that's good, I guess, but you're moving awfully fast, considering your current physical condition and your doubts about my story."

"I'm not moving fast enough. I can hear a clock ticking, Amelia."

For some reason the cold certainty in his voice unnerved her more than anything else he had said. On the positive side, whatever had happened in the service lane tonight had convinced him she was not delusional and that she really was in danger.

"I can hear that clock, too," she said. She set the half-finished glass of wine on the kitchen island. "There are some pictures I want to show you. Don't worry, they aren't aura or energy photos. I'll be right back."

He said nothing but she was aware of him watching her as she walked across the living room and around the corner into the small entryway at the front door. She continued on down the hall to the darkroom.

Opening the door of the former walk-in closet, she flipped the light switch and went inside. The envelope that contained prints of the photos from the Night Island investigation was on the workbench. She grabbed it and started back toward the door. On impulse she paused, opened a drawer, and picked up the baggie that contained the badly charred hotel room key.

When she returned to the living room, she discovered that Gideon hadn't moved. He continued to occupy her recliner as if he owned it. It occurred to her that she had no practical means of evicting him from her apartment. She was getting the feeling she was stuck with him, at least for the near future.

"We don't have a lot of solid leads, but my friends Talia March and Luke Rand returned from Night Island with a few photographs," she said. "The photographer was a researcher who had a special interest in fungi, so most of the photos are pictures of weird mushrooms, but he also took some shots of the interior of a laboratory on the island. One in particular interests me. I used a computer program to enhance it."

Gideon took the black-and-white photo without a word and considered the image for a long moment.

"It looks like the corner of a box of laboratory chemicals or medication," he said.

"We—my friends and I—think it might be a box that contained the drugs that were used in some of the experiments."

She waited, wondering if he would question the conclusion.

"I can make out three letters on the side," he said. "'Aur.'"

"Yes," she said. At least he wasn't dismissing the small bit of evidence. "We're hoping those are the first three letters of the name of the firm that shipped the drugs to Night Island. Our producer, Phoebe, is doing a deep dive into the dark web to look for a lab or compounding pharmacy with 'Aur' in the name, but so far, no luck."

"Needle in a haystack," Gideon said. He looked up from the photo. "Anything else in the way of physical evidence?"

"There's a photo of two men who were involved in the Night Island experiments. Both have disappeared. Talia and Luke are working that angle."

"Is that it?"

"Probably."

Gideon's brows rose. "Probably?"

She handed him the baggie with the key inside. "I've made several trips to Lucent Springs. On one of them I found that room key in the ruins of the old clinic. As you can see, there was a plastic tag attached at one time that may have had some identification on it. You can make out the number ten and what looks like a partial sketch of a barrel cactus."

"Does it look like an old Lucent Springs Hotel key?"

"No. I've come across a few of them in what's left of the lobby. They are very different in design."

Gideon studied the key for a moment and regarded her with a thoughtful look. "What made you think it might be important?"

"I'm not sure," she admitted. "Probably the fact that I found it in the burned-out clinic and it's charred. That means it was dropped before the fire, not by some curiosity seeker who arrived afterward. For some reason—"

"For some reason you thought it might be important. Sounds like you're going on intuition, and that's more than enough to make me think this key is important."

"Really? You trust intuition that much?"

"Oh, yeah."

"So does Aunt Cybil."

"Good for Aunt Cybil. I hate to be a demanding houseguest, but would it be too much to ask for a blanket?"

It occurred to her that he was rapidly taking control of everything, including her apartment.

"This is a one-bedroom unit and my sofa is too small for you," she warned, clutching at straws.

"I don't need a bed. This chair will work just fine." He settled deeper into the recliner. "Very comfortable."

She cleared her throat. "Look, I'm grateful for the new information you just gave me and I am very sorry you were injured tonight, but let's be honest. You are in no condition to continue working my case."

"Someone tried to kidnap you or maybe intended to murder you."

"*Murder* me?"

"Neither would have been a good outcome. You were right when you said you needed a bodyguard."

She swallowed hard, grappling with the possibility that the stalker might want to kill her. "You're not exactly the bodyguard type, are you?"

"I realize I have failed to make a good impression but I'm not quite as pathetic or useless as I appear."

"What's that supposed to mean?"

"There's a reason I was on Uncle Shelton's list," Gideon said. "He was conducting research, remember?"

"Yes, but—"

"He needed a control subject, someone he knew for sure possessed genuine paranormal talent."

She got an electric ping. "So?"

"So, he used me as his control."

"And just how did your uncle prove you had some measurable paranormal ability if he didn't have a reliable way of actually measuring it?"

"Unlike a lot of talents, mine is fairly easy to demonstrate."

"Is that right?" She folded her arms. "What do you do? Bend spoons or talk to ghosts?"

"When you opened the door tonight you asked if I had fallen down the stairs. I told you that you should see the other guy."

"What happened to him?" she asked, suddenly uneasy.

"He's in a coma." Gideon finished the last of the cognac and lowered the glass. "He may or may not wake up."

She stilled.

"Did you hit him with something?" she asked.

"Yes," Gideon said. "But not with a physical object."

Her breathing got very tight in her chest. "Are you saying you used your talent to put him into a coma?"

"He hit his head when he went down," Gideon said. "That won't improve his chances for recovery. But, trust me, he was out before he fell."

She stared at him, trying to read his unreadable eyes. He did not sound triumphant, she decided. He wasn't boasting. He wasn't trying to impress her. His voice had a bleak, resigned quality. Whatever the truth of the matter, she did not doubt that he believed every word he had just said.

She unfolded her arms and tried to unobtrusively wipe her suddenly damp palms on her jeans. The assailant had no doubt hit his head very hard when he fell. That would explain his unconscious state. For the first time she wondered if Gideon was the one who was delusional.

"I'm not sure I understand," she said carefully.

Gideon's eyes got a silvery sheen that iced her nerves. Energy shivered faintly in the atmosphere.

"Be grateful you only see auras, Amelia," he said. "There are more complicated talents."

Aunt Cybil's advice rang in her ears. *Trust your intuition. Some things you know are true.*

In that moment she decided she believed Gideon.

"I'll get a blanket for you," she said.

CHAPTER NINE

FOR THE FIRST time in months she turned off most of the lights before she got into bed. The exceptions were the bathroom fixture and the plug-in night-lights scattered throughout the apartment. Her stupid phobia seemed less intense tonight. She was pretty sure that was because of the battered private investigator sleeping on her recliner. He was a train wreck, but something about his energy suggested competence. At least he finally believed her.

She changed into her customary nightgown, brushed her teeth, and sat down on the edge of the bed. She opened a drawer in the nightstand and picked up the small black velvet pouch. Opening the bag, she removed the three crystals and set them out in a row on top of the nightstand.

She sat quietly for a time, taking in the soothing vibe of the crystals. Silently she chanted the mantra her aunt had given her: *I am calm. I am serene. I am centered. I exhale the bad energy and inhale the good.*

After a while she settled under the covers and reflected again on the fact that she knew almost nothing about her uninvited houseguest. His prints and his aura would be visible in the shadows now that most of the lights were off. It wouldn't hurt to take a quick glance. In fact, it was the smart thing to do. She needed information about him.

She waited a few more minutes, absorbing the silence. When she was satisfied that he was probably asleep she eased the quilt aside and got out of bed.

She opened the door of her bedroom and padded softly down the hall. Her bare feet made almost no noise on the imitation wood floor. When she reached the entryway at the front door, she stopped. As long as she did not take a few more steps and go around the corner into the main room Gideon could not see her from his position on the recliner. She waited again.

Silence.

She went into her other vision and studied the splashes of energy on the floor. A nearby night-light cast a weak glow that muted but did not entirely mask the pools of paranormal radiance.

Gideon's prints burned quicksilver-hot in the shadows.

Instinctively she took a step back. She was still struggling to read and interpret energy prints but she knew raw power when she encountered it. She was locked in for the night with the man who had laid down the tracks on her floor.

She took a deep breath. Okay, maybe Gideon did have some serious talent, but that didn't mean he could actually render someone unconscious with a psychic punch. Did it? How could she possibly know? This was uncharted territory. She was still in the process of trying to cope with her own rapidly evolving senses. Still afraid of what the future might hold for her.

But although her nerves were shivering with acute awareness, she was not getting the dreaded vibe of an oncoming anxiety attack.

There were none of the icy chills she had experienced when she had viewed the stalker's disturbing prints the previous night. None of the ominous vibes she had detected in the prints left by Irene Morgan's undercover cop boyfriend.

"See anything interesting?" Gideon asked from the living room.

She yelped, caught her breath, composed herself, and walked around the corner. There was enough ambient light slanting through the windows to reveal the recliner and its occupant.

Gideon's aura—fierce, powerful, and fascinating—blazed in the shadows. She should have been afraid. Instead, she was *thrilled*. There was no other word for her response.

She ignored his question and asked one of her own instead. "Did you really put that man into a coma tonight?"

"Yes."

"How?"

"Trust me, you really do not want to know."

"Screw it," she said. "It's bad enough that I've got a beat-up investigator who ought to be in an ER. I don't need one with a depressing, cryptic attitude."

"What the hell?"

"Right now the only reason you've got my case, Gideon Sweetwater, is because you have apparently condescended to take my claims about the paranormal elements involved seriously. I realize that most professional investigators would not get that far. So, yes, I'm stuck with you. That doesn't mean I will put up with a bad attitude."

Gideon pressed the recliner button. The chair brought him to an upright position. "What is your problem?"

"As my Aunt Cybil would say, get over yourself. You're not the only one who got saddled with a dumbass talent. At least you've found a way to make what appears to be a very good living with yours. I, on the other hand, am trying to pay the rent and stay out of an asylum."

"An asylum?"

"Good night."

She stalked back into the bedroom, closed the door with some force, got under the covers, and once again opened her senses to the gentle vibes of the three crystals.

I am calm. I am serene. I am centered. I exhale the bad energy and inhale the good.

CHAPTER TEN

THE VOLUMINOUS, LACY, pearl-studded bridal veil was crumpled into a big, frothy heap on his doorstep.

"Well, shit," Gideon said. "Talk about lousy timing." Bracing himself on his cane he leaned down and scooped up as much of the netting as he could grasp in one hand. He held it out to Amelia. "Would you mind holding this while I unlock the door?"

"Uh. Okay." She stared at the veil for a beat and then looked at him. "Is there anything you want to tell me about your personal life before we leave town?"

"Not right now. Long story. I'll tell you all about the bride who goes with the veil after we get on the road."

"Okay," she said again. "I guess."

He got the door open and ushered her into the hall. She stepped inside, moving cautiously. The veil spilled over her arms and trailed on the terra-cotta floor.

"Just dump it on a chair," he instructed. He gestured toward the living room. "I'll be back in a few minutes. I appreciate the shower at

your place, but now I need to change clothes and pack an overnight bag."

She looked down at the heap of gossamer netting in her arms.
"Okay," she said.

He hesitated and then reminded himself he did not have time to
waste on explanations just then.

He left Amelia standing in the middle of the tiled floor, her arms
full of wedding veil, and went down the hall to his bedroom. It didn't
take long to pull on a fresh shirt and trousers. He took a few more
minutes to toss some clothes into a duffel bag and grabbed a wind-
breaker. It could get chilly at night in the desert at this time of year.

He was pleased to note that he was moving fairly well in spite of
the scene in the service lane. To his surprise, he had gotten some de-
cent, nightmare-free sleep in the recliner and his pain levels were
minimal this morning. There were a few fresh bruises, but evidently
he had not done any additional damage to the leg or the ribs.

He was, in fact, feeling better than he had any right to be feeling
considering his recent activities. It helped that he had a new, very interesting case, but there was another element in play—the new, very
interesting client.

So many questions.

His phone rang. He took it out, saw his uncle's name, and took
the call.

"What have you got?" he asked.

"I finally found my notes about the various individuals on that old
list," Shelton said. "I'll send them to you but I'm not sure how helpful
they will be. I marked a handful as unstable. But I don't think you
need to worry too much about them. That sort might end up as low-
level criminals, possibly quite violent. Enhancing their paranormal

senses, however, would also exacerbate the underlying instability. Even if they could tolerate the increased sensory input, they would lack the control required to plan and carry out an elaborate scheme involving kidnapping and illegal experiments."

"They might make useful enforcers for whoever is running the project."

"Maybe, at least for a while." Shelton paused. "If you were going to use that type as muscle you'd want to be damned sure you could control them. They would be likely to turn on you in a heartbeat."

"Got it." Gideon zipped the bag shut. "The Frankenstein theory in action. Sooner or later, the creatures you create will destroy you. Anything else of interest in your notes?"

"Yep. The people on that list you really need to worry about are the subjects who tested as latent or semilatent but stable. If the full power of their paranormal senses was unleashed suddenly by a drug or trauma or some other means, they could become very dangerous, very fast."

"I understand."

"Here's the important news, Gideon. Your new client is one of the test subjects I marked as stable and, therefore, potentially dangerous."

Gideon smiled. "You have no idea."

"What?"

"Never mind. I've got to run. Send me those notes."

He ended the call, gripped the handle of the duffel, and used his cane to thud-thud-thud his way back down the hall and into the living room. Amelia was waiting. The wedding veil was piled on the seat of an armchair.

He looked at the yards of netting and groaned. "I've got an engraved wedding invitation and a bouquet of dead flowers to go with the veil."

"That sounds . . . complicated."

"Like I said, it's a long story, but it's not complicated. I've got a stalker, too."

CHAPTER ELEVEN

ABOUT THE BRIDAL veil," Amelia said. "And the invitation and the dead bouquet."

She was sitting in the passenger seat of Gideon's steel-gray SUV. She had volunteered to drive but it was clear he had been irritated by the offer.

"I am not completely incapacitated," he had growled.

Men and their egos. But she could take a hint. He was a professional private investigator and he insisted on being treated with some respect. He definitely did not want to be coddled or pitied. To his credit, he had single-handedly foiled an attempt to kidnap or murder her during the night. That was definitely a point in his favor.

And it wasn't as if she had a lot of options. There weren't any other convenient PIs on the list, and after the events of the night she had to assume that what her intuition had been screaming at her for days was the truth. Time was running out.

"Right," he said. "A month ago the parents of a teenager asked me to extract their son from a cult called The Colony."

Amelia studied the highway taking them into the mountains that separated the urban sprawl on the coast from the vast expanse of desert on the other side. A memory stirred.

"I remember seeing something about the arrest of the leader and a few others involved with a cult based just outside of San Diego," she said. "I think the leader died in custody. Suicide."

"His name was Ian Luxford."

"I admit I didn't pay much attention. My friends and I have been busy with our investigation."

"Luxford called himself Merlin."

"How original."

"Most of his followers were young people in their late teens and early twenties who were living on the streets. Cult leaders are natural-born con artists and Luxford was no exception. But he had a few additional skills. He was charismatic and he had a genuine talent for hypnosis."

Amelia turned in the seat, startled. "Are you telling me it was a *psychic* talent?"

"Unfortunately, yes. Not that the police or anyone outside the cult believed he had any psychic ability. Because, you know, only charlatans, frauds, and deluded people actually take the notion of the paranormal seriously."

She made a face. "Don't remind me. But you knew Luxford was the real deal?"

"It wasn't hard to figure out," Gideon said. "It was the main reason I took the case."

She got another one of the intuitive pings that told her there was more to the story. "The *main* reason you took the case?"

"Well, that, and I felt sorry for the parents. They are good people and they were devastated by what had happened to their son."

"Wait a second," she said, holding up one hand. "Are you telling me you specialize in cases that you suspect have a paranormal angle?"

"I do."

She caught her breath. "Like *The Lost Night Files?*"

"I'm a licensed investigator," he said evenly. "I'm not in the business of providing entertainment."

She summoned up her sweetest smile. "As opposed to *The Lost Night Files?*"

He flexed his hands on the wheel. "I think we can agree that true crime podcasts walk a very thin line between fiction and reality. I believe the term is 'infotainment.'"

"*The Lost Night Files* is not infotainment."

"Do you want to hear the rest of my story or not?"

"Keep talking."

"Turned out Luxford was more than just a con with some talent. He had bought into his own press. He was convinced he had a world-changing destiny and he was determined to build an army of followers. He didn't care who he hurt in the process. He did a lot of damage."

"How did you rescue your clients' kid?"

"I coordinated with the local police and went in wearing a wire. Confronted Luxford. Told him that I was taking over the cult."

"*What?*"

"The only thing people like Luxford fear is strength. I was stronger than him, but things got messy for a while because he had a security detail and his enforcers were definitely not kids. They were hard guys and they had guns."

Gideon's matter-of-fact, business-as-usual tone chilled her. She sat very still in the seat and did not take her eyes off the road. "What happened?"

"I cornered Luxford in his office. He tried to take me out with his talent. When that failed he panicked and called in a couple of his thugs. Told them to execute me. I got that on the recording, by the way, and it is what gave the cops grounds for arrest—not the fact that he was running a cult. Anyhow, the enforcers arrived. Shots were fired. One of them hit my leg."

"That's how you were injured."

"What can I tell you? I got careless."

"You could have been killed."

"I wasn't," he said, "and fortunately the police were standing by, waiting to move in. That's the thing about being a serious, licensed investigator. You can liaise with regular law enforcement."

She opted not to take the bait. "What about your clients' teenage son?"

"He's in therapy but everyone seems to think he'll be okay," Gideon said. "Mostly I think he's just embarrassed that he got taken in by a con."

"So who is stalking you?"

"For the most part, Luxford's hold over his followers ended with his suicide. But one young woman is still under his spell. Evidently Luxford told her that she was to be his number one bride. She's determined to avenge him."

"That is so sad. Do you know the identity of the woman?"

"No. There was a lot of chaos and confusion after the police arrested Luxford and the enforcers. Several of the followers simply disappeared."

Amelia shivered. "That means your stalker could be almost any woman of the right age you happen to pass on the street."

"Theoretically. But sooner or later the bride will make herself known. Stalkers always escalate."

"You don't sound especially worried."

Gideon's mouth kicked up in a rare, wry smile. "I'm good at compartmentalizing. Ask any of my exes."

"Ex-wives?"

"None of my relationships got as far as marriage."

She contemplated the subject of his exes and decided she really did not want to know anything more about them. Then she remembered the paintings on the walls of his home. He might be good at compartmentalizing, but he was paying a price.

"Are all of your cases as exciting as the Colony cult case?" she asked.

"No, fortunately."

"I couldn't help but notice that you seem to be very successful in the private investigation business. I always assumed the good money in that line came from corporate security work. But your website states that you don't take those kinds of jobs."

"I prefer to work with private individuals. People like you. People who can't or won't go to the police."

"I see."

His mouth kicked up a little at the corner. "You want to know where my money comes from."

"You mentioned that you have been successful with your investments."

"My talent has one useful side effect," he said. "It gives me a certain insight into the financial markets."

"Convenient. Wish my talent had an upside like that. How does your special insight work?"

"I know what spooks individuals and markets," he said, his voice tightening. "With that kind of information it's not hard to decide where to put your money."

"You make it sound so easy."

Gideon did not respond.

"I get the feeling making money is boring for you," she said.

"I've got bills like everyone else."

"Your investigation work is your true passion, isn't it?"

He seemed surprised by the question. "I've never thought of my investigation work as a passion, but it feels like I'm doing what I'm supposed to be doing. You could say it's a branch of the family business."

"What, exactly, is the family business?"

"Sweetwater Security. It's a consulting firm. Does mostly extremely boring work for the government and one or two outside clients. What about you? Are you passionate about photography?"

Okay, that was a quick change of subject. She got the feeling he did not want to go too deeply into the work his family's firm did for the government. Probably classified.

"I'm drawn to photography," she admitted. "But I can't seem to find the right niche. I'm getting by, barely, on real estate shoots and CEO headshots and pet portraits, but I don't love that work. I failed at fashion photography. I don't have the artistic vision it takes to make it in the art world. I'm not interested in videos. And to make life even more difficult, I prefer to work with old-school prism-and-mirror cameras and black-and-white film."

"What do you like to shoot?"

"I love photographing abandoned buildings that have an interesting past. Hotels. Spas. Asylums. Hospitals. So much atmosphere. But that's about it, really, and there's not much money in that end of the market. As far as I can tell, my stupid talent doesn't come with a useful side effect." She paused. "Unlike, say, a psychic feel for the financial markets."

"You're not going to let that go, are you?"

"Probably not."

CHAPTER TWELVE

THE EARTHQUAKE DID a lot of structural damage," Amelia said, "but it was the fire that gutted the central section of the hotel, where the clinic was located."

"I can see that," Gideon said.

He and Amelia were standing in what had once been the sweeping front drive at the entrance to the Lucent Springs Hotel. The ruins stood alone in the desert, a few miles outside the small community of Lucent Springs. The structure was a sprawling two-story monument to the 1930s Southern California architectural mash-up of Art Deco and Hollywood's version of Spanish Colonial architecture.

Amelia had explained that the hotel had originally been built as an upscale sanatorium for wealthy patients suffering from tuberculosis. The medical theory at the time had held that the warmth of the sun and the dry air of the desert were the best therapies for the disease.

By the 1940s the hotel had been converted into a luxury resort that catered to the rich and famous. In its day it must have been an impressive destination, he thought. Nevertheless, in the end the rich and famous had chosen Palm Springs, Burning Cove, and Phoenix for their winter playgrounds. Several attempts had been made to renovate the hotel in the ensuing years but they had failed.

The gardens had long since disappeared beneath cacti and tumbleweeds but some of the colonnaded walkways still stood. Most of the windows in the central structure and the two side wings were either studded with jagged shards of glass or empty entirely. The remaining room doors hung on rusted hinges. The walls were crumbled in places and badly charred in others.

The history of the hotel was interesting, but in that moment he was focused on Amelia's reaction to the ruins. Her tension level had increased with each mile of the trip from San Diego to Lucent Springs. It had probably been a mistake to tell her about his stalker, but he'd had no choice. He'd had to explain the wedding veil.

He knew she was exerting a lot of willpower now in an attempt to appear calm and in control. He wondered if she was going to have an anxiety attack and then he wondered what he could do if she did. He had some skills, but offering comfort was not one of them. He could send her straight into a nightmare but he did not know how to pull her out of one.

And she thought she had a depressing talent.

"Walk me through everything you can remember about the day you arrived here for what you thought was a job interview," he said.

She gave a small start, as if she had been somewhere else in her head.

"Right," she said, recovering quickly. "Talia, Pallas, and I had never met before we arrived that afternoon. We had each received an invitation to take a contract with a hotel corporation that planned to renovate the property and turn it into a destination spa. Pallas is an interior designer. She was going to restore the interiors to their former glory. Talia was supposed to chronicle the history of the place with a view toward marketing. I was asked to do a series of before-and-after photographs to record the transformation."

"How were the business arrangements handled?"

"Everything was done online until the day we met here. There was a professional website that made the hotel company look legit. The corporation claimed that it owned several luxury resorts in Asia and the South Pacific."

"Were all the supposed holdings offshore?"

"Yes. This was supposed to be their first American property." Amelia shook her head in disgust. "Later, of course, we realized we had been scammed. The business existed only on the internet. Afterward every trace of the company vanished. The website, the emails, the texts, the electronically signed paperwork and the drafts of the contracts simply disappeared. Our producer, Phoebe, is very good with tech. She's trying to find whatever may be left in the way of digital tracks."

"Has she picked up any leads?"

"Nothing we've been able to use," Amelia said.

Her fury and frustration were unmistakable but so was her fierce determination. He resisted the impulse to give her a reassuring hug for two reasons. The first was that he did not have anything to offer in the way of actual reassurance. The second was that it was always bad policy to hug a client. Not as dumb as having an affair with a client but still a really, really bad idea.

"Tell me the rest of what you remember," he said. He knew he sounded brusque and unfeeling but that seemed like the best way to handle the fraught moment.

She squared her shoulders. "I have no clear memories of what happened after we walked through the front door. Talia, Pallas, and

I woke up early the next morning strapped to gurneys inside the old sanatorium clinic."

He studied the dark entrance of the lobby. "Where is the clinic?"

"At the rear of the center section of the hotel. I'll show you."

She started toward one of the outdoor colonnaded walkways. He followed, interested by how confidently she moved through the ruins.

"Looks like you know your way around," he said.

"I've been here a number of times in the past several months," she said over her shoulder. "My friends think I'm obsessing on this damned hotel and they're right. But I keep returning because I'm certain I'm overlooking something important."

"In addition to the key?"

"Yes."

"Any idea what that might be?" he asked.

"No."

She stopped at the far end of the central building and indicated a shattered window.

"We woke up inside that room," she said. "The ground was still shaking. We could hear things falling and crashing around us. The fire was already going strong. We could smell the smoke. It was nearly dawn."

He walked to a shattered window and studied the interior of the burned-out space. The walls were blackened with soot. Ash covered the floor. The sight of the charred and twisted gurneys lined up against one wall sent an icy rage splashing through his bloodstream. Amelia had been strapped to one of those gurneys.

"How did the local police respond?" he asked.

He did not realize that he had allowed some of his emotional reaction to seep into his voice until he saw Amelia flinch. Great. Now he was frightening the client. *That is not good for business, Sweetwater.*

"The authorities did not believe us," Amelia said, her voice far too neutral. "They assumed the three of us had come out here to do some designer drugs or get drunk and accidentally started a fire."

"Was there an investigation?"

"No. Lucent Springs is a very small town. The fire department is staffed by volunteers. There are no investigators. Not that the local authorities saw any reason to conduct an investigation."

"Let's see if we can find the origin point of the fire."

They went back along the walkway, checking the interiors of the various rooms they passed. The burn patterns led to a room in the middle of one of the wings.

"This is where it started," Gideon said.

"Earthquakes often spark fires," Amelia pointed out.

"Not in this case," he said. "Someone set this one. Kids, maybe, or a transient."

"Okay, assuming you're right, what does that tell us?"

Gideon looked at her. "It tells us there may have been a witness to what happened to you and your friends that night."

"Whoever it was didn't come forward at the time. Probably afraid they would be blamed for the fire."

"It doesn't mean we can't persuade an eyewitness to talk," he said.

Amelia brightened. "With a bribe, you mean. I hadn't thought about that approach."

"Neither had I," he admitted.

"What?"

"I was thinking of a more straightforward method of convincing someone to talk," he said. "But you're right, bribery is a much better idea."

Her momentary flush of enthusiasm faded almost immediately. "I don't have a lot of cash. Business has been a little slow in the past few months. What do bribes cost?"

"Let's worry about that if we come up with an actual eyewitness."

She sighed. "What are the odds?"

"We won't know until we start looking. We'll start with our best lead."

"Which is?"

"The key you found in the ashes. I think it's a good bet that it opens a room in a small single-story motel, one that hasn't bothered to go to the expense of upgrading to key cards. We can probably assume that management didn't want to pay a locksmith to rekey the room. The place we're looking for will be somewhere nearby, because whoever booked it wasn't looking for a luxury destination resort. They wanted a location that was convenient to the Lucent Springs Hotel."

She blinked. "You're sure that key belongs to someone who was involved in what happened to Talia, Pallas, and me, aren't you?"

"Yes."

"Why?"

"Because your intuition is telling you that it is connected," he said, striving for patience.

"That's enough for you to go on?"

"For now." He frowned. "What? You don't trust your intuition?"

"Seven months ago, my intuition is what convinced me to apply for the job here at the Lucent Springs Hotel."

"Well, there's no such thing as one hundred percent certainty."

"That is not reassuring."

"Best I can do for now." He walked toward the SUV. "Let's go find the motel room that fits this key."

"How do you plan to do that? Drive to every motel and resort in the area and try the key in all the rooms that have a number ten on the door? We'd probably get arrested."

"We'll limit our search to the motels that meet our criteria," Gideon said. "Small, located nearby, minimal security, few amenities, and—"

"And what?"

"There may or may not be a cactus garden on the premises."

She raised her brows. "Is your intuition telling you there may be a cactus garden because of the partial sketch of a barrel cactus on the key?"

"I admit I'm winging it with the cactus garden guess."

CHAPTER THIRTEEN

Cutler Steen stood on the wide deck of the big house, clenching the railing with both hands. The warm California sun shone down on the calm waters of the cove and sparked diamond-bright on the vast expanse of the Pacific beyond. He was always uneasy when he left the security of his island fortress but this time the sensation of hypervigilance was worse than usual. He had become an insomniac.

He refused to consider the possibility that he was fighting off panic. He was a survivor. He did not panic.

He had done his best to secure the house here on the Southern California coast but there was no avoiding the fact that he was far more vulnerable than he was on the island.

He traveled as infrequently as possible because the risks were many and varied. A man in his business accumulated dangerous clients, competitors, and enemies. The safest place from which to operate his global security network was his headquarters on the island. There he was in control of everything, including the local government and the police.

Here on the California coast his control was far more limited. Yes, he had sophisticated security tech installed inside and around the walled-and-gated compound that surrounded the cove house, and yes, he was accompanied by a small contingent of his carefully selected security team. But whenever he left the island he was acutely aware that he no longer exercised the power he wielded at home.

He'd had no choice but to risk the journey. Time was running out. The entire project was in danger of blowing up in his face—all because of three women, three *failures*—who had launched a fucking podcast.

He had been assured that Amelia Rivers, Pallas Llewellyn, and Talia March had failed to respond either positively or negatively to the formula. Yes, they had survived a dose of the drug, but there had been no indication that the enhancing serum had been successful, no sign that they had developed any strong psychic senses. Instead, their personal lives had fallen apart. Their relationships had soured. Their careers had gone off track.

According to the medical records he had hacked into, they had sought help from therapists for complaints ranging from amnesia and sleepwalking to nightmares and hallucinations. Luckily, their memories of their lost night had not returned. But they had managed to find others who had been used in the trials.

When they fired up the *Lost Night Files* podcast it was as if the three witches had put a curse on him. His expensive, carefully planned projects had started to disintegrate.

In hindsight it had been a mistake to entrust the drug trials to his three offspring. It was rapidly becoming evident that they were failures, too.

He had never thought of Benedict, Celina, and Adriana as his children, but rather as his longest-running experiments. Each was the product of a different union, their mothers selected because they appeared to exhibit some genuine psychic ability.

He had hoped that his own talent—a gift for strategy coupled with the ability to manipulate others—would be enhanced genetically in his progeny if he mated with females who also possessed a sixth sense. Each woman had conveniently disappeared shortly after giving birth. He had taken care of that part of the process personally to make certain the bodies would never be found. And then he had proceeded to place his three infant test subjects into the hands of nannies, tutors, and the best private schools.

Until recently he had been satisfied with the results. His offspring had, indeed, inherited some paranormal talent from him as well as from their mothers, although it had manifested in different ways in each individual—nothing extraordinarily powerful, but enough to give each of them an edge against the competition in a tough world.

And then, a little over a year ago, the directors of a small offshore pharmaceutical lab had approached him with an offer to provide him with access to a drug they claimed enhanced the psychic senses. There was, of course a catch. The drug was in a highly experimental stage. Results were dangerously unpredictable. Human trials were needed to fine-tune the formula and determine a profile of the ideal candidates—those who could both tolerate the drug and benefit from it.

The directors had guaranteed him access to the final version of the formula provided he arranged for the drug trials to be conducted. He had jumped at the opportunity. A drug that could generate or enhance paranormal sensitivity promised incredible potential. So much more efficient than trying to breed for strong paranormal senses.

He had envisioned expanding his elite mercenary forces with psychically talented spies and assassins. Their services would be for sale to dictators, warlords, and others willing to pay top dollar for discretion and efficiency.

And then there was the dazzling prospect of being in a position to market the promise of genuine psychic talent to those who could afford the astronomical prices he would charge.

But mostly he was obsessed with the prospect of enhancing his own natural talent. He would found a dynasty. His name and his bloodline would become legend.

Now three women threatened his dreams of an empire. Rivers, Llewellyn, and March should not have become a problem, but here he was—with a problem. The fucking podcast was getting too close.

"Falcon is here to deliver his report, Mr. Steen."

Cutler flinched violently, startled by the sound of the voice. He immediately regained control but he was aware of the ominous tremor that flickered at the edge of his awareness. *Not panic,* he assured himself. A searing jolt of fury shot through him. He wanted to yell at the guard, fire him on the spot. Hurl him over the railing onto the rocks below the cliff.

You're overreacting, Steen.

He pulled hard on his control and managed to rein in his temper.

He turned to look at the armed man in the black uniform standing in the doorway. "About time he showed up. Send him out here, Twitchell."

"Yes, sir."

Twitchell inclined his head and went back across the great room of the big house. A moment later Falcon walked out onto the deck.

"Nice day," Falcon said.

Cutler ignored the pleasantry. Until two months ago Falcon had been properly respectful. A loyal subordinate who would take a bullet for his employer. When Cutler had hired him, Falcon had been on the run and pathetically grateful for the opportunity. But his attitude had begun to change after he had been given the first dose of the new version of the drug. He was starting to assume a certain equality between the two of them. Acting as if they were business partners, not employer and employee.

The situation was annoying but Cutler was aware that he could not afford the time it would take to get rid of Falcon and find someone else who could tolerate the drug. One of the things he had discovered in the course of the research trials was that many people could not handle the serum. They either died immediately or spiraled rapidly into insanity and death.

"What the fuck went wrong this time?" Cutler asked.

"There was an unexpected twist," Falcon said. He lounged against the railing. "The target hired a PI named Sweetwater. Took me a while to put it together. Yesterday I followed her to his address. I checked him out. He's licensed. But I didn't think he would be a problem until last night. No homeless guy could have taken out Hurnley. Must have been Sweetwater. Probably had some martial arts training."

"Sweetwater?" Cutler frowned. He had memorized every name on the list. "Gideon Sweetwater?"

"Yeah." Falcon's brows rose. "You know him?"

Cutler shook his head. "Never met the man, but he's on the list of potential candidates for the drug."

Falcon's expression hardened. "Did he receive a dose?"

"No. I considered him briefly at one point but I put him at the bottom of the list."

"Why?"

Cutler pulled up memories of the background checks he had done on each of the names on the list. "The family business is a security consulting firm. Government contractor. If something happened to Gideon Sweetwater, people with some serious connections would probably start asking questions. I don't want that kind of attention if it can be avoided."

"This particular Sweetwater operates a small-time, one-man investigation agency, but he managed to interfere in the pickup. He took Hurnley by surprise. Knocked him down. Hurnley hit his head pretty hard. He's still unconscious. Weaver says he thinks Hurnley is in a coma. Says he needs an ER."

"We can't risk it."

"You said the drug doesn't show up on blood tests."

Cutler grunted. "Because no one outside the need-to-know circle is aware the serum exists. You can't test for what you don't know about. But if Hurnley wakes up in a hospital there will be a lot of questions. He'll be confused and disoriented. If he's questioned he might talk."

"You think he's a security risk in his current condition?"

"Unfortunately, yes." Cutler sighed. "Fucking shame. He was a valuable asset. It won't be easy to replace him."

"Because he was one of the few who could handle the drug," Falcon said. He gave it a beat before adding, "Like you and me."

There it was again, a subtle reminder that Falcon no longer viewed himself as a subordinate. Cutler told himself to let it go. He needed to keep Falcon close, keep him loyal. For now.

In the wake of the Carnelian disaster and impatient with the slow progress of the trials, Cutler had decided to experiment on someone he *knew* possessed a degree of paranormal talent—himself.

He had been thrilled with the results initially. His natural ability for strategy and manipulation had been greatly enhanced. He could identify an individual's strengths and weaknesses with astonishing accuracy. Talk about knowing what buttons to push. He could pinpoint weaknesses and exploit them with ruthless precision.

That was just the beginning. As the weeks went by and he had settled into his heightened talent he had learned how to identify and short-circuit vital wavelengths in an individual's aura. When he had taken out one of his competitors at a cocktail party hosted by a warlord, leaving no evidence, he had realized he could kill with his enhanced paranormal senses. The discovery had been intoxicating.

That was when he had decided to risk another dose of the drug. He had not only survived; he had become even stronger.

He had repeated the experiment with Falcon. The results had been equally satisfactory. Falcon's natural speed, physical coordination, strength, and keen eyesight combined with a ruthless, sociopathic personality had made him a lethal human predator. The serum had turned him into a superb assassin.

On the basis of that success Cutler had given the drug to a few more of his most trusted security people.

It was only after they had all been injected with the second dose that they had begun to experience the side effects. Some were tolerable—night sweats, insomnia, bad dreams, short-term fevers. But those had been followed by a disturbing restlessness and agitation. In the past his three offspring had never questioned his decisions, but now he caught them studying him covertly. He knew that look. They were searching for signs of weakness.

When the new talents began to fade and he and Falcon and the others had started to deteriorate he had demanded an explanation from the directors of the pharmaceutical lab. They had concluded that continuous boosters were required to maintain peak efficiency of the serum.

So now they were all on a three-week schedule. That meant they were dependent on an offshore lab—location unknown—for a continuing supply of the drug. It was intolerable.

"By the way, I'm almost due for another booster," Falcon said.

Cutler shot him an irritated look. "We all are. Don't worry, I've got the next round of doses. I'll give you what you need for yourself and the others. Hurnley won't be needing his."

"We can't go on being dependent on that fucking lab," Falcon said. "We've got to get our hands on the formula and set up our own in-house facility."

"I'm working on it." Cutler grimaced because he could feel the acid of his frustration eating up his insides. "But we need a stable version of the drug and the only people who have the knowledge required to create it are the directors of that lab. Grabbing the current formula would leave us in the same situation we face now."

Falcon grunted. "I know."

"Meanwhile, we have another priority. Pick up Rivers. No more mistakes."

"What about Sweetwater?"

"If he gets in the way again, get rid of him. We'll have to risk it. Try to make it look good. I'd rather not attract attention but I'm running out of time. I can't afford to stay here in California a minute longer than necessary."

"Understood."

This time Falcon sounded a little more subdued. That was good,

Cutler thought. Evidently the man had remembered that his boss was the one who had access to the directors of the lab and, therefore, access to the boosters.

One thing was certain. Whoever controlled the serum was the one with the power.

CHAPTER FOURTEEN

HE CACTUS GARDEN Motel was a sun-bleached relic from another era. *Make that another century,* Amelia decided. It looked
like it dated from the 1950s, but if it had set the standards for the
architectural style known as mid-century modern, the trendy look
would never have been revived.

There was no golf course, no spa, no restaurant, no bar, no security cameras. The desert surrounded it on all sides, crouched and
ready to take over the property on short notice. The sole amenity
was a small swimming pool in the courtyard. The landscaping consisted of some scruffy palms, a handful of bushy paloverde trees, and,
yes, a cactus garden—assuming you counted two ocotillo and three
barrel cacti as a garden.

There were only a handful of vehicles in the parking lot behind
the rooms. The space marked number ten was empty. On the way
to the manager's office Gideon casually inserted the mystery key
into the lock. The door opened easily.

"Damn," Amelia said. She watched him relock the door. "You're
good at this investigation stuff."

"Glad you're impressed." Gideon dropped the key into a plastic baggie and slipped it into the pocket of his trousers. "But it wasn't hard to figure out that this motel is exactly what I would have been looking for if I needed a place to stay while I conducted some illegal experiments at the Lucent Springs Hotel."

"This is a huge leap forward," Amelia said, anticipation spiking. "I knew that key was important. I just didn't know why. I hope we can get a room here for tonight."

"Rooms," Gideon corrected absently.

She flushed. "Of course. That's what I meant. Rooms. Two of them. Absolutely."

"With connecting doors," Gideon added. "I'm supposed to be your bodyguard, remember?"

"Right." She hesitated. "What if they don't have two rooms with connecting doors?"

"We'll go somewhere else if necessary."

"Sharing a room wouldn't be the end of the world," she ventured. "We're adults. Who cares how it looks? Besides, it's not as if we haven't spent a night under the same roof. You slept in my living room last night."

"That was different," he said.

His stubborn refusal to consider sharing a hotel room was starting to irritate her. You'd think she was suggesting a hookup.

"How is it different?" she demanded.

"Never mind." He stopped in front of the door marked *Manager*. "You've got our story straight?"

"Of course I do," she said. "I'm the one who invented it, remember?"

Great. Now she was snapping at him. What was happening here? She needed to stay in control.

Either Gideon did not notice her small flash of temper or else he chose to ignore it. He opened the door of the manager's office and followed her inside.

"NO PROBLEM WITH connecting rooms," the manager said. He had introduced himself as Pete Ellerbeck. He was middle-aged, partially bald, and endowed with an outgoing, friendly manner. "Most of 'em connect. Double beds in each room. Take your pick. We're not very full tonight. You'll probably want to be close to the pool."

"How about a couple of rooms near the ice machine?" Gideon asked.

Amelia glanced at him, surprised. She had assumed he would request room number ten.

"Let's see, that would be ten and eleven," Pete said. "Here you go." He put two keys on the counter.

Okay, Amelia thought. She had to hand it to Gideon. That had been a very slick maneuver.

"You say you're in town to do a photo essay on the old Lucent Springs Hotel?" Pete asked, lounging against the counter.

"That's right," Amelia said. "I'm a photographer. Gideon is my assistant. We're working on a series on abandoned hotels of the West Coast. You'd be surprised how many there are scattered around the area, especially out in the desert. They've all got a history, and several have ghosts."

Pete snorted. "The Lucent Springs Hotel has a few stories, I can tell you that. Lot of movie stars stayed there in the old days. Wouldn't be surprised if there are a couple of ghosts hanging around as well."

"You sound like you know a lot about the hotel." Amelia gave him her shiniest smile, the one she used when she was trying to get

CEOs to give her a warm and friendly expression for the company's annual report. "We would love to interview you while we're here."

"Sure," Pete said. "Glad to help out."

"We're in a rush because we recently found out that the hotel is going to be demolished," Gideon said.

"That's the word around town," Pete said. "Some big international hotel chain picked it up real cheap over a year ago. Talk was they planned to renovate it. But there was an earthquake and a fire a few months later. Did a lot of damage. The company has concluded it would cost too much to rebuild so they're going to take it all the way down to the ground. As it stands now, those ruins are a big liability. Lawsuit city if someone gets hurt out there."

"Probably a magnet for kids looking for a place to hang out with their friends," Gideon said.

Pete nodded. "Oh, yeah. Kids. Transients. Idiot tourists. The fire was caused by some out-of-town visitors who were fooling around with a drug party out there."

Amelia froze.

"Is that right?" Gideon said easily. "What happened?"

"No one knows exactly," Pete said. "Some women decided to have themselves a little fun. Got high. Must have started a fire to keep warm. There was an earthquake and the fire got out of control. The women panicked. They were lucky to make it out alive."

"You're sure they were doing drugs?" Gideon asked.

"Oh, yeah," Pete said. "No doubt about it. And whatever they were using must have been some strong stuff. I talked to Wilton, the police captain at the time. He told me the women were hallucinating like nothing he'd ever seen before. Totally bonkers."

Amelia fought the urge to jump the counter and wrap both hands around Pete's throat.

"Were they talking about UFOs and little green visitors from outer space?" Gideon asked with a chuckle.

"No." Pete snorted. "Even better. They claimed they had amnesia. Couldn't remember anything after they walked into the lobby of the old hotel but they were sure they had been kidnapped. Wilton said they sobered up real quick when he threatened to throw them in jail on suspicion of arson."

Another wave of outrage slammed through Amelia, threatening to overwhelm her. It took every ounce of control she possessed to keep from losing her temper. She wanted to scream at Pete Ellerbeck. *No one believed us and now my life and the lives of my friends are in danger. Someone tried to kidnap or murder me last night because no one believed us seven months ago. My life has been put on hold for seven months because no one believed us. I'm as afraid of the dark as a five-year-old child because no one believed us.*

Gideon must have sensed her inner turmoil, because he closed a hand around her arm in what probably looked like a casual gesture. It was anything but. His touch sent an electric shock through her. She did not have to be a mind reader to get the message. *Keep it together. We're making progress here. Don't screw this up.* Or maybe that was her intuition warning her to get a grip on her emotions.

She managed another, not-so-shiny smile for Pete. "We look forward to doing the interview with you."

"Anytime," Pete said, oblivious to the undercurrents in the atmosphere.

Gideon picked up the two keys. "Got any recommendations for dinner?"

"Closest place is the restaurant at the Sunrise Springs Lodge. A couple of miles back toward town. Can't miss it. There's also a pizza place that will deliver. The number is in the room. You don't need to worry about breakfast. It's free with your rooms. Six a.m. to ten. Served out on the pool patio in good weather. Indoors if it's too chilly."

"Thanks," Gideon said. He looked at Amelia. "Let's go get settled."

"Sure," she muttered.

She waited until they were unloading their luggage from the back of the SUV before she spoke again.

"There was no need to worry," she said, slinging the strap of her camera bag over her shoulder. "I wasn't going to cause a scene."

"I know," he said.

"No, you didn't know. You were afraid I would blow our cover."

"Not for a minute," Gideon said. He unlocked the door of room ten and disappeared inside with his duffel.

She set her teeth but she did not call him out on the lie. Okay, maybe she had been a little tense there in the office for a minute or two. She'd been under a lot of stress lately.

Opening the door of room eleven, she hauled her stuff inside and set the bags on the floor. A quick walk-through assured her that the place was clean. There were two double beds and a connecting door, as promised. In addition to the parking lot door, there was another one on the far side of the room that opened onto the courtyard.

The amenities consisted of a table, a television, a small coffee maker, and a little refrigerator. The price list for the various items in the refrigerator was taped to the top.

She went to the connecting door and unlocked it. Gideon did the same on his side. When he opened the door she found herself looking into a mirror image of her own room.

"I've got to hand it to you," she said. "Your request for a couple of rooms next to the ice machine was brilliant."

He looked amused. "Thanks. That means a lot coming from you. I know you haven't been too impressed with my investigative skills."

She flushed. "Don't push it, Sweetwater. I've been under a lot of stress lately."

"Understood."

She looked past him into room ten. "So that's the room that goes with the key I found in the ruins. Creepy, isn't it?"

"Thanks for putting that idea in my head," Gideon said. "I hadn't thought of it that way until you mentioned the creep factor."

She frowned. "Are you sure you want to sleep in there? We don't know what happened to whoever lost the key that I found."

"Are you sure you're not in the ghost-hunting business?"

She glared. "I'm serious."

"Relax." Gideon set his duffel on the luggage stand and looked around. "This room has probably been rented out hundreds of times since the person who lost that key was here."

She sighed. "I'm overreacting, aren't I?"

"Yes, but you're entitled."

"Thanks. Okay, we've got access to room ten. Now what?"

"The next step is to check the motel files to see if I can get a name and an address of the individual who stayed in this room around the time you were kidnapped."

She chilled. "You're talking about breaking into the manager's office, aren't you?"

"Don't worry, I'm good at that kind of thing."

She straightened away from the doorframe and swept out her hands. "What if you get arrested?"

"That won't happen." He glanced at his watch. "It's after five. I can't do anything useful until later tonight. We've got time to kill.

We might as well drive to that nearby resort the manager mentioned and have dinner."

Dinner. Out.

Amelia glanced at the window. Twilight was rapidly descending. By the time they got to the restaurant it would be dark. Her night vision would be at full strength.

"Something wrong?" Gideon asked.

"No," she said quickly. "I was thinking pizza. The manager said there is a place that delivers. Besides, I didn't bring any clothes suitable for going out to dinner at a resort."

"This is Southern California and we're in the desert. What you have on is fine."

She glanced down at her black jeans and long-sleeved black tee. "The thing is—"

"Are you afraid you'll run into someone who remembers you from what happened seven months ago?"

"That's unlikely," she said, thinking about it. "The only people who might recognize me on sight are the medics at the local clinic who treated Pallas and Talia and me after we escaped, and Wilton, the police captain. But he retired months ago. Oh, the reporter who covered the story for the local paper would probably remember me. But Talia, Pallas, and I did not hang around. It was pretty clear everyone blamed us for the fire."

"You said you've been back here several times."

"Yes, but only long enough to walk through the ruins and take some photos. I've never stayed overnight. To be honest, I don't trust anyone in Lucent Springs. I've always had the feeling that someone knows the truth about what happened out at the hotel. Whoever it is didn't come forward afterward, so I assume they are part of the cover-up."

"Or they were too frightened to talk to the authorities."

"Or that," she agreed.

Gideon looked at her. "All the more reason for us to go out to dinner and be seen. We want people to take an interest in us. We're looking for the eyewitness who was at the hotel that night."

He was right. Amelia steeled herself. She could do this. The night before last she had made it downstairs and out into the gardens of the apartment complex to take the photographs. True, she hadn't slept well for the rest of the night, but she had made it through until morning without succumbing to a panic attack. That was a positive sign. Dr. Pike would have been proud.

"Amelia?"

She realized Gideon was watching her a little too intently. She pulled herself together. Just a quick dash outside to the car, another short walk into the restaurant, and then back to the motel. She wouldn't be alone. Gideon would be with her.

How bad could it be?

She smiled what she hoped was a confident smile. "Sounds like a plan."

CHAPTER FIFTEEN

I RENE MORGAN WAS on her laptop checking email and doing a little shopping when she heard the muffled footsteps on the stairs. A thrill of sensual anticipation whispered through her, kicking up her pulse. Falcon was here.

As she had told Amelia, he had a real name, but his code name, Falcon, suited him. Amelia had guessed correctly. Falcon was dangerous. Irene looked at Daisy and Dahlia, who were cruising serenely past the little bubble-blowing diver on the bottom of the aquarium.

"That's what makes him so much fun," she said.

The goldfish ignored her, as was their habit. They only took a serious interest in her when they spotted her approaching their water world with a jar of fish food. They had priorities. She respected that. She had priorities, too.

She closed down the laptop and got to her feet. Falcon was the polar opposite of the boring men who drifted in and out of her life. With the notable exceptions of a special forces operative and a race car driver—both of whom had been brief, whirlwind affairs—she invariably found herself in the company of singularly dull males. Tech bros. CEOs. Politicians. They all had three things in common: they were narcissists to the core, they expected her to do all of the work in bed, and they got fever-hot when she put on the leather gear and pulled out the dominatrix paraphernalia.

Falcon was different. Sure, he was a narcissist, but he had a real edge. He wasn't looking for someone to whip him into an erection. He liked to be in charge.

Three sharp raps sounded on her door. She made her way across the living room. She was very certain that Falcon was on the other side of the door, but she was a single woman living alone. She took a moment to check the peephole.

Falcon in all his leather glory was in the hallway. She was suddenly a little breathless.

She opened the door. "Come in. I'll be ready in a minute."

Falcon moved through the doorway and gave her a head-to-toe assessment, taking in the teal-green slip dress and the high heels. His mouth curved in a satisfied way and his eyes narrowed.

"Nice," he said. "Very nice."

"Thanks. You look good, too." She picked up the small handbag and the gossamer cashmere wrap and went back toward the door. "To tell you the truth I expected you to cancel tonight. When you texted earlier you said there had been a glitch in your current project."

"Things got fucked up last night but I'm in the process of getting the situation back under control," Falcon said. "There's going to be a delay but the end result will be the same."

"You're not worried?" she asked, moving past him into the hallway.

"No, I'm dealing with an amateur," Falcon said. "Amateurs are unpredictable, and that can complicate things, but amateurs are weak. Soft. And they have no idea what's really going on."

Something in his voice sent a flicker of anxiety through her. She was attracted to Falcon because of his dangerous edge but she did not fear him. From the outset she had been confident that in the final analysis she was the one in control. She was, after all, a lot smarter.

She remembered what she had told Amelia about her father. *He always thought he was the smartest one in the room. Until he wasn't.*

CHAPTER SIXTEEN

A MELIA WALKED THROUGH the resort parking lot like a woman walking a gauntlet. Tense, a little shaky, but resolute.

Gideon watched her out of the corner of his eye as they made their way toward the brightly lit entrance of the resort. When they reached the rectangular reflecting pool in front of the glass doors she visibly relaxed.

He stopped as if pausing to admire the brightly illuminated fountains that ran the length of the pool. Amelia halted and gave him an inquiring look.

"Something wrong?" she asked.

"I think so," he said. "This isn't about you being nervous because you're afraid you might run into someone who remembers you, is it?"

"I'm not sure what you mean—"

"A moment ago I was afraid you were going to have a panic attack. Do you want to explain why?"

"Lucent Springs holds a lot of bad memories for me."

"You were doing okay this afternoon at the ruins. Tonight you almost fell apart in a parking lot. What's wrong with this picture?"

"I did not fall apart, damn it."

"No, but it was touch-and-go there for a while."

"That is not true," she said. She sounded like she was talking through clenched teeth. "You're imagining things."

He turned away from the pool and looked at her. "There's something else going on here, and under the circumstances, I think I've got a right to know."

"What circumstances give you that right? Let's be honest. The only reason you took my case is because your uncle is responsible for that stupid list and you want to know who is doing what with it. Fine. That's a perfectly reasonable motive and your goals align with mine, at least for the moment, because I want answers, too. We are working together because we need each other for the time being but that doesn't give you a right to ask personal questions."

"Correction. I took your case because of you, not the list."

"Hah."

"Okay, maybe the list was a factor, but it wasn't the only factor. Let's get something to eat. Also, I need a drink."

He tightened his grip on his cane and started toward the glass doors. Behind him Amelia did not move. He stopped and turned around but this time he kept his mouth shut.

"If you must know, I've developed a phobia about night," she said, not meeting his eyes. "That's why I was seeing Dr. Pike."

"The therapist who wanted you to book evening appointments? The guy who might be your stalker?"

"Yes."

"That's it? That's why you were shivering back there in the parking lot?"

"You make it sound like it shouldn't be a problem. Obviously you live a phobia-free life. How nice for you."

"What, exactly, are you afraid of?"

She glared at him for a long time before she answered.

"I see things after dark," she said, her voice low and tight. "Things I don't want to see. It's as if I'm catching glimpses of other peoples' dreams and nightmares in their auras and energy prints. Sometimes I wonder—"

"If you're going insane?" he asked.

"Well, yes."

In the shadows her eyes glittered with unshed tears. Anger, he decided. Frustration. And fear. But the emotional storm was aimed inward. She was furious with herself. And she was scared.

He knew a lot about fear.

"Welcome to the dark zone," he said. He took her arm. "Every talent has one. Let's go get a drink and I will explain a few of the paranormal facts of life to you."

CHAPTER SEVENTEEN

I T'S ALL ABOUT control," Gideon said. "What was your core talent, the one you possessed before you were enhanced?"

"I was—I *am*—a pretty good photographer," Amelia said. "Not amazing, but pretty good. I've always been able to sense a vibe of energy around my subjects and shoot for it. Or not, depending on the vibe in question."

"And now?"

She sighed. "Now, after dark, I don't just pick up a vague feel for an individual's energy field. I *see* it in living color. And I'm talking about colors that don't have any names because they aren't on the normal spectrum. Going outside at night or entering an unlit room is like walking into another dimension. A ghost world."

She was beginning to relax, she realized, not just because of the wine but because she was starting to conclude she had hired the right private investigator after all. In the parking lot his aura and his prints had appeared reassuringly strong and stable.

She was also feeling quite pleased with herself. She had survived the harrowing journey across the parking lot without succumbing to an anxiety attack. She had to give Gideon credit for pushing her out of her comfort zone. The realization that she had not fallen apart when she was confronted with the murky fog of glowing energy prints on the pavement had boosted her self-confidence as nothing else had since the stupid phobia had taken root.

They were seated in a cozy booth that overlooked the illuminated swimming pool and the night-darkened golf course beyond. The restaurant decor was desert-style resort casual—lots of colorful tile work, dark wood, and ocher-colored walls. The menu was modern eclectic, leaning Mediterranean. The room was comfortably busy but not crowded and she was aware that, for the first time in days, she was hungry.

You ought to see me now, Dr. Pike, she thought. *I'm out at night and acting normal.*

"When did you first realize you had a core talent?" Gideon asked.

She nibbled on a chunk of herbed focaccia dipped in olive oil and sprinkled with coarse salt while she considered the question. "I'm not sure," she said finally. "I didn't think of it as a psychic ability. It was just something I gradually became aware of as I grew older. By the time I was in my late teens I was obsessed with old-school photography."

"Right," Gideon said, "you grew into your talent gradually as you grew into adulthood. Figuring out how to handle your ability was a process. There's a learning curve."

"And then one day I walked into an abandoned hotel, got slammed with a bout of amnesia, lost an entire night, and woke up the next morning with a whole new level of my basic talent," she said.

"You would have been just as shaken, just as unnerved, if you had gone to sleep one night and awakened with a sense of hearing that allowed you to listen to conversations taking place at the end of the block or across the street."

"I would have been seriously rattled. Probably would have wondered if I was delusional."

"Exactly." Gideon reached for another slice of focaccia. "My point is that it's all about control. It takes time to adapt to a powerful talent. It also helps if you have some guidance along the way. Evidently you and your friends did not have those benefits."

"No." She swirled the wine in her glass and met his eyes across the table. "Sounds like you did, though."

"There's a strong psychic vibe in the Sweetwater bloodline," Gideon said with a casually dismissive gesture. "Has been for decades. Centuries, actually."

"You're serious, aren't you?"

"Yes."

She took a moment to absorb that information. "Do all of your blood relatives have your talent?"

"Paranormal abilities take different forms in different people. No two talents are identical. But, historically speaking, the Sweetwaters tend to wind up in careers that involve criminal investigation and security."

"Why is that?"

His eyes heated a little. "Probably because we are very, very good at hunting bad guys."

She got a ping warning her that he was telling her the truth but not the whole truth. "You said your family business involves security work for the government?"

"Mostly."

Fascinated, she leaned forward and started to ask another question, but the server, a cheerful woman in her early twenties, chose that moment to arrive with the main courses. She set the plates down and smiled enthusiastically.

"I hear you two are in town to photograph the old Lucent Springs Hotel," she said.

"Word travels fast," Amelia said.

"Yeah, well, small town and everything. Pete Ellerbeck, the guy who owns the Cactus Garden Motel, talked to my boss late this afternoon and said you might be in for dinner. My name is Madison, by the way. Pete also said you were planning to talk to people who have stories about the hotel."

"That's right," Gideon said. "Do you know some of the history of that place?"

Madison chuckled. "Not the kind of history you're probably looking for. When I was in high school my friends and I used to go out there to party sometimes, but I don't think that happens much anymore. Things changed after that big hotel company bought the property and put up all the No Trespassing signs."

"I never knew a No Trespassing sign to stop people looking for a party," Gideon said.

Madison rolled her eyes. "The cops started paying more attention after three dumbass tourists went out there to do drugs one night and managed to start a fire. The hotel company is afraid someone will get hurt, so they're going to take the place down to the foundation and try to sell the property."

"We heard that," Amelia said. She would ignore the *dumbass* crack, she told herself. Priorities.

Gideon gave her an approving look, which only served to further annoy her.

Madison opened her mouth to say something else but a man seated on the other side of the room caught her eye.

"Gotta go," she said. "Enjoy your dinner."

There was a short silence. Amelia looked at Gideon. There was a thoughtful stillness about him.

"What?" she said.

He picked up his fork. "There's no record of the offshore hotel company existing and yet the rumor here in Lucent Springs is that the nonexistent corporation is planning to go to the trouble and expense of demolishing a property that has no value. Why bother? Why not walk away and let the hotel rot into the desert? It's not as if injured parties would be able to track down a phantom company and sue."

"Okay, good question. Do you have an answer?"

"Maybe. It looks like you and the *Lost Night Files* podcast team have become more than a nuisance to whoever is behind the experiments."

"That may explain why they tried to grab me but it doesn't tell us why the fake company would schedule the demolition of the Lucent Springs Hotel."

"I can think of one very good reason why someone might want those ruins razed to the ground."

"What?"

"It would be the only way to be sure that all the evidence was erased."

"But there is no evidence out there in the ruins," she said. "I should know. I've spent hours looking around and photographing that damned hotel."

"You found that key," Gideon reminded her.

"But that's all."

"There's a chance there's more evidence. I'm talking about the paranormal kind."

"If there is, I haven't been able to sense it."

"You told me your talent works best at night. Ever been out there after dark?"

She stopped breathing. Her throat got tight. The back of her neck was suddenly ice-cold.

"No," she admitted. "But I really don't think that's a good idea."

Damn. Now she sounded weak.

"If you want evidence of the sort you can perceive with your talent you'll need to look for it in the ruins at night."

She cleared her throat. "This is the desert, remember? There's a lot of nightlife. Scorpions, snakes, spiders."

"We've got flashlights and boots."

She did not like the casual way he brushed aside her very legitimate concerns. "You're kind of a hard-ass, aren't you?"

"When I'm working I tend to be very focused."

"I noticed." She couldn't blame him. When she was working with a camera she was focused, too. She swallowed hard. "Are we going out there tonight?"

"No, tonight I'm going to take a look around the manager's office at the motel, remember? I want to try to ID the individual who lost the key to room ten in the ruins."

She relaxed a little. She had a twenty-four-hour reprieve. "Right."

Gideon frowned, as if he had finally realized just how unenthusiastic she was about an after-dark tour of the scene of her lost night.

"You won't be alone out there," he said. "I'll be with you."

She turned that over a few times in her head. The thought of a night visit to the old hotel was daunting, but he was right. Maybe she had missed some important evidence because of her phobia.

"I know," she said, resigned.

"I wouldn't ask you to do this if I didn't think it's a way to get some answers."

She gave him a steely smile. "Enough about me. Let's talk about you. You haven't explained how your own talent works."

"Trust me, you really don't want to know."

"Yes, Gideon, I really do want to know."

He took a moment to consider her demand and then he evidently came to a decision. "I can't view auras or prints the way you do, but I'm good at picking up certain currents in the human energy field. Currents that come from a very specific portion at the far end of the spectrum."

She watched him for a moment, wondering what he wasn't telling her. "What portion?"

"I sense the energy that generates dreams," he said in an unnervingly neutral voice. "Nightmares, to be precise."

Her mouth went dry. "Nightmares?"

"According to Uncle Shelton, dream energy is the likely source of all the psychic senses. When you use your talent you tap into the dreamstate."

"While you're awake?"

"That's right," he said. "And that's what makes it so damned tricky to handle a strong psychic vibe. If you can't control the dream energy while you're awake it will overwhelm your normal senses. It can literally drive you insane. Think hallucinations. Voices. Visions. Delusions."

"Are you telling me you see other people's nightmares?"

"No, for which I am profoundly grateful. I don't even want to think about what it would be like to have a front-row seat for other people's nightmares." Gideon ate a bite of the fish he had ordered. "My own are bad enough."

She speared some of her roasted yellow cauliflower and thought about the paintings on the walls of his library. "That must be a very . . . *annoying* talent."

The words *terrible* and *awful* and *scary* came to mind but she didn't think it would be polite to go there. The conversation was weird enough.

Gideon watched her with a look that told her he knew exactly what she was thinking.

"My talent occasionally has its uses," he said.

"In your work as an investigator, do you mean?"

"Yes. You see, I'm not just good at picking up the currents of a person's nightmares. I can trigger them."

She put down her fork with great care. "You could send me into a nightmare? While I'm awake?"

"While you're awake."

She swallowed. "What would happen?"

Gideon's eyes got a faint, silvery sheen. He watched her intently. She knew he was waiting to see how she would react to what he was telling her.

"Turns out the human mind can't deal with that kind of sensory overload," he said quietly. "It shuts down. Sometimes permanently."

"Are you telling me you can *kill* someone with their own nightmares?"

"I can use your own nightmares to scare you to death, Amelia."

CHAPTER EIGHTEEN

ER PHONE RANG.

Amelia flinched. *Of course I flinched*, she thought. *The man on the other side of the table just informed me that he could murder me with my own dreams.*

So much for concluding that she had hired the right investigator. Was he telling her the truth? Was murder by nightmares even a thing? Was he delusional?

She reminded herself that the strength in his energy field had been rock-solid stable.

The phone rang again. The couple at a nearby table glared. She raised a hand in apology and yanked the device out of her bag. She expected to see Talia's or Pallas's name but she flinched again when she saw the identity of her caller. She started to decline but, on impulse, changed her mind.

"Why, hello, Dr. Pike," she said, lowering her voice and infusing it with all the cheery warmth and charm she could summon. "I wasn't expecting you to call. I'm afraid this isn't a very convenient time."

On the other side of the table, Gideon's brows rose. She could not tell if he was amused or merely curious. Maybe both.

"Amelia, where are you?" Norris Pike's voice was sharp with what was probably concern, but his authoritative tone was irritating, nonetheless. "I've been worried about you. You're not at home. That's not like you."

She tightened her grip on the phone, aware that Gideon was close enough to hear both ends of the conversation.

"How do you know I'm not there?" she asked, replacing the warmth and charm with ice.

"When you didn't answer my earlier calls I started to wonder if you were in trouble," Norris said. "Anxiety attacks can be quite debilitating. I was afraid you might be dealing with depression. I dropped by your apartment to check on you."

"You went to my apartment?"

Norris ignored the outrage. "As your therapist, I had every right to be concerned. One of your neighbors heard me knocking on your door. She told me she saw you leave this morning with a male friend and a suitcase. She suggested you might have taken off for a couple of days, but she had no idea where you were."

"Sounds like you talked to Irene," Amelia said. "You'll be delighted to know that she was right. I'm out of town with a friend. At the moment we're having dinner in a very nice restaurant, so I'm going to hang up because it's rude to take calls in restaurants. Goodbye, Dr. Pike."

"Are you telling me you're on a date?" Norris demanded, sounding stunned. "At night?"

"I know, I'm a little surprised myself. But, yes, it's a real date and it is definitely night. Progress, Dr. Pike. There's hope for me after all. Bye."

"Wait, don't hang up."

She ended the call and dropped the phone into her bag. When she turned back she found Gideon watching her with a speculative expression.

"You're wondering if Norris Pike is my stalker, aren't you?" she asked.

"You said you had never had an opportunity to view his aura or see his prints after dark, so you haven't been able to compare them to the photos of the stalker's prints."

"True," she said. She smiled.

"What?" Gideon asked.

"Nothing." She forked up a bite of her cauliflower.

He gave her a knowing look. "You got a kick out of letting Pike think that you were on a date, didn't you?"

"I did. Give me a break. This is the closest I've come to anything resembling a real date since my lost night."

Gideon's eyes gleamed with what looked like genuine amusement. "Should I feel used?"

She managed a smile but the little rush of satisfaction she had experienced when she told Norris Pike she was out on a date at night was already dissipating. In its place was the realization that she was sharing connecting rooms with a man who claimed to be able to kill with psychic powers.

Her life had gotten complicated.

CHAPTER NINETEEN

IDEON BROUGHT THE SUV to a halt behind room ten of the Cactus Garden Motel and shut down the engine. Amelia unclipped her seat belt, collected her tote, and prepared to open the door.

It had been a mistake to tell her the truth about his talent, Gideon thought. He should have known better. He *did* know better. What had he been thinking? That was just it. He hadn't been thinking. He had taken the leap of faith on impulse, driven by the irrational hope that she would not only believe him but accept his talent.

At least he wasn't getting the vibe that told him she was afraid of him. That was good. Maybe she simply didn't believe him. The real problem was that he could not tell what she was thinking.

He knew she had indulged in a short-lived rush of triumph when she had informed Pike she was on a date, but the dose of endorphins had faded fast. She had gone very quiet after the phone call. He had hoped that the successful navigation of the gauntlet journey back across the resort parking lot would give her another mood boost, but she had remained locked in her quiet zone.

From out of nowhere he was hit with a sense of weary resignation bordering on despair.

He had been a fool. He should not have told her about his talent.

There had been a few occasions in the past when he had let down his guard and tried to explain his paranormal abilities to someone outside the family. The results had never been good. People either didn't believe him and concluded he was a fraud and a con or they decided he was delusional.

Amelia did not seem to have fallen into either of those two categories, but her ongoing silence was not a good sign. Maybe she had decided to take a pragmatic approach. It wasn't as if she had much choice. They both knew there were not a lot of private investigators who would take her case seriously.

"Shit."

He did not realize he had spoken aloud until Amelia paused in the act of opening the car door and turned toward him.

"Something wrong?" she asked.

"I was just wondering if you're going to fire me," he said.

"What? Oh, no, of course not."

"Because you don't have any other viable options?"

"No." She cracked open the door, jumped down to the pavement, and turned to look at him. "Because I've seen your aura and your energy prints. I'm not afraid of you, Gideon, if that's what you're worried about."

"You trust your ability to read energy well enough to make a decision like that?"

"Call it my photographer's intuition."

"Then why the silence after dinner?"

"No big deal. It's just that after Pike called it occurred to me the best way to determine whether or not he's the stalker would be for me to make an evening appointment with him. I'll need to get him into a dark place, but that shouldn't be too difficult. A lot of restaurants are dimly lit, and then there are parking lots and the gardens at my apartment complex."

He thought about that for a beat. "That's not a bad plan, as long as I'm with you or close by when you meet Pike."

"Thanks." She smiled. "I came up with the idea all by myself."

"Is that the only thing you've been thinking about for the past half hour?"

"Well, no. But trust me, you really don't want to hear about the other stuff."

He took a breath and exhaled with control. "I think I do want to hear about the other stuff."

"Are you sure? You won't like it."

"We're working as a team. It's best if I know what you're thinking."

"Okay, if you insist. Promise you won't get mad?"

"I never lose my temper." He paused. "Hardly ever."

"Right, the compartmentalizing thing. Well, the truth is, I was thinking about your talent."

He groaned. "I had a feeling that might be it."

"It must be a very difficult ability to live with," she said gently. "I don't enjoy reading auras and prints. I can't even imagine how awful it would be to pick up the vibe of other people's nightmares. I imagine that kind of energy affects your own dreams. No wonder you're big on control and focus and compartmentalizing. It explains your paintings, too. I'll bet they are how you cope with the bad stuff. Worst of all, your talent must be murder on your personal life."

Blindsided, he stared at her, struggling to recalculate. "Are you telling me you feel sorry for me?"

"Sympathetic," she corrected quickly.

"I don't need sympathy, damn it."

She held up a hand. "I warned you that you wouldn't like the answer to your question."

He pulled himself together and opened his door. "You've got that right. I sure as hell don't want you feeling sorry for me."

"Look at it this way. We're even now."

He climbed out of the car, reached back inside for his cane, and looked at her across the width of the cab. "What's that supposed to mean?"

"Don't tell me you weren't feeling sorry for me earlier tonight when you practically had to carry me across the restaurant parking lot. Do you think I liked that? I was mortified. Humiliated."

"I was trying to be supportive."

"Bullshit," she shot back. "You felt pity for me."

"That is not true."

"Your talent might have a dark side but mine is downright embarrassing. Do you know what it's like to become a recluse at night because you're afraid of the dark? Try explaining that to a potential date or your friends. You start making up excuses, but they don't work. Everyone tells you that you need therapy but what they're really thinking is that you're weak-minded. Prone to phobias and fears."

"Have you considered that you may be overreacting?"

"After a while your friends stop calling. Stop visiting. Stop inviting you to join them for drinks at the neighborhood tavern because they know you'll say you have to wash your hair instead. My talent is ruining my life. And I don't like knowing people feel sorry for me any more than you like knowing they feel sorry for you."

She shut the door of the vehicle with a forceful *ker-chunk* and stalked toward her room.

He closed his own door and went after her. "Hang on, we need to talk about this."

"Some other time." She jammed the key into the lock of her room door. "I'm not in the mood. I prefer to wallow in self-pity."

She moved into the room, flipped the light switch, and shut the door in his face. He heard the bolt slam into place.

Clients. Can't live with them. Can't run an investigation business without them.

CHAPTER TWENTY

GIDEON WAS RIGHT. She was overreacting.

Amelia went to the connecting door and yanked it open. She heard the sound of his key in the lock of the parking lot door just as she looked into his darkened room.

An ankle-deep fog of murky energy seethed on the floor. The spectral mist created by the layers of paranormal radiance was similar to what she had glimpsed in her own room a moment ago before she switched on the lights. It would disappear as soon as Gideon turned on the lights.

She was not surprised to see his prints glowing hot and silver in the fog. She would know them anywhere.

She pushed the door all the way open, crossed the threshold into room ten—and stopped, frozen with shock.

The large pool of luminous dark energy seethed on the carpet near the entrance to the small bathroom. The radiation wasn't fresh but she knew the cause; knew that it would take a long time to fade—years maybe. She had occasionally viewed similar stains in houses she had photographed for her real estate clients. She hated those jobs.

"Oh, shit," she whispered.

Gideon got the outside door open, moved into the room, and hit the wall switch, flooding the space with normal light. The fog of paranormal energy and the unnerving stain on the carpet disappeared.

"Amelia?" Gideon came toward her, his eyes tight with concern. "What's wrong?"

She took another breath. She was not alone and the man with her did not think she was mentally unstable. He believed she was merely having a little trouble learning to control her other vision. He seemed to think it was perfectly normal for her to be unnerved from time to time. Hey, it could happen to anyone.

Control.

She wrapped her arms around her midsection. "I think something terrible happened in this room."

He did a quick, thoughtful survey of the space and then looked at her again. "What did you see a moment ago when the lights were off?"

"Hang on, I need to be sure."

She unfolded her arms and went back into her room. Opening the camera bag, she took out the old Nikon. Immediately her nerves steadied. She could do this.

She went back to the doorway. "Please turn off the lights again."

Without a word, Gideon moved to the wall switch and flipped it, plunging the room into darkness. The gray fog flooded back, drifting low across the worn carpet. The terrible stain near the bathroom radiated an eerie light.

She examined the scene through the viewfinder. Now, thanks to the camera lens, she could make out the details. There was no longer any doubt.

"What do you see?" Gideon asked quietly.

She lowered the camera. "Someone died here. Not natural causes. Murder."

CHAPTER TWENTY-ONE

ECENTLY?" GIDEON ASKED.

He was not questioning her statement, she realized. Just looking for more information. Knowing that made it easier for her to concentrate.

"Good question." She raised the camera again and focused on the disturbing pool of paranormal radiance. "Not recently as in last night or last week. I think we're talking months, not years. That's not very helpful, is it?"

"You never know. Every data point matters."

"Like you said, there's a learning curve when it comes to talent." She started to lower the camera but a flicker of energy at the edge of her vision made her stop. She focused again and turned slowly in a circle, taking a close look at the rest of the room.

"What do you see?" Gideon asked.

"There are some weird prints around the minibar," she said. "They look like they date from about the same time as the murder stain but they are still unusually hot." She lowered the camera. "They shouldn't be so hot."

"Unless they were laid down with a lot of intense emotion."

"Yes." She brightened. "Yes, that makes sense." Intrigued by the notion, she raised the camera again. "Hmm. I think you're right. Whatever it is, it's not a happy vibe, I can tell you that much. More like frightened. Panicky."

Gideon crossed to the small refrigerator and opened the door. "Any prints inside?"

She walked closer to the minibar and examined the interior through the camera lens. "Yes, but not the same as those on the outside. It looks like whoever left the hot prints was trying to move the minibar."

"Let's take a look."

Gideon switched on the lights and went back to the small refrigerator. He leaned his cane against the nearby table, gripped the minibar on either side, and eased it away from the wall.

He checked the back. "There's a piece of white cardboard taped to the rear panel."

Amelia watched him remove the cardboard. When he straightened she saw that he was holding one side of what had once been a small white box. She moved closer to get a better look. Aurora Islands Pharmaceutical Laboratory was emblazoned in blue on one side. Stunned, she looked at Gideon.

"It's the same as the box in the photograph that came from Night Island," she said. "The first three letters are identical. 'Aur.' It can't be a coincidence."

"Trust me, I'm not about to argue. I agree with you." Gideon turned the cardboard over and looked at the other side. "It gets better. Take a look."

He gave her the small piece of cardboard. There was a short, hand-printed note on the back. She read it aloud. "'My name is Dr. S.

Fulbrook. If you find this message it means I'm dead. This company murdered me.'"

"You were right," Gideon said. "The photo of a portion of a box that your friends brought back from Night Island was a lead."

"Yes." Amelia looked up from the note, excitement sparking and flashing across all of her senses. "I knew it was important. But I would not have found that note if it hadn't been for you."

"You're the one who tracked it down."

"Only because I'm starting to think in terms of focus and control," she said. "That's your doing. I've got a long way to go but I can see a path forward. I must admit I've made more progress in the past twenty-four hours, thanks to you, than I did after a month of appointments with Dr. Pike."

Gideon gave her an unreadable look. "Yeah, well, that's great."

"You know, this could be a new career path for you."

"Advising people on how to cope with their suddenly enhanced paranormal senses? Somehow I don't think there would be much demand for that particular service. It's not like there are a lot of newly minted psychics running around, and I don't think I'm cut out to be a counselor."

"It could be a sideline."

"Forget it." He switched his attention back to Fulbrook's note. "We need to find out whatever we can about this pharmaceutical company."

"Right," she said. "I'll call Phoebe in Seattle right now and have her get started on a search. Trust me, she's got a real talent for that kind of thing."

"Tell her she can probably assume it's an offshore operation."

"What makes you think that?" she asked, curious.

"Aside from the fact that it is most likely engaged in some very illegal activities, you mean?"

"Well, yes."

"The name of the company," Gideon said. "The Aurora Islands are phantom islands off the coast of South America. Supposedly they've been sighted a couple of times over the centuries but no one has ever found them. Looks like whoever named the lab is into irony."

"I get it. Fake islands, fake pharmaceutical company."

"I'm sure the lab is real. It's just not going to be easy to find."

Amelia looked at the carpet near the bathroom door. A somber knowing whispered through her. "Please turn out the lights. I need to take another look at something."

Without a word, Gideon switched off the lights again.

She raised her camera and studied the luminous dark energy on the carpet. When she was certain of her conclusion she lowered the camera.

"The person who died over there on the floor is the same individual who left the prints on the minibar," she said. "Dr. Fulbrook did not make it out of this room alive."

CHAPTER TWENTY-TWO

I T WAS ONE o'clock in the morning. The rooms in the Cactus Garden Motel were dark except for the thin edges of light that framed the shade covering the window of Amelia's room. There was not a lot of nightlife in the town of Lucent Springs to keep visitors out late, and evidently none of the handful of motel guests were insomniacs, Gideon thought.

He made his way to the manager's office through the shadowy parking lot. Pete Ellerbeck's truck was parked in back of his residence but the windows were dark. There were no flickering lights indicating late-night television or internet activity.

The lock on the back door of the office succumbed to the pick. There was no alarm system. It was easy to get careless about security matters when you lived in a small town.

He stood quietly for a moment, absorbing the feel of the empty space before he went behind the counter, took out a penlight, and started going through files.

It did not take long to find what he was looking for. Satisfied, he went back out into the night.

An electric frisson of awareness whispered across the back of his neck. For a moment he went very still in the shadows, his senses wide open.

Nothing moved. No one jumped out from behind a parked car. But he had done enough watching from the shadows to know when he was the one being watched.

CHAPTER TWENTY-THREE

Amelia was on the phone with Phoebe when she heard Gideon let himself into the other room.

"Hang on, he's back," she said. "Maybe he found the information we need. I'll put you on speaker."

"Excellent," Phoebe said, her voice infused with anticipation.

Amelia went to the opening between the two rooms. Gideon was in the process of locking the back door.

"Any luck?" she asked. She held up the phone. "I've got Phoebe here."

Gideon turned away from the door. There was a cold heat in his eyes. "Hello, Phoebe. Nice to meet you."

"Same," Phoebe said. "Amelia told me about the box with the logo of the pharmaceutical company and she gave me the name of the man who wrote the note."

"Good," Gideon said.

Amelia smiled at him. "You found something, didn't you?"

"Maybe," he said.

"My room." She turned and led the way to the small table near the window.

He followed and sat down across from her. She put the phone on the table.

"Okay," she said. "We're listening."

"Dr. S. Davis checked into room ten two nights before the day that you and your friends were kidnapped," Gideon said. "There is no question that Davis is Fulbrook."

"I *knew* there was a connection," Amelia said. A thrill of satisfaction snapped through her. The scorched key, like the photo of the pharmaceutical box, was an important clue. Her intuition had not betrayed her.

"You're sure that Dr. S. Davis is S. Fulbrook?" Phoebe asked.

"I checked the handwriting on the registration form," Gideon said. "Davis and Fulbrook are one and the same. He paid cash up front, so there's no credit card trail. I'm sure the address on the form will turn out to be a fake, but the manager made an interesting note—Davis lost his room key. He was issued a second key."

"*Yes,*" Amelia said softly.

Amusement flashed briefly in Gideon's eyes. She ignored him.

"Here's what I've got so far," Phoebe said. "There was a Dr. Scott Fulbrook who was the director of research at a small startup pharmaceutical company in Silicon Valley. The startup got bought out by one of the big pharma companies but it looks like Fulbrook was not part of the deal. In fact, he was fired."

"The acquiring company did not keep the startup's director of research?" Gideon asked. "That's unusual."

"I think I've found an explanation for why they dumped Fulbrook," Phoebe said. "There's a reference to a government investigation into his research results. He was suspected of fraud."

"Was?" Amelia asked. "Past tense?"

"He seems to have dropped out of sight about a year ago," Phoebe concluded.

"Anything yet on Aurora Islands Pharmaceutical Laboratory?" Gideon asked.

"No," Phoebe said. "Pretty sure it's not a U.S.-based company, as you suspected, but that's all I can tell you. I need more time."

"Call as soon as you have any information," Amelia said.

"Will do," Phoebe said.

"Can you update the others for me?" Amelia asked. "I'm sure Talia and Luke and Pallas and Ambrose must be wondering what's going on."

"I'll bring them up to speed when they check in. At the moment they are all still off the grid. No cell phone service for any of them."

"All right," Amelia said. "Thanks, Phoebe."

She ended the call and looked at Gideon. "What aren't you telling me?"

He cranked back in the chair and stretched out his injured leg with some caution. "What makes you think I'm not telling you everything?"

"Maybe I'm getting to know you."

"Huh. Maybe you are. Okay, here's what I didn't tell Phoebe. I'm pretty sure someone is watching us."

Amelia went cold. "The gang that tried to kidnap me?"

"That's definitely a possibility. But there are others."

"Such as?"

"We've attracted some attention here in Lucent Springs. One or more of the locals may be taking an interest in us."

"I wish we knew who."

"Maybe Pete Ellerbeck," Gideon said.

"The manager?"

"Think about it. He's closer to the situation than just about anyone. If you're right, if someone was murdered in my room—"

"I'm certain of it."

"He has to know something about what happened, even if he doesn't realize it. We'll see what we can get out of him when we interview him." Gideon gripped his cane and pushed himself to his feet. "Meanwhile, we both need some sleep. Neither one of us got a lot of rest last night and today has been a very long day."

Alarmed, she stood quickly. "Where are you going?"

He turned in the doorway and looked at her in mild surprise. "I thought it was obvious. I'm going to bed."

"You can't sleep in that room."

"Why not?"

She swept out both hands. "Because someone died in there. Obviously."

Gideon glanced into his room and then looked back at her. "Assuming your analysis is correct, that happened seven months ago."

"Trust me, there's still way too much negative energy in that room. It's not just the vibe of the actual death, it's all the panic and horror and desperation. The whole room is saturated with it. Now that I've seen it with my other vision I can't unsee it."

"I understand," he said. "But you're a lot more sensitive to that kind of energy than I am. There's no reason it will bother me."

She folded her arms and raised her chin. "Just because you don't sense it in your waking state doesn't mean it won't affect your dreams. You're the one who gave me the lecture on how dreamstate energy is the source of all the psychic senses. If that's true, it's vitally important to practice good sleep hygiene."

He looked at her as if she had just dropped in from another dimension. "Sleep hygiene?"

"Never mind." She unfolded her arms and waved at the bed nearest the closet in her room. "You can have that one. I prefer the one closest to the window."

Gideon glanced at the beds. "There may be something to your theory about negative energy affecting the dreamstate, but I don't think it would be a good idea for me to accept your offer."

"Why not? You slept in my living room last night. This isn't much different."

"It's different."

"Why? Because we would be sharing the same room? Separate beds, Gideon. We're adults. It will be like camping out in the same tent. Sort of."

His jaw tightened. "It would be different."

"How?"

He braced a hand against the doorframe and looked at her with slightly savage eyes. "Earlier this evening you felt sorry for me because you assumed my talent probably complicated my relationships."

"And you got pissed because you didn't want me offering sympathy."

"I don't want your sympathy any more than you want me thinking you're weak because your talent has made your life difficult. But you were right about one thing. My psychic vibe definitely screws up personal relationships."

"Meaning?"

"Meaning I can't sleep with someone else in close proximity."

She reflected on that for a beat. "Because other people's dreamstate energy affects your own dreams? I can see where that might be a problem."

"No, Amelia, the problem is that I give other people nightmares."

"That's hard to believe."

"Trust me, you do not want to run the experiment to find out if I'm telling you the truth."

She tilted her head slightly to one side. "Why do you give other people nightmares?"

Gideon groaned. "Let's save this discussion for morning, okay?"

"No. I want to know the answer."

"Fine. You want to spend what's left of the night discussing paranormal biophysics? You've got it. Uncle Shelton thinks the basic problem is that I can't control my dreamstate when I'm asleep the way I can when I'm awake. The dream energy in my aura overwhelms anyone with the bad luck to be sleeping nearby."

"Huh."

"You think the vibe from the murder in the other room might give me nightmares? It's nothing compared to what I can do to your dreams."

"Interesting. When did your sleep issues first appear?"

He stared at her in disbelief. "What the hell? Are you trying to psychoanalyze me?"

"I'm curious, okay? Hey, I've got sleep issues, too, remember?"

"My issues appeared at about the time my talent reached full power. That was in my early twenties. Look, I'm not here for therapy. I'm trying to explain why I don't think it would be a good idea for me to sleep close to you."

"Separate beds," she pointed out.

"So?"

"So, it's not the same thing as sleeping in the same bed."

"Amelia, in case you haven't noticed, the two beds in this room are only a couple of feet apart."

She glanced at the double beds. He had a point. "Have you run the experiment?"

He frowned. "Sleeping in separate beds?"

She waved at the doubles. "In close proximity like this."

"It never seemed like a good idea."

"How do you explain your sleep issues to others?"

"Mostly I avoid the conversation," he said.

There was a cold edge on the words. She pretended not to notice.

"You must have tried to tell people about your little phobia," she said gently.

"It's not a phobia, damn it." He made a visible effort to get control of his temper. "If I can't avoid it I tell people I've got a form of PTSD that makes it impossible for me to sleep in the same bed."

She flushed. "As I keep reminding you, we're talking about separate beds, not the same bed. Have you ever had an opportunity to run the experiment with someone like me? Someone with a strong paranormal vibe?"

She was sure he would say no.

"Yes," he said. "A few years ago I met Caroline. She's a botanist, a scientist who has devoted her life and her psychic talent to discovering new plants that might have potential medicinal properties."

"I see," Amelia said. Ruthlessly she tried to suppress her disappointment. "So she's really, really smart?"

"Brilliant," Gideon said. "And beautiful."

"Uh-huh," Amelia said. Great. The competition was a psychic Barbie botanist devoted to saving the world.

"Before you ask," Gideon continued, "things did not end well with her, either. It was only one bad night, but she experienced a nightmare. I believe it involved giant carnivorous plants."

"Wow. Carnivorous plants?"

"It took me a while to awaken her. During that time she was trapped in that in-between state—not quite awake but not really asleep. Paralyzed. Terrified. When she finally did come fully awake she went straight into a panic attack."

Amelia had to fight the urge to hug him. "That can't have been good for your ego."

"No shit."

"That is a very sad story, and I'd tell you that you have my sympathies, but we both know you don't want them so I won't."

"Good plan." He pushed himself away from the doorframe and turned, clearly intending to escape into his room. "Good night, Amelia."

"Wait. Nothing you've told me changes my conclusion. I still think it would be a very bad idea for you to sleep in room ten and I honestly don't believe there will be any problem with us sharing this room."

He glared at her over his shoulder. "What makes you so sure of that?"

She smiled, confident now. "I've seen your aura and I've viewed your prints. You may be strong, Gideon Sweetwater, but you are not scary. Not to me. Like I said, you can have the bed nearest the closet."

"What if you're wrong?" he asked. "What if you wake up in a nightmare?"

"Try to keep some perspective here. I see weird things in the dark. I've got a stalker and someone tried to kidnap me last night. Seven months ago I was drugged and forced to become an involuntary test subject in a dangerous experiment involving an unknown paranormal serum. I lost a night of my life to amnesia. Don't you worry your pretty little head, Gideon Sweetwater. If I have a nightmare I've got a long list of people and events to blame it on. Currently, you are at the bottom of that list."

He stared at her. "My pretty little head?"

"Excuse me. I'm going to brush my teeth."

CHAPTER TWENTY-FOUR

AMELIA DID NOT wake up in a screaming nightmare.

That was a shock, Gideon decided, but not nearly as surprising as it was to discover that he had not had any bad dreams, either.

He opened his eyes and lay quietly for a moment, giving himself time to assess the facts on the ground. He was lying on top of the bed, fully clothed, but there was a blanket over him. He had no memory of the blanket, so at some point Amelia must have gotten up and covered him with it. Morning light was peeking in around the edges of the window shade and he could hear the shower running in the bathroom.

What's wrong with this picture?

It was all so astonishingly normal. That's what was wrong. He did not do normal when it came to relationships. Then again, Amelia had been very clear about their association. They were not in a relationship.

His leg protested when he tried to swing it over the side of the bed. He took a minute to let the pain retreat and then he reached for his cane and got to his feet.

He looked at the three crystals sitting on the small table that separated the two beds. Amelia had set out the stones just before turning off the light. When he had asked her why, she had said her aunt, the maybe-not-so-fake psychic currently giving performances on a cruise ship, had given them to her and that they helped her sleep.

He did not entirely discount the possibility that some crystals had paranormal properties—his mother was convinced they could exert a calming influence on the nerves—but he had always suspected that any therapeutic benefits were due to the placebo effect. He did believe in the power of suggestion. It was just one step away from hypnosis, after all.

Regardless, the bottom line was that he had not caused Amelia to wake up in a nightmare. Granted, it amounted to a one-off experiment. Still. The rush of relief and satisfaction surging through him was more energizing than a triple-shot Americano. He was not in the mood to give the crystals any credit.

He headed for the connecting door, intending to use the shower in room ten.

The envelope was on the floor in front of the parking lot door in his room. There was a note inside. He read it and got another shot of satisfaction, the kind Sweetwaters got when they knew they were closing in on the bad guys. He picked up his shaving gear.

AMELIA WAS WAITING in her room when he returned. She was wearing what he was coming to think of as her uniform—black jeans and a black tee—and her hair was caught up in a casual twist. She looked ready and eager to plunge into another day of investigation. There was no indication that she had spent a dream-troubled night.

She gave him a disapproving glare. "I can't believe you went back into that room," she said.

"All my stuff is in there," he reminded her. "So is the other shower. I keep telling you the vibe doesn't bother me the way it does you."

"I still think it would be a very bad idea for you to sleep that close to such bad energy."

"You might be right," he admitted. He paused. "You seem to be feeling rather chipper."

"Yep. Best night's sleep I've had in a long while."

"Seriously? No bad dreams?"

"Nope," she said. She gave him a smug smile. "You?"

"Well, no."

"I told you so."

"Nobody likes an I-told-you-so, Amelia."

"Get used to it." Her expression turned serious. "I've been think-ing about your dreamstate issues. I didn't want to mention my the-ory last night because you were not in the mood to hear it, but have you considered the possibility that your phobia is somehow con-nected to sex?"

"*Sex?*" He was stunned. Outrage struck next. He took a step closer, closing the distance between them. "You know, I woke up feeling surprisingly good. Damned near normal. But you just blew my sunny mood to hell."

"Think about it." She took a quick step back, very earnest now. "My theory explains everything. I think you probably had a few bad experiences early on and concluded that you couldn't spend the night with a date. Now you've got a full-blown phobia about sleeping with someone."

He took another step toward her. "Stop trying to analyze me."

"My theory also explains why neither of us had any issues last night."

"It does?"

"Yes. We're working together, see? We're not dating." She moved back a pace and stopped when she came up against the wall. She swept out her hands. "No sex, no problem."

Gideon leaned in and flattened one hand on the wall beside her head. "This would be a very good time for you to stop talking about my sex life."

"Okay. I understand you're a little upset, but promise me you'll at least think about my theory."

"I promise I will do my damnedest to forget it." He took his hand off the wall, stepped back, and held out the envelope. "Not to change the subject, but to change the subject, someone took our bait. I found this under the door. We've got a meeting with a possible informant."

"Seriously? Why didn't you say something?"

"You were too busy doing all the talking."

Amelia snapped the envelope out of his fingers, removed the note, and read it aloud. "'I know why you're in town. I was there that night. I have information. The old hotel, eleven tonight. Five hundred cash. Tell no one.'"

"It might not be legit," Gideon warned. "Just some local who thinks they can spin a story and collect a quick five hundred."

"If it's just an opportunist, why the secret meeting out at the ruins?" Amelia said. "Why not approach us here at the motel or meet us at a restaurant?"

"Maybe our informant is into drama," he said. "But this note feels real. I think whoever slipped it under the door doesn't want to be seen chatting with us."

"Well, we are planning to go out to the ruins tonight anyway. You said I should view the scene with my other vision, and that requires darkness."

A flicker of dread came and went in her eyes. His irritation faded, replaced with guilt. "I know this is going to be hard for you."

"I'll be okay." She gave him a forced smile. "This will give me an opportunity to work on my own phobia issues. There's just one problem. I don't have five hundred in cash on me. Nobody carries that kind of money around these days."

"Except drug dealers. Don't worry, we'll find an ATM."

Amelia sighed. "This is going to hit my bank account hard. I'm still waiting for payment on my last real estate shoot. I'll have to go into my savings. Again."

"I'll take care of the five hundred tonight and put it down under expenses."

She flushed. "It's okay. My friends will reimburse me at the end of the month. We've agreed to split up the expenses involved in the investigation."

"I said I'll take care of the five hundred."

"That's very generous of you, but—"

He took her arm and steered her toward the door. "I'm hungry. Let's get our complimentary breakfast."

"Are you pissed?"

"Me? Pissed? Of course not. I'm used to dealing with difficult clients. Goes with the territory."

"I am not a difficult client."

"Trust me, you are a difficult client."

CHAPTER TWENTY-FIVE

THE COMPLIMENTARY BREAKFAST consisted of an assortment of day-old doughnuts, hard-boiled eggs, cold cereal, and bananas. This was the Southern California desert, Amelia thought. There should have been oranges and grapefruit. But, hey, the repast was free.

It was not an exciting display but the patio setting was pleasant. The morning sun shone down from a perfect blue sky, and the wild expanse of the elemental landscape stretched out to the mountains.

She and Gideon joined the short line of guests at the buffet table. Gideon made his selections—two doughnuts and a banana—and started to move on to the coffee machine. She knew the exact instant when he realized he could not manage a coffee cup, not when he was holding the plate with the doughnuts and banana in one hand and gripping his cane in the other hand.

"I'll get the coffee," she said.

"Thanks," he muttered.

"You're not a morning person, are you?"

He ignored the comment and made his way to a table for two on the outer edge of the patio. She listened to the muffled thuds of his cane on the tiles and knew that, in spite of his claim to being adept at compartmentalizing, the injury annoyed and frustrated him. Maybe he was wondering if he would ever be able to get rid of the cane.

She went back to considering the doughnuts. None looked worth the calories. She was reaching for a hard-boiled egg when she heard a soft chuckle beside her and turned to see a woman dressed in tight yoga pants, a snug halter top, and a light zip-up hoodie. Her mane of sunny blond hair was caught up in a perky ponytail. She looked like she had just finished her Sun Salutation poses.

"It's a free breakfast, what do you expect?" the woman said in a low, conspiratorial voice. "I figure the convenience outweighs the problem of having to drive somewhere to find a restaurant that is open for breakfast."

Amelia smiled. "You're absolutely right. And this patio is a very nice place to drink morning coffee."

"Definitely. My name is Katy, by the way. Katy Shipley."

"Amelia Rivers."

"I'm here to relax and unwind." Katy took a doughnut. "Something about the desert gives a person a different perspective."

"Yes, it does. Come here often?"

"My first time. I usually go to Palm Springs for my desert fix. Thought I'd try a more laid-back experience this time. You?"

"I've been to Lucent Springs before but this is my first time at this motel."

"Vacation?" Katy asked.

"No. I'm here to photograph what's left of the old hotel on Spring Road before it's demolished."

"Really?" Katy looked intrigued. "What's so special about it?"

"It's got a history. It was originally an expensive sanatorium and then it became a failed resort. That was followed by a series of hotel and resort failures. The nineteen-thirties-era architecture makes it special and worth recording."

"Are you here on your own?"

"No, my assistant is with me." Amelia angled her head toward the table where Gideon sat contemplating the desert. "I do the photos. He handles the background research."

"I see," Katy said. "Sounds interesting."

The wistful note in her voice made Amelia pause.

"What about you?" she asked.

"Signed the divorce papers last week. My friends were tired of watching me mope around, so I figured I'd take a vacation and give them a break."

"Good idea."

"I got in last night," Katy said. "This is my first full day here. I intend to spend it sitting in the shade beside the pool, reading a book."

"Enjoy."

"I will," Katy promised.

Amelia filled two large cups with coffee, snapped on the plastic lids, and set them on a small plastic tray. She added the egg and a banana and picked up the tray.

Pete Ellerbeck appeared with a platter of replacement doughnuts for the buffet table.

"Good morning, Ms. Rivers," he said. "Great weather for a photo shoot today."

Amelia smiled. "Unfortunately, sunshine doesn't provide the right atmosphere for what I'm trying to capture. I'm after the hotel's history. Night shots will provide more emotional depth."

"I get it," Pete said. "You're going for creepy."

"Something like that, yes."

"I should have time to do that interview today after the morning rush," Pete said.

"That would be great," Amelia said. "Thanks."

She made her way to the table where Gideon waited and sat down across from him.

He reached for a cup of coffee. "Who were you talking to?"

She looked at him, surprised. "Pete Ellerbeck."

"I meant the woman."

"Oh, she's a guest here at the motel. Her name is Katy something. Shipley, I think. She's here on her own. Recovering from a divorce." Amelia cracked the egg against the table and started to peel it. "Why?"

"At this stage we can't trust anyone," Gideon said.

"Wow. You are even more paranoid than I am. I honestly don't think we need to worry about Katy, but whatever. By the way, Ellerbeck wants to do the interview later this morning."

"That works."

She finished peeling the egg, sprinkled a little salt on it, and took a bite. "Out of curiosity, how are you going to ask Ellerbeck about a death in room ten without letting him know we think Dr. Fulbrook was murdered in that room?"

Gideon snapped the lid off his coffee. "I can be subtle."

"Really? I hadn't noticed."

Gideon picked up one of the doughnuts and got a determined expression. "About last night."

"Oh, joy. I love conversations that start with 'about last night.' What can possibly go wrong?"

"I want to make it clear that I do not have a phobia."

"I didn't say you did." She finished the egg. "I said it was a theory."

"You are not qualified to offer an opinion."

"Okay, how would you describe your little problem with sex?"

Gideon choked on the bite of doughnut. He coughed a few times, glanced around to make sure nobody had overheard her question, and then looked at her, his eyes very fierce. He lowered his voice to a dangerous level.

"I do not have a problem with sex," he said, spacing each word out. "I have issues when it comes to sleeping with someone. It's complicated, damn it."

"I dunno. Sounds pretty straightforward to me." She picked up the banana and set about stripping off the peel. "You've had a few unfortunate experiences and you've developed a fear of falling asleep in close proximity to someone you're sexually attracted to. Ergo, you've developed a phobia. Perfectly understandable."

"There's just one problem with your theory."

"Yeah? What's that?"

"It's true that you did not wake up in a screaming nightmare last night."

"Which proves my point. No sex, no problem."

Gideon watched her insert the tip of the banana between her lips.

"We did not have sex," he said evenly. "But do not assume that I did not want to have sex. With you."

She felt as if she had been zapped by a bolt of lightning from the clear blue sky. Her front teeth clamped down on the tip of the banana. Gideon winced.

She tried to swallow and gagged instead. She grabbed a napkin, aware that a few heads were turning her way—some in concern, some in curiosity. She knew she was turning red.

Gideon gripped his cane, got to his feet, and slapped her lightly on the back a few times. "Breathe."

She swallowed, took a breath, and managed to pull herself together.

"You're embarrassing me," she hissed.

He sat down and picked up his coffee. "Just trying to clarify a point."

She leaned forward and lowered her voice another notch. "Are you telling me that you wanted to have sex last night?"

"Yep. Sort of blows your theory all to smithereens, doesn't it?"

She narrowed her eyes, trying and failing to suppress the heady little rush his news gave her. She'd had a few heated fantasies of her own last night but she had told herself the attraction was one-sided. What if it was mutual?

"I suppose it's been a while for you, what with the trauma of the cult case and your injuries," she said.

"Believe it or not, I was doing just fine until you showed up."

"Actually, I think you were sort of depressed."

"You're a photographer, not a therapist."

"I was just trying to be helpful. As someone who has also experienced an unusual phobia, I can understand—"

"Excuse me." Gideon grabbed his cane and propelled himself to his feet. "I need another doughnut."

She munched the rest of her banana and watched him make his way back to the buffet table.

The attraction was mutual.

The thought dazzled.

CHAPTER TWENTY-SIX

AMELIA HAD TO admit she was more than a little awed by how smoothly Gideon conducted the "interview" with Pete Ellerbeck. He really was a pro, she thought.

They met with Ellerbeck in his small office behind the front desk. He poured glasses of iced tea, left the door open in case a guest entered the lobby, and then leaned back in his chair.

"Nope, you're not the first folks to take an interest in that old hotel," he said in response to one of Gideon's casual questions. "We've had some curiosity seekers drop by to ask directions. They usually call it the Lost Night Files Hotel. Evidently the place was featured on a podcast or something. Took me a while to figure out what they were talking about."

"Forget the tourists," Gideon said. "We're here to get the facts. We know the basics of the early history of the hotel but we haven't been able to find out much about the fire seven months ago."

"Well, like I told you before, most of the locals assume those three women who decided to party out there started the fire to keep warm and it got away from them. That's the scenario the former police captain went with, and I admit that's the most likely explanation."

Amelia pretended not to notice the warning glance Gideon sent her way. She would not lose her temper. She could be cool.

"You sound like you have another theory," Gideon said to Pete.

"Between you and me, I've always kind of wondered if it might have been arson," Pete said.

"A firebug?" Gideon asked.

Ellerbeck shook his head. "Insurance fraud."

"Really?" Amelia asked, deliberately widening her eyes a little. "What gave you that idea?"

Ellerbeck shrugged. "The place was beyond renovation. Trust me. I've done enough construction to recognize a teardown when I see one. I think the hotel company didn't know what it was getting into when it bought the property and in the end decided the quickest, cleanest way out was a fire."

"Fascinating," Amelia said.

Gideon made a note and looked up, frowning a little. "We hadn't heard that theory. Were any of the company officials in town around the time of the fire?"

"No." Ellerbeck drank some of his tea and lowered the glass. "I've never seen any of the hotel execs. Course, if they did show up they would have stayed at one of the big resorts. But no one mentioned they were in town, and news travels fast around here."

Gideon watched Pete with a knowing look. "You think you know who the arsonist was, don't you?"

"Maybe." Pete leaned forward a little and lowered his voice, although there was no one else except the three of them within hearing distance. "A guy claiming to be a doctor checked in a couple of days before the fire. He wanted directions to the hotel. I asked him why he was interested in that run-down property. He said something about its history as a sanatorium."

Amelia stilled. "Someone else was exploring the story of the hotel? Maybe we should interview him, too."

Ellerbeck shook his head. "Afraid I can't help you there."

"Of course not," Gideon said. "There are customer confidentiality issues. We understand."

"Well, that, too, naturally," Ellerbeck said. "But there's another reason you can't talk to him. He left early the morning of the fire. Took off before dawn. I wasn't too concerned at the time because he'd paid cash in advance for the room. But he must have been in a rush, because he left some clothes behind in a drawer. When I tried to contact him I found out that the name, address, and phone number he'd put down on the registration form were fake."

Gideon made a note. "Now, that is interesting."

"The day before the fire, he told me he'd lost his key and needed a replacement," Ellerbeck said. "I've been meaning to rekey the room but haven't gotten around to it." He peered at Gideon. "He was booked into your room, by the way. Number ten."

"Okay, that's a little disturbing," Amelia said. "He gave a false ID and then disappeared shortly after the fire? I can see why you had some questions about him."

"You bet I did," Ellerbeck said, warming to his topic.

"Did you mention your suspicions to the police captain?" Gideon asked.

"Sure, but he was convinced those three women were responsible. A drug party gone bad."

CHAPTER TWENTY-SEVEN

AFTER THE INTERVIEW they made their way back to their rooms via the central courtyard. Katy Shipley was ensconced poolside on a lounger. She had a book in her hand. An ice-filled glass of some sparkling drink was on the table beside her. An umbrella shielded her from the sun. She glanced up and waved when she saw Amelia.

"You should join me," she said. "Great day to read a book by the pool."

"Maybe later," Amelia said. "Working now."

"Right," Katy said. "How goes the photo project?"

"Still doing research," Amelia said. "Enjoy the day."

"Thanks, I will."

Gideon waited until they were back inside their separate rooms and then he spoke from the connecting doorway. "Looks like you've got a new friend."

"Who? Katy?" Amelia took off her sunglasses and set her tote down on the table. "She seems harmless. Pete Ellerbeck is a lot more interesting, if you ask me. By the way, I take back what I implied earlier about your lack of subtlety. You did a great job interviewing Ellerbeck today. Nice work."

"I'm glad you feel you're finally getting your money's worth in a private investigator," Gideon said.

"Definitely." She decided to pretend she had not picked up on the sarcasm. Evidently he held a mean grudge. So much for trying to do the man a favor by diagnosing his phobia. No good deed goes unpunished. "Do you think he really does not know that Fulbrook was murdered in your room?"

"I think he told us what he believes to be the truth," Gideon said. He used his cane to make his way to the one chair in her room. His jaw hardened a little when he sat down, but his stoic expression returned immediately. "His logic works. If Fulbrook was the arsonist it makes sense that he would have vanished after the fire. But the fact that some clothes were left behind indicates that's not how it went down. No professional arsonist would be careless enough to leave anything behind in a motel room."

"And we know that Fulbrook was murdered in your room. That leaves us with a lot of questions. Who killed Fulbrook and what happened to the body?"

"It's likely two killers were involved," Gideon said.

"Two?"

"It would have been easy for a lone killer to smuggle the body out the back door, load it into a vehicle, and then dump it. There's a lot of desert around here. No problem digging a grave that was unlikely to ever be found. Alternatively, they could have hauled the body up into the mountains and tossed it into a canyon. But that leaves the problem of getting rid of Fulbrook's car. It had to disappear."

"I see what you're saying. If there were two killers, one could have packed up the room and driven away in Fulbrook's car while the other person used a second car to get rid of the body." Amelia thought about that for a moment. "I wonder why they killed him."

"Probably for the usual reason," Gideon said.

"What is the usual reason?"

"Fulbrook knew too much. They were afraid he would talk."

"Makes sense," Amelia said.

She walked to the front window and looked out at the courtyard. Katy Shipley was no longer alone. A couple of other guests had joined her at poolside. They were all chatting amicably.

"See anything interesting?" Gideon asked.

"Looks like Katy Shipley won't be spending the day moping around by herself." Amelia turned away from the window. "She's talking with some of the other guests at the pool. I'm so glad."

Gideon's brows rose. "You feel sorry for her, don't you?"

"Grieving a divorce can be as traumatic as grieving a death. Some people say it's worse because there's no real closure the way there is with death."

"Let me guess, you googled that?"

She sighed. "Yes."

"Why? Did you go through a divorce?"

"No, my parents did."

"It was not an amicable separation, I gather?"

"I doubt if there is any such thing."

"Probably not," Gideon agreed. "Well, that explains the book Shipley is reading."

"You saw the title?"

"*When Life Gives You Lemons: Ten Steps to Moving On.*"

CHAPTER TWENTY-EIGHT

G IDEON BROUGHT THE SUV to a stop in the driveway of the abandoned hotel and cut the lights. The desert night, star-studded and lit with a brilliant moon, closed in immediately.

Amelia unclipped her seat belt and leaned forward to get a better view of the ruins.

"I was right when I told Pete Ellerbeck that a night shoot would be the best way to photograph this place," she said. "Talk about creepy."

The full moon illuminated the partially destroyed hotel in shades of gray that ranged from skeletal-pale to impenetrable shadow. She dreaded getting out of the car.

"See anything?" Gideon asked.

She raised the camera and studied the scene through the wind-shield. As expected, a low-lying fog of old energy drifted around the lobby entrance, but there were several splashes of recent prints. They phosphoresced in the night, seething with nameless colors. Some were familiar. Gideon's tracks were everywhere.

"The windshield is distorting things somewhat," she said. "But I can see your prints from our first visit. There are others that are new, though."

"What about your own prints?" Gideon sounded genuinely curious.

She shrugged. "For some reason I can't see my own prints. Can't photograph them, either."

"Makes sense. You probably can't see your own aura."

"Very true. I never made that connection. How did you come up with it?"

"Blame Uncle Shelton."

"Right," she said. "That would be the Sweetwater family genius who got my friends and me into this mess."

"Under the circumstances, I think that's a little unfair. Tell me about the new prints at the entrance."

"I think someone went into the lobby not too long ago."

"Sounds like our informant has arrived," Gideon said. "But he's not rushing out to meet us. I wonder why."

She raised the camera and peered through the viewfinder. "I think there's something very wrong with whoever left those prints."

Gideon did not take his attention off the lobby entrance. "Define 'wrong.'"

"I can't be certain but I have a sense that whoever went into the lobby earlier is in pain. Ill, maybe. Weak."

"Any exit tracks?"

"Good question." She studied the prints again. "No. But the person could have left through another doorway. There are a lot of rooms in both wings and each one has a door that opens to the outside. And then there are all the empty windows."

"Stay here, doors locked. I'll see what's going on."

Ice touched the back of Amelia's neck. The thought of getting out of the SUV was disturbing, but she could not let Gideon venture into the hotel alone. She needed to do this.

"I'm coming with you," she said.

"You'll be safer in the car. Get into the driver's seat and be ready to fire up the engine if anyone other than me comes out of the lobby."

"Whoever left those tracks could be anywhere inside. You shouldn't walk in cold. You need me to read the prints. Also, I know the layout of the hotel."

"No."

She took a breath. "I've got a feeling, Gideon."

He hesitated and looked at her. "A feeling?"

"My intuition tells me I should go in with you."

He considered that, his eyes heating in the shadows, and then apparently came to a decision. "You may be right. Stick close and stay behind me."

"I understand." She steadied her nerves and glanced down at the penlight in his hand. "Uh, shouldn't you have a gun?"

"I hate to break this to you, but I don't have a gun."

"I see." She dove into her tote. "Fortunately, I've got my Taser."

"Have you ever actually fired that thing at someone?"

"Well, no, but don't worry, I've done some target practice."

She opened the door and jumped down to the ground. No longer muted by the windshield, the mist of prints laid down over the years abruptly became heavier and more ominous. The seething currents swirled around her ankles. The paranormal fog was cold.

A flash of primal fear warned her that if she fell into the ghostly river she might never get back to the surface. She froze, staring at the lobby entrance. The last time she had walked into the darkness she had lost a night of her life to amnesia.

"Amelia."

Gideon's voice was low and sharp with command. She responded instinctively, clamping down on her flaring senses. *Control.* She had to get stronger if she wanted to get her life back. *Focus.* She was a photographer. She understood the concept.

She concentrated, pushing back against the unwanted visions generated by her imagination. The mist faded, no longer threatening to pull her down into the depths.

"I'm okay," she said.

And she was. Mostly. Gideon was right; she wasn't tipping over into madness. She was adjusting to her new normal. She had to stop fighting it and embrace her new senses. She was the same person she had always been. Yes, the special sensitivity she had taken for granted all her life had been enhanced. But she could handle it. She was not going mad.

Gideon came around the front of the vehicle. "Are you sure you want to do this?"

"Yes."

She focused again on the recent energy prints that led into the dark lobby. Her newfound assurance gave her the confidence to pay closer attention to her intuition. She examined the pale currents in the footsteps. They rippled with an alarming vibe.

And suddenly she knew what she was looking at.

"We have to hurry," she said. "Whoever went into that lobby tonight is badly injured. Maybe dying."

Gideon did not question her analysis. Instead, he switched on the penlight and swept the narrow beam across the entranceway. Amelia got another rush of anxiety when she noticed the dark spots on the concrete.

"I think that's blood," she said.

"I think you're right. And it's fresh."

Gideon moved to the side of the doorway and aimed the light into the midnight shadows of the old lobby.

"My name is Gideon Sweetwater," he said, raising his voice. "I'm a private investigator. It looks like you've been injured. Do you need help?"

There was no response. Gideon edged into the shadows. Amelia followed. Something small skittered away from the light. Scorpion. She tried not to think about what other creatures might be hiding in the ruins. She was wearing boots, she reminded herself. She would be okay. Probably.

She focused on the prints. Pale and luminous, they led across the lobby to the arched entrance of the east wing.

"To the right, Gideon," she said. "That hallway."

Gideon aimed the flashlight at the cracked and chipped floor tiles. More splashes of blood led to the second guest room in the corridor. The sagging door stood ajar.

Gideon motioned Amelia to stay out of the line of sight and then he eased the door open.

"Gideon Sweetwater," he said quietly. "Amelia Rivers is here with me."

There was no response. He went into the room. She followed. The beam of the flashlight speared a man who was huddled on the floor, partially propped against the wall. His head was sunk on his chest. He was dressed in faded jeans and worn boots. He was nude from the waist up. He clutched what appeared to be a wadded-up shirt against his side. The garment was dark with blood.

Metal glinted in the beam of the flashlight. There was a gun on the floor beside the collapsed man.

Gideon started toward him. "Call nine-one-one," he said to Amelia.

She already had her phone out of her pocket.

The injured man raised his head and opened his eyes partway. "Won't do any good. No service out here."

Amelia glanced down at her phone. "He's right, Gideon."

"We'll have to get him into the car," Gideon said. "But before we move him we need more pressure on the wound. I've got a first aid kit. I'll get it."

"I'll hold his shirt in place," she said.

She dropped her phone back into a pocket and hurried forward to crouch beside the bleeding man. He groaned when she adjusted the makeshift bandage in an attempt to pack the wound more firmly.

"I'm sorry," she said.

Gideon disappeared out the door and returned a moment later, kit gripped in his free hand. Balancing himself with his cane, he opened the container and set it on the floor.

"Can you keep the pressure on while I get the dressing ready?" Amelia asked.

"Yes." Gideon lowered himself down on one knee and took over the task of pressing the crumpled shirt against the wound.

Amelia ripped open several packages of sterile bandages. She thought the injured man had lapsed into unconsciousness but he stirred when she began wrapping the gauze tape around his chest to secure the thick dressing.

"Run," he said, the words thick in his mouth. "Get out of here be-fore they come back."

"Before who comes back?" Gideon said.

"Drug gang. Go. Now."

But the muffled rumble of a heavy engine told Amelia it was too late to run.

CHAPTER TWENTY-NINE

GIDEON PUT HIS hand on the injured man's shoulder. Amelia felt energy shiver in the atmosphere.

"How many?" Gideon asked.

The man rallied as if drawing strength from Gideon's powerful aura. Or maybe he simply realized there was some hope after all, Amelia thought.

"Three, I think," he mumbled. "Maybe four. They wanted information before they finished me but one of 'em said he could see the lights of your car. That's when they took off."

The effort to speak exhausted him. His eyes closed and his head lolled to one side.

Gideon picked up the informant's gun, checked it with a crisp, efficient motion that made it clear he knew how to use it, and then grabbed his cane and levered himself to his feet.

He handed the weapon to Amelia. "If you have to pull the trigger, do it. Don't hesitate."

"You should take it," she insisted, fumbling with her phone's flashlight. "I've got a Taser."

"Don't hesitate," he repeated evenly. "Do you understand?"

"Yes," she whispered. She was way out of her depth now. A Taser was one thing. A gun was something else altogether.

Gideon went to the doorway and turned back briefly to look at her. In the darkness his eyes burned with a silvery energy. Probably just her imagination, she thought. Or maybe a trick of the light.

"Stay here," he said. "Do not come out until I tell you. Shoot anyone who comes through that doorway who isn't me. Clear?"

She tried to swallow and discovered she could not. Her mouth was too dry. "Clear," she croaked.

"Turn off the light."

She obeyed. He switched off his penlight at the same time. The room was abruptly suffused in the ghostly light of the moon streaming through the empty window. Her senses, already operating in the red zone, shot up another level. The ankle-deep miasma of energy in the space glowed with an eerie radiance. *Focus*, she thought. *Control*. She could do this. She had to do this. There was no alternative.

Gideon vanished into the night-drenched hallway. Outside, the heavy vehicle slammed to a stop. Car doors opened. There was a lot of commotion at the lobby entrance and then voices.

"Freeze," a man shouted. "DEA. Come out with your hands on your head."

When he got no response, he tried again.

"I repeat. We are DEA. You are under arrest. Come out with your hands on your head and you will not be hurt."

"Sweetwater and the woman probably took off down one of the hallways when they heard us," a second man said. "They could be hiding in any of the rooms in one of the wings."

"All right," the one in charge said. "Kirby, clear the hallway on the left. Sage, you've got the other wing. Deacon, go back outside. If they get out of here they'll run for the vehicle. Assume Sweetwater is armed. Take him down on sight. Remember, we need the woman alive."

Heavy boots thundered on the old tile floor. Amelia's pulse beat wildly. She wondered if she was about to go into a panic attack. Then she wondered if the fear of having a panic attack would bring one on. *Focus, woman.*

"Kirby," the boss snapped, "what are you waiting for? I said clear that hallway. Sage, get moving. If we lose her again there won't be any more boosters for either of you."

The screaming started then. Horrified yells that could have frozen blood reverberated down the hallway. Amelia shuddered. In that moment it would not have been difficult to believe that the gates to hell had just opened out in the lobby.

The screams stopped abruptly and somehow that was more shocking than the panic-stricken shrieks had been. She heard a heavy thud and knew that someone had fallen hard on the cracked tiles.

"Kirby's down," Sage yelled. "What happened? What's going on?"

"Forget Kirby," the boss shouted. "Get Sweetwater."

"Fuck, he could be in any of those rooms." Sage raised his voice. "Deacon, where are you? Cover me."

Deafening shots roared in the hallway.

Amelia heard footsteps pounding outside the room where she and the injured man were hiding. Through the partially open door she glimpsed the hot, unstable aura of one of the attackers. That had to be Deacon, she thought. He had entered the east wing from one of the rooms farther down the hall. He was heading toward the lobby.

Gideon was occupied with the boss and Sage. He would not be aware of the man rushing up on him from behind until it was too late.

Gun clutched in both hands, she lurched through the doorway, out into the darkened hall. The attacker was a few steps ahead, moving fast. She raised the gun and then realized Deacon was between Gideon and herself. She was no marksman. If she tried for a shot she could easily hit Gideon by accident.

"Gideon," she shouted, "behind you."

She fired into the ceiling, hoping to distract Deacon. The thunder of the weapon deafened her but it got the attacker's attention. He spun around. Moonlight gleamed on the pistol in his hand.

She had time to realize she was going to die before Gideon loomed in the shadows. His eyes blazed molten silver.

The tsunami of glacial energy struck before she had time to process what was happening. She fell headlong into the hallucinatory world of a nightmare.

The shards of the dream hurtled toward her with the force of a hurricane.

She walks into the shadowed lobby. Pallas and Talia follow her. There are three men waiting inside. She can't see their faces. One of them is standing back, observing. She gets the impression he's in charge.

The other two approach. They are smiling but she can sense the energy around them and she knows something is terribly wrong. They move forward as if to shake hands. That is when she sees the syringes.

She screams, trying to warn Pallas and Talia, but it is too late. They are screaming, too. The men plunge the needles into them. She turns to run but the one who greeted them when they arrived wraps his arm around her throat, choking her, as he stabs the syringe into her upper shoulder.

She sinks into the darkness but the nightmare does not end . . .

She is aware of being lifted onto a gurney. A man in a surgical mask and gown appears . . .

CHAPTER THIRTY

AMELIA, WAKE UP. Do you hear me? Wake up."

Gideon's dark voice cut through the nightmare. The words were a command but she sensed another element embedded in them—a desperate plea.

She pushed the last fragments of the dream aside and opened her eyes. She was aware of a strange silence and then she saw Gideon looking down at her. His aura blazed in the shadows.

Reality slammed back. She became aware of the hard tiles beneath her, the darkness and the eerie silence.

She sat up abruptly, automatically pushing hair out of her eyes.

"Oh, crap," she whispered, scrambling to get to her feet. "Are you okay?"

"Me?" Gideon sounded confused by the question. "Yes. What about you?"

"I'm all right. I think." She looked around and saw the crumpled figure on the floor. "One of them was sneaking up on you. I thought I might be able to stop him but I was afraid I might shoot you instead. You turned around, I saw your eyes, and then I was suddenly in a dream."

"A nightmare," Gideon said in a grim voice. "I know."

Her senses were spinning. She shook her head in an instinctive effort to clear it but that motion made things worse. Her stomach protested. For a few precarious seconds she thought she was going to be sick. She pressed a hand to her stomach.

"Are you sure you're okay?" Gideon demanded.

"I'm a little dizzy, that's all." She took a couple of steadying breaths. "What just happened?"

"I'll explain later. Do you think you can help me get our informant into the car? I'm not sure I can manage it alone, not with this cane."

Her stomach was calming and the world was no longer whirling. She was still shaky but she knew she had to hold it together long enough to get the injured man into the SUV.

"Yes," she said.

It was a struggle, but between the two of them they got the informant on his feet, his arms draped around their shoulders. He groaned but he tried to do what he could to aid in his own rescue. The three of them staggered past the crumpled Deacon.

Amelia's senses were still frazzled. She could not focus her talent, but when she and Gideon steered the injured man across the lobby she saw the silhouettes of two more attackers sprawled on the floor.

"That makes three," she said. "Are they—?"

"No," Gideon said.

She tried to sort out her chaotic memories. "There was a fourth."

"The guy in charge got away," Gideon said. "I recognized his voice. He was the one driving the van the night they tried to kidnap you. Pretty sure two of the others were with him. I didn't recognize the fourth guy."

"Thank God you're all right. I was so afraid they would kill you."

"I told you to stay in the room with the informant," Gideon said.

"Really? You're going to do this now? You're going to lecture me about a failure to follow orders because I tried to save your life?"

"Later."

"Damned right, later," she muttered. "Like never."

"You're pissed? After I saved *your* life?"

"I was feeling grateful but you just ruined the mood."

The informant raised his head slightly. "Could you two finish this conversation some other time?"

"Yes," Amelia said. "Where's the nearest hospital?"

"This town doesn't have a hospital," the man said. "Emergency clinic next to the fire station."

"Got a name?" Gideon asked.

"Mayfield. Joe Mayfield."

Amelia helped Gideon wedge Mayfield into the rear seat of the SUV. Gideon got behind the wheel and fired up the big engine. She climbed into the passenger seat, fastened her seat belt, and gripped her phone.

She waited tensely for service. It seemed to take forever for the bars to appear. She called nine-one-one.

When she finished dealing with the operator, she ended the call and twisted around in her seat to look at Mayfield.

"The operator said the medics will be waiting at the clinic when we get there," she told him.

He was slumped into the corner of the seat. He opened his eyes partway.

"Sorry I got you two into that mess," he mumbled.

Acting on impulse, Amelia unclipped her seat belt, knelt, and reached out to put her hand on Mayfield's leg. Once again he rallied.

"You're going to be okay," she said.

Mayfield opened his eyes again. "Everyone knows that the local kids sometimes go out to the hotel to party and do a little dealing but I wasn't expecting to run into a professional drug gang."

"Are you sure that's who those guys were?" Gideon asked. "Drug dealers?"

"Who else?" Mayfield said.

"Why did you set up the meeting with us tonight?" Gideon asked.

Mayfield looked at Amelia. "I know who you are. You're one of the women who do that weird podcast."

"*The Lost Night Files,*" Amelia said quietly. "How did you know?"

"I never miss an episode. You're still looking for answers, aren't you?"

"Yes," Amelia said. "Do you have some for us?"

"I was there that night," Mayfield said.

Gideon glanced at the rearview mirror. "You're our eyewitness, the one who started the fire."

CHAPTER THIRTY-ONE

STARTED DOING some new mushrooms the night it all went down," Mayfield said. "I'm writing a book, see, and I needed a little inspiration. But it was heavy stuff. Got lost in the visions for hours. I don't remember when the big car arrived. They never knew I was there. I had parked my bike in the old groundskeeper's shed."

"What did you see?" Amelia asked.

"I thought I heard voices but I couldn't be sure of anything. I was convinced I was traveling in another dimension. I remember trying to cook up some more mushrooms and then the earthquake hit. I thought it was the end of the world. The crack of doom, or whatever. I remember getting out of the room through the window. I had some crazy idea about escaping the apocalypse. I dunno. I was really flying."

"Keep talking," Gideon said.

Amelia shot him a warning look. The last thing they needed to do now was frighten Mayfield. Gideon did not appear to get the message. Fortunately, Mayfield was too weak and woozy to do anything except follow orders.

"When I got to the shed where I left the bike, I looked back. The flames were sweeping through one wing of the hotel. I saw people running to their cars. I took off. I swear I didn't realize you and your friends were still inside. All I could think about was getting away. I was sure I was seeing the fires of hell."

"I understand," Amelia said.

"I got on the bike and gunned it. Don't know why I didn't crash. Just dumb luck, I guess. It took a few days for the mushrooms to wear off. By then you and your friends were long gone and there were all kinds of rumors going around the valley. A lot of folks were sure you and your pals had been doing drugs and set the hotel on fire."

"You didn't clarify things with the police, did you?" Gideon said, each word a shard of ice.

"No." Mayfield groaned. "I should have but I couldn't be sure of my own memories. Couldn't separate the mushroom visions from reality. Everything was jumbled up together."

"And you figured you'd be blamed for the fire," Gideon added.

"Well, yeah." Mayfield focused on Amelia. "But after I started listening to the podcast I was able to piece things together, at least somewhat. When I heard you had checked in at the Cactus Garden and were asking around for stories about the old hotel I decided to talk to you."

"For five hundred bucks," Gideon said.

"Just seemed like good business," Mayfield said. "I'm sort of broke. But don't worry, you two saved my life and I think I've finally nailed the plot of the book I'm writing, so I figure we're even now. No charge."

"No shit," Gideon said.

He pulled into the driveway of the small clinic. Two medics

greeted them with a gurney. They extracted Mayfield from the rear seat.

"We called in the Air Evac team," one of them said. "They're on the way." He looked at Gideon. "Every cop on the force is on the way out to the old hotel right now, but the captain said to tell you two not to leave town until he's had a chance to talk to you."

"Understood," Gideon said.

He climbed back into the front seat. Amelia watched the medics wheel the gurney through the glass doors of the clinic. She realized she could make out the energy prints on the sidewalk. Her senses were returning to normal. She could focus again.

"We have to go back out to the hotel," she said. "Now. While it's still night."

Gideon started the engine and drove onto the main road. "I agree. I want to talk to the cops. But why are you so enthusiastic about the idea?"

"Because I need to get a look at the prints before the police have trampled all over them."

Gideon shot her an unreadable look. "Are you sure you're feeling okay?"

"Yep, I'm fine. You can relax, Gideon. You didn't traumatize me tonight. Well, maybe a little, but only temporarily. I got sideswiped by that storm of energy you used to take down Deacon, didn't I?"

Gideon drew a breath and exhaled deeply. "Yes. You did. You should have been . . . overwhelmed. Comatose. Like those three we left at the hotel."

"Well, I'm not, so stop worrying. Here's the interesting bit. It's true you threw me straight into a nightmare, but in the process, you helped me recover a few memories. I remembered at least some of what happened after Pallas, Talia, and I walked into the lobby of the hotel seven months ago. Enough to be certain of one thing."

"What?"

"I need to get back into that dream again. I'm pretty sure you're the only one who can take me there."

"No." Gideon clenched the steering wheel. "Absolutely not."

"We'll talk about it later."

"Forget it. We've got a more immediate problem. We need to get our story straight before we talk to the cops. We do not want to have the authorities blow us off or conclude we were anything other than innocent bystanders."

"I agree. So how do you suggest we handle this?"

He told her.

CHAPTER THIRTY-TWO

THEY ARE ALL dead?" Amelia asked. "I don't understand. I'm sure those three men were alive when we left to take Mayfield to the clinic."

She looked and sounded stunned, Gideon realized. She turned to him for confirmation.

"They were alive, weren't they?" she said. "All three were alive."

"Yes," he said, "but there were a lot of bullets flying around. We didn't check those men to see if they'd been badly injured. We were too busy trying to escape and take Mayfield with us."

Silently he tried to send her the message, *Stick to our story*. But at the moment, she was clearly shocked. People in shock did not focus well.

He and Amelia and Richards, the head of the Lucent Springs Police Department, were gathered at the entrance of the hotel lobby. They were not alone. The medic at the clinic had been right. Every cop in the small Lucent Springs Police Department—all six of them, counting the captain—appeared to be there. The scene was illuminated by the glaring headlights of the various vehicles parked in the vicinity. Inside the lobby, officers milled around with military-grade flashlights.

He was trying to concentrate on getting answers from Richards, but he kept getting distracted by Amelia. Her shock at the news of the three deaths aside, she really did seem to be okay. Amazing.

She gave Richards a fierce look. "They were alive when we left, Captain."

"I believe you," Richards said. "No way was this a DEA takedown, either. Relax, I'm not looking to pin this on the two of you. But you said one got away. We think he waited until you and Mayfield left. Then he returned to execute the others. He must have concluded they weren't worth saving and he needed to make sure none of them talked."

Richards was in his early forties, solid and compact, his hair trimmed in a number one buzz cut. There was a wedding ring on his finger. Everything about him suggested that he was a smart, competent veteran of law enforcement. It was, Gideon reflected, a field in which experienced professionals preferred the Occam's razor approach to crime solving. The right answer was usually the one with the least number of possible elements. Why look for complicated conspiracies involving illegal medical experiments with exotic paranormal drugs, kidnappings, and amnesia when everything at the scene indicated a routine drug deal gone bad?

The wisest course of action was to let Richards run with his own theory of the crime, Gideon thought. That was working out fairly well—so far.

But what was up with Amelia?

When he realized she had been caught by the edges of the energy he had used to take down Deacon he had been prepared for her to plunge into a nightmare and then retreat into unconsciousness. And she had apparently entered a dreamscape for a short time—but she had snapped out of it almost immediately.

She should be having an anxiety attack whenever she looked at him. Not only had she witnessed what he could do with his talent, she had experienced it firsthand. By now she had to understand how truly dangerous he was. Why wasn't she treating him as if he was a monster? Why wasn't she putting distance between them; flinching whenever he got close? As far as he could tell she wasn't even nervous around him.

"We were lucky," Amelia said to Richards. "I'm sure the one who took off would have tried to kill us, too, if we had been here when he returned."

Good, Gideon thought, relieved. She was back on track with the story they had invented for Richards. There was a practiced ease in her voice now that impressed him. It was clear this wasn't the first time she had dealt with law enforcement.

"The fourth man is in the wind," Richards said. "I'll get the word out. We haven't had gang or cartel problems here in Lucent Springs. We're too far away from the big-city drug markets. I hope this is a one-off and not the start of something more serious."

"What do you know about Mayfield?" Gideon asked.

"Everyone around here figures he's harmless." Richards shrugged. "Claims he's writing a book."

"He had a gun," Amelia pointed out.

"So does everyone else in town," Richards said. "Look, I'm going to need a statement from the two of you, but it can wait until morning. Right now I need to lock down the scene."

"We're staying at the Cactus Garden Motel," Gideon said.

Amelia gave Richards an ironic look. "I imagine everyone in town knows that."

"If they don't already, they will by morning," Richards said.

He crossed the fractured entranceway to join his officers inside the lobby.

Gideon looked at Amelia. She had turned around and was now staring at the cracked pavement behind the patrol cars and out of the range of the headlights.

"What is it?" he asked quietly.

"There's no point going inside. Too much light. But there are some prints over there. I need to take a closer look."

"All right, but let's try to make it seem as if we're just getting out of the way."

"Don't worry," she said. "I'm not about to tell Richards that I'm looking for paranormal footprints. I'm well aware that law enforcement doesn't welcome input from people claiming psychic talents."

"There are a few exceptions, but generally speaking, you're right."

They moved into the deep shadows behind the lights. He heard Amelia take a sharp breath.

"Oh, shit," she whispered.

"See something important?"

"Yes," she said. She swung around. "Let's get out of here. I need to make a call and there's no service out here."

He did not argue. They went back to the SUV and climbed inside. He started the engine and drove toward the main road.

"What's the rush?" he asked.

"I know the identity of the man who escaped tonight, the one who was in charge," Amelia said. She clutched her phone in both hands as if she could will the bars to appear. "He's dating my neighbor."

CHAPTER THIRTY-THREE

. . . Irene, this is Amelia. I have to talk to you as soon as possible. It's very important. Please call me as soon as you get this voicemail."

Amelia ended the call and lowered the phone. She fixed her gaze on the strip of headlight-illuminated pavement visible through the windshield. "This is horrible. I can't leave a message telling her I think she's dating a killer because he might be with her when she listens to her voicemail. She might panic and he would realize why and . . . Shit. What are we going to do?"

Gideon did not take his attention off the road. "Are you certain those prints you saw back at the hotel belong to the man your neighbor calls Falcon?"

She summoned up the memory of the hot, unstable prints. "Yes."

"What do you know about him?"

"Just what Irene told me. She thinks he's exciting. Claims he's an undercover cop working vice. I've never met him. He rarely visits her at her apartment. He usually picks her up in the parking lot or she meets him somewhere. But a few days ago he came by to see her late at night. I was awake, as usual. I heard him on the stairs. After he left I went outside. I could see his prints on the sidewalk."

"How would you describe them?"

She concentrated. "They were hot but not like yours."

"My prints are hot?" Gideon asked.

His voice was a little too even, she thought. She glanced at him. In the shadows it was impossible to read his hard face, but she didn't have to go into her other vision to know that there was a lot of cold tension in his energy field. She could feel it electrifying the atmosphere.

"Yes," she said. "But with a different kind of heat. His look—I don't know—feverish."

"How does your intuition interpret 'feverish'?"

She thought about that for a moment. "I'm not sure. My first impulse is to say there's something wrong with the person who laid down those prints."

"Huh." Gideon took a beat. "Do you think he's ill?"

"Maybe, but not in the normal, physical sense. Falcon isn't weak. But maybe there's something wrong with his nerves?" She broke off, frustrated. "I just don't know. I saw something similar in the prints of the stalker. I tried to capture the vibes in the photographs I took but they didn't come out very well."

"Cameras aren't built to take paranormal photos."

She groaned and folded her arms across her midsection. "Talk about a useless talent. I'm starting to feel like Cassandra. I can point to a bad guy and tell people he's dangerous, but no one will believe me, at least not without conventional evidence. Just imagine how Richards would have reacted tonight if I had tried to tell him about Falcon's prints."

"Welcome to the wonderful world of paranormal investigation, the ideal career for psychics who can't figure out any other semi-honest way to make a living with their talents."

She glanced at him. "Don't you find it frustrating?"

"Oh, yeah."

"But you keep doing it."

"My uncle would tell you that's how it is with a sixth sense. There's a need to use it. Not using it would be like going through life with gloves on so you couldn't access your sense of touch."

"Great. I'm a photographer who is stuck with a talent that lets me see things I can't photograph. Just great."

"You'll find a way to use your new abilities."

"Since when did you become Mr. Sunshine?"

"Maybe when I realized you weren't going to go into a coma or freak out after I slammed you into a nightmare tonight? I have to tell you, a lot of people would have some serious qualms about getting anywhere near me after an experience like that."

"Are you kidding? Thanks to you, I got some of my memories back."

"Tell me about those memories."

"I remembered the men who were waiting for Talia, Pallas, and me in the lobby. They grabbed us and injected us with some kind of knockout drug. One appeared to be a doctor or someone with medical training." Amelia paused. "Maybe that was the man who died in room ten."

"Fulbrook?"

"He signed himself *Dr. S. Fulbrook*, remember? In addition to him I think there were three others. Something about one of them was familiar. I got the feeling I should recognize him but I couldn't get a clear vision."

"Keep in mind that you were hallucinating, Amelia. Your mind was generating scenes from a dreamscape."

"They were real memories," she said. "I'm sure of it. What's more, I'm almost positive that if I go back into the dream, there's a good chance I'll be able to see the face of the one who looked familiar. I'll be prepared this time. I can focus on him."

"The answer is still no. We can't risk it. You might not come out of it this time."

"You're the one who claims that managing the psychic senses is a matter of control. You sent me into that nightmare once and you pulled me out of it. I don't see any reason why you can't do it again."

He glanced at her, startled. "What do you mean I pulled you out of it? How did I do that?"

"You called my name, remember?"

"Your name," he repeated. He shook his head. "I don't understand."

"There is a lot of power in names, Gideon."

CHAPTER THIRTY-FOUR

'M TELLING YOU, this is a really bad idea," Gideon said. He wheeled the SUV into the parking space behind the Cactus Garden Motel, braked to a sharp halt, shut down the engine, and turned in the seat. "You don't know what you're suggesting. You saw what I did to those men back there at the hotel."

"Calm down and think about this," Amelia said.

"Do not tell me to calm down. You're the one who is going off the deep end here."

"You said that handling our psychic senses is all about control."

"Yes. Exactly."

"Have you ever tried to put someone into a lucid dream? The kind of dream the dreamer controls?"

"I don't even know what you're talking about."

"Have you ever tried to make someone hallucinate on demand?"

"It's not the kind of talent you can run experiments with."

"You don't know that because you've never tried to run the experiments," she said. "I'm suggesting that we could work together to guide me through my lost memories."

"What the hell makes you think that's possible?"

"I'm almost certain your talent is a form of hypnosis. That's why you were able to pull me out of the nightmare using my name. If I'm right, you have more control over your talent than you realize."

"What the hell makes you think that?"

"I've seen your aura, Gideon. I'm looking at it right now. My intuition tells me you have all the power you need to control your psychic senses."

He was aware that his left hand was clenched very tightly around the steering wheel. But she was getting to him. How many times had he wondered if there was some other use for his talent?

"What if you're wrong?" he asked quietly.

"We'll take it slow. You'll be in control. If you think things are going sideways you can just stop."

"My talent doesn't work that way."

"Here's the thing that I'm pretty sure will make all the difference: I won't be a target. I will be a willing participant in the experiment. Hey, I survived one test run tonight and it worked. I got some memories back accidentally. Imagine what might be possible if we worked together to recover the rest."

"Damn it, Amelia—"

"Please, Gideon. Just give it a try. I'm begging you. Tonight, at the hotel, I almost saw the face of the man who stole a night of my life. A man who is responsible for killing who knows how many people in the course of his so-called experiments. And now he's trying to kidnap me. I need answers. So do my friends."

He ought to say no. He knew that. But she was right about one thing. She had bounced back swiftly tonight after he had hit her with a shot of his talent—and she had recovered what she was certain were genuine memories. If they went about it slowly he might be able to calibrate his talent.

"This is a really stupid idea," he said.

Amelia glowed. "I knew you'd agree. Don't worry. It will work."

CHAPTER THIRTY-FIVE

S HE SAT ON the edge of the bed in her room. Gideon took the
chair. The lamps were off but the connecting door was open,
allowing some light from room ten to slant across the floor. She
was nervous. Anxious. Excited. But she knew Gideon was in a far
worse state. His aura flared in the shadows. He was terrified that he
might hurt her.

"It's okay," she said. "I'm not fragile."

"You're sure you want to do this?"

"Wait." She jumped to her feet. "Hang on, I want to get something."

She hurried to her tote, took out the velvet pouch, and removed
one of the crystals. She went back to the bed, sat down, composed
herself, and tightened her grip on the stone.

"Go," she ordered.

A silvery sheen illuminated his eyes. She realized she could see
the heat because she was in her other vision. Tendrils of energy
shifted in the atmosphere, reaching out to close around her and draw

her down into the depths. She resisted the urge to push back, trying instead to open herself to the escalating currents.

She slipped beneath the waves and searched for the partial memories she had recovered earlier.

The crystal heated in her hand. Without any warning she was suddenly deep in the nightmare . . .

. . . There's an arm around her neck. The needle stabs into her upper shoulder. She sinks into the darkness. A man in a surgical mask and gown appears . . .

. . . She feels the gurney move as if it is riding a wave.

"Shit. A fucking earthquake?" the man in charge says.

"Sir, this place is coming down around us. There's a fire. I can smell the smoke. We have to get out of here . . ."

"What about the subjects?" the man in the surgical mask and gown asks.

"There's nothing we can do," the one in charge says. He's angry. "The experiment is terminated. We have to get out of here. Don't worry, the fire will take care of the evidence and the subjects."

The men are leaving now. The one in charge looks back at her. For the first time she sees his face . . .

"Amelia. Wake up."

Gideon's command pulled her out of the dreamscape. A euphoric rush of certainty hit her like a powerful tonic. She opened her eyes.

"It worked," she said. "I saw him and I know where I've seen him before."

Gideon watched her as if she was some fey creature who had materialized in front of him. "Are you all right?"

"Yep, and the good news for you is that it's obvious you can control your talent more than you realized. You can use it for something other than scaring bad guys. Don't get me wrong—as far as I'm concerned that's a fine, respectable, socially acceptable career path, but now you know you've got options."

Gideon sat, unmoving. "What are you talking about?"

"Think about it. With your ability and some practice you might be able to assist the police in interviewing crime scene witnesses. Or maybe help people deal with night terrors and bad dreams. Who knows?" She widened her hands in a sweeping gesture. "There are all sorts of possibilities."

"Before you waste any more time trying to give me career counseling advice, why don't you tell me what you saw in your dreamscape?"

"I told you, I saw the man who was in charge that night." She jumped to her feet and went to her tote. She pulled out the Night Island photos and held up the one that showed the two men on the boat dock. "That's him. The older one. I'm sure of it. He was involved with the Night Island experiments and he was at the old hotel when my friends and I were kidnapped. He was the one giving the orders."

Gideon sat forward and took the photo. He studied it for a long moment and then looked up. "You're sure?"

"Positive. I may not be the best photographer in the world but I've got a good photographer's eye."

"Okay, you've tied him to the case, but it doesn't help us identify him."

"I recognized someone else, as well. Falcon was there that night."

"We've got three dead bodies and a couple of attempted kidnappings courtesy of Falcon," Gideon said, "and the only thing we know about him is that he's dating your neighbor."

"Irene can help us identify him."

"She thinks he's a cop, remember?"

"Yes, I know," Amelia said. "But—"

Her phone rang. She whirled around and grabbed the device. When she saw the identity of the caller she put the phone on speaker.

"Irene," she said. "Thank goodness you got my message. Where are you? Are you okay?"

"I'm fine," Irene said. "I should be asking you that question. It's almost three in the morning. I know you're a night owl, but you don't usually leave messages for me at this hour."

"Are you alone?"

"Yes, unfortunately. Falcon is away on a mission. What's going on?"

"Falcon is the reason I'm calling. Your new boyfriend murdered three people tonight and I'm pretty sure he would have killed me and my assistant, too, if he'd had the opportunity."

There was a short, shocked silence on the other end. When Irene spoke she sounded very worried.

"Amelia, are you on something? Please don't tell me you are doing drugs on the first date you've had in months."

"Gideon is my assistant, not my date. We're in Lucent Springs on an investigation for the podcast but everyone here thinks we're doing a photo essay of the ruins of an old hotel and—damn it, never mind. The point is, we had a meeting with an informant tonight but it looks like we interrupted a major drug deal gone bad. Falcon was there. He got away."

Okay, it wasn't the whole truth, but it was simpler this way. She had to make Irene take her seriously, and this was not the time to try to explain that bad guys were after her because she had been subjected to some bizarre paranormal experiments.

"Wait, you're certain it was Falcon?" Irene asked.

"Yes, he shot three people in cold blood, Irene."

There was another short silence on the other end of the line before Irene spoke again.

"Are you saying he killed three members of a drug gang?" she asked.

"Yes."

"That doesn't mean he's one of the bad guys," Irene said. It sounded as if she was trying to reason with herself. "I mean, isn't that what an undercover cop would do if things went south with an operation? Shoot the real bad guys?"

It dawned on Amelia that Irene had a certain amount of logic on her side. "The local police said the three men looked as if they had been executed."

"You said Falcon got away. Did you actually see him shoot those three people?"

Amelia closed her eyes. "No."

"Are you even sure Falcon was there? You've never met him. How did you recognize him?"

Amelia opened her eyes and tried to think of a reasonable explanation. "I saw him from a distance once when he was leaving your apartment."

"Did you see his face?"

"Well, no, but—"

"Look, we both know you've been under a lot of stress lately." Irene's voice gentled. "We also know that, aside from the therapist you were seeing for a while, I have been the primary focus of your social life lately."

"Irene—"

"Don't get me wrong. I am very grateful for our friendship. I enjoy our pizza and wine and movie nights, too. But I know that you have a problem with me dating Falcon. Ask yourself if you're jealous because I've been spending so much time with him."

"It's not that."

"I'm horrified that you and your new friend got caught in what sounds like a very dangerous situation tonight," Irene said. "I was pleased when I saw you leave with him and a suitcase. I assumed you were starting a new relationship. I told myself that was a good thing. But now I'm concerned. How much do you really know about your so-called assistant?"

"Irene, I understand that you don't want to believe me. I can't give you the proof you want. The best I can do is tell you that I'm sure Falcon is not who he says he is. Please be careful."

"It sounds like you're the one who should be careful, Amelia. My turn to give you some advice. Ditch that assistant and come home."

"Irene, please."

"In the meantime I'm going to get some sleep. You should, too. Good night, pal."

The phone clicked off. Amelia looked at Gideon.

"Obviously that did not go well," he said.

"No. It didn't. My Cassandra talent in action." She got to her feet and put the phone on the table. She realized she was still clutching the crystal. She set it on the nightstand. "Irene was right about one thing. I can't prove Falcon was there tonight. Actually, she was right about something else, too. Maybe he really is an undercover cop and maybe he did execute those three men to protect his identity and the mission. It was brutal, but everyone knows the drug business is horribly violent."

"This is no time to doubt yourself or your conclusions. I don't believe in coincidences, so I don't think that gang from out of town just happened to show up at the ruins on the same night that we were to meet our informant. You heard what Richards said. Lucent Springs hasn't had any major problems with the narcotics trade until now."

She stopped, turned around, folded her arms, and raised her chin. "You're absolutely right. I *did* see Falcon's prints at the scene of the killings tonight, and I believe you when you say someone tried to kidnap me. I've got to develop more confidence in my own talent. It's just that for weeks now I've been wondering if it's driving me mad. I've started to question a lot of things."

Gideon gripped his cane and got to his feet. "Remember, it's all about control. You can handle your new senses."

"Thanks for the encouragement." She managed a shaky smile. "And thanks for restoring some of my memories. I can't wait to tell the others. They hate the amnesia as much as I do. They'll want you to do your dream therapy with them, too."

Gideon groaned. "I'm not some kind of dream therapist."

"Maybe not professionally," she said. "Not yet, at any rate. I realize you need some practice. But I'm happy to let you run a few experiments on me. I'm sure it won't take you long to get the hang of it."

"The hang of what? Helping people recover lost memories? I am not going down that road. Can you imagine the potential for lawsuits?"

"Oh. No, I hadn't considered that angle."

"I investigate certain kinds of crimes, Amelia. That's what I do."

"I understand," she said. "I'm not suggesting that you give up your work as an investigator. But you might want to think about broadening your range, so to speak."

"Right now, all I want to think about is you."

A thrill swept through her. "Me?"

"Yes, you. I need to know why you were so certain I could pull you out of the trance."

She winced. "So this is about you, not me."

He frowned. "Now what? Are you pissed?"

She gave him a bright, shiny smile. "Who, me? Pissed? Why would I be pissed? Moving right along, the answer to your question is that I knew you could do it because *you did it accidentally back there in those freaking hotel ruins when you used my name.*"

"You *are* pissed. Why the hell are you mad at me?"

"Figure it out for yourself, Mr. Psychic Private Investigator."

"I asked an honest question," he said. "I've got a right to an honest answer."

"No, you don't have any rights. However, being the gracious person I am, I will give you an answer. Last night I deliberately let my ex-therapist think that I was on a real date. This morning at breakfast you indicated that you were attracted to me. Tonight my neighbor told me she assumed that you and I were hooking up. And then, a moment ago, you said 'all I want to think about is you.' Silly me, I thought maybe you meant it. That maybe we were at the start of something."

Gideon did not move but his eyes gleamed with a little silver. "If I had meant it, how would you have responded?"

Another heady jolt of excitement lifted her senses.

"I ought to say it's too soon," she whispered. "We barely know each other. We don't have anything in common except that we both happen to have some weird psychic talents. Also, we recently survived a life-and-death confrontation with some very bad people, so there's probably a lot of excess adrenaline flooding our system. And maybe some other hormones, as well."

"Are you actually going to say all that bullshit?"

"No." She moved to stand directly in front of him and planted her hands on the front of his shirt. "It's all true, but right now I don't care."

"Neither do I, because I wanted you that first day when you walked into my house and hired me. Before I knew you had a paranormal vibe. Before we survived the shoot-out tonight. Before the adrenaline rush."

He meant it. She was certain of that. No, he hadn't dated in a while, so that was probably a factor. Yes, he had made it clear he had problems with intimate relationships. But tonight she was sure he was telling her the truth. He wanted her. Maybe that was enough. For now.

The tide of heat swept back in, stronger than ever. She was shivering, but not with panic. This was what true sexual desire felt like. Talk about an enlightening moment. She had never experienced anything like this intoxicating anticipation; this sweet, aching hunger.

She clenched the fabric of his shirt in her fists. "I want you, too."

Gideon leaned his cane against the table, braced his injured leg against the bed, and wrapped his arms around her. His mouth came down on hers in a kiss she sensed he intended to be a controlled burn. But they were both already smoldering. The physical contact sparked a wildfire.

She got the front of Gideon's shirt open and off. He struggled with her sweatshirt. She froze when she heard him draw a sharp breath.

"Your leg," she said, suddenly anxious.

"Forget my leg."

"All right, if you're sure."

"I'm sure, damn it."

"Okay, okay. Give me a minute."

She freed herself to turn down the bed. He sank onto the chair and set about removing his low boots. She sat on the edge of the bed and took off her own boots. By the time she finished he was back on his feet.

He started to unbuckle his trousers. She watched, riveted. It was the sexiest thing she had ever seen a man do in her entire life.

Without warning a shot of electricity snapped through her—and not in a good way. She went cold.

Gideon paused in the act of unzipping his trousers.

"Having second thoughts?" he asked.

She could tell he was braced for rejection. She felt the heat rising in her face and was grateful for the shadows.

"No," she said.

But that was a lie. The truth was that she was suddenly feeling rattled. Unsettled. Nervy. Anxiety was setting in fast.

Shit. Not now. Not a panic attack. Not tonight.

She turned away, scrambled awkwardly out of her clothes, and then got quickly into bed. She grabbed the top sheet and yanked it up to her shoulders.

Now she was shivering.

What she was experiencing was connected to Gideon. She was certain of it. Yes, it had been a long time since she'd been intimate with a man, but that didn't explain the nerves. What was wrong with her? She was not afraid of Gideon. The opposite was true. She trusted him.

A disturbing thought struck: she did not trust herself.

What if her reaction to the prospect of a sexual encounter tonight was a side effect of her recently enhanced senses? What if her new vision was going to ruin the possibility of ever having a love life?

Gideon got out of his trousers and sat down on the edge of the bed.

"Amelia, tell me what's going on," he said quietly.

"That's just it," she managed. "I don't know. I can't stop shivering. I thought it was the result of coming down off the adrenaline jag but I'm pretty sure that's not it. I think my intuition is trying to tell me something important."

Gideon watched her with eyes that were no longer heating with desire. Instead, she sensed grim resignation.

"Your intuition is telling you that going to bed with me would be a very bad idea," he said. "It's probably right."

"No, that's not it."

"Yes it is. After what happened back there at the hotel you finally understand what I can do with my talent. Your intuition is warning you not to get any more involved with me. You should listen."

He started to push himself up off the bed. His aura was still igniting the space, but she knew he was in complete control.

And just like that, comprehension struck.

She sat up and clamped a hand around his arm. "Sit down. This is important."

Her senses were going off like fireworks, and the physical contact intensified everything. She uttered a shocked gasp. Gideon flinched. She knew he had experienced the little jolt of lightning, too.

"Sorry," she said. She yanked her fingers off his arm. "That was my fault."

"What is going on?" he rasped.

She took a deep breath. "I think that this"—she waved one hand to indicate the bed—"you and me together. Like this. In bed—"

"Can you slow down and clarify for me? It's been a difficult night.

I thought I knew where this was going but now I have absolutely no idea."

"Right," she said. She pulled herself together. "Okay, here's my problem. I think there is a strong possibility that sex with you would be dangerous. Not for me. I'm afraid you're the one who will get burned. I'm talking literally, Gideon. Or at least semi-literally."

CHAPTER THIRTY-SIX

L ET ME GET this straight," Gideon said. "You think you might accidentally shock my aura if we have sex?"

"Something like that," she mumbled. She was mortified. "This is absolutely the most awkward pre-sex talk I've ever had, but I don't know what else to do. I don't want to be responsible for damaging your energy field."

"Pretty sure my energy field will survive, but I can't guarantee that my ego will make it through this conversation."

"I'm serious, damn it." She realize'd she was starting to get mad. "I'm trying to do the right thing here. I've always had problems with . . . intimacy."

"Sex."

"Whatever. It's like a part of me is always standing back. Observing. Waiting for something big to happen."

Gideon's mouth twitched. "Are you trying to tell me you like to watch? There's a word for that. Voyeurism."

"That is not what I meant and you know it," she snapped. "Looking back, I think my core talent has affected my whole life. It explains why I chose photography as a career. That way I'm always the one who is behind the camera. I'm not part of the action. Maybe it's the reason I've never been able to fall in love."

"Uh-huh."

"I don't know how to be in the moment. Maybe I'm afraid to be there because when I've tried, things have not gone well. Dr. Pike said he thinks that because of my past failures I've let my risk-averse tendencies take control."

"Forget Dr. Pike," Gideon ordered.

"Okay, but what if he's right?"

"Until tonight, have you ever had an anxiety attack before having sex, or am I a first?"

"I am not having an anxiety attack. I told you, my intuition is trying to warn me that I might injure you."

"How?"

"Well, I don't know, exactly," she admitted. "You told me that your talent has a negative effect on your relationships. I think I'm in the same situation."

He smiled. "Welcome to my world."

"I mean it, Gideon. I'm scared."

Another flash of silver lit his eyes. "This is your lucky night, Amelia Rivers, because I'm not scared."

Outrage splashed through her. She clutched the sheet to her breasts. "You aren't taking this seriously, are you?"

"Nope. You have allowed yourself to fall down the rabbit hole of catastrophizing. You're afraid of your new talent. I get that. But what you need is practice, and that requires a suitable test subject, one who isn't afraid of your psychic side."

"You?"

"Me."

He leaned toward her, yanked the sheet out of her fingers, wrapped an arm around her, and hauled her against his chest.

"Your ribs," she gasped.

"To quote someone I know, don't you worry your pretty little head about my ribs."

She gripped his shoulder. "Gideon."

He kissed her, effectively silencing her. His mouth was warm, sensual, compelling. She got another lightning-sharp thrill, but it felt different this time—a shock of intense awareness. Recognition. Rightness. It was as if his energy field was whispering to her, reassuring her. Seducing her. She sensed that her aura was doing something similar to his.

The feeling of intense intimacy was beyond exciting. Beyond arousing. It was joyful.

When he finally raised his head she saw that the energy in his eyes was molten. She was still shivering, but not with anxiety.

"What if things go horribly wrong?" she said.

"Then we will practice until you get it right."

She gave a choked laugh. Maybe there was nothing to fear. Maybe she was overthinking things.

And then she stopped thinking altogether because he was easing her down onto her back. He got up long enough to unbutton his shirt and take off his briefs. She glimpsed his fierce erection before he climbed into bed and got another rush. He definitely wanted her.

The weight and strength and heat of him thrilled her senses as nothing else ever had. Her entire body tightened.

She wrapped herself around him and abandoned her senses to the rising tide of urgency. His mouth moved to her throat. His hand went to her breast. One of his legs tangled with hers.

"Amelia."

He whispered her name in a way that was both demand and desperate plea, as if he not only wanted her but needed her. No man had ever said her name in such hoarse, harsh, heartfelt tones.

His hands traveled over her in a journey of discovery and pleasure. In return she explored him, sliding her palms down his chest. When she found the rigid length of his erection he groaned and closed his hand over hers, easing her away.

"I'm too close," he growled against her shoulder.

"You worry too much about control," she said, struggling to free her hand.

"Think so?"

"Definitely."

"Let's see how good yours is."

He wedged one thigh between hers, opening her for his touch. She almost stopped breathing when he found all the exquisitely sensitive places. She was suddenly drenched.

"Come for me," he said against her mouth.

And she did. She was shocked by the intensity of her release. She never climaxed without a vibrator.

At some point he lifted himself away from her long enough to sit up on the side of the bed. She watched him take a small foil packet out of his trousers. He sheathed himself and then he reached for her again.

"My turn," she said.

He allowed her to push him onto his back. When she came down astride him he groaned. His fingers dug into her thighs. She moved slowly, letting herself adjust to the width and breadth of him; setting the pace until she could no longer control herself or him.

His release pounded through both of them, triggering a second climax for her. Energy flooded the room, charging the atmosphere.

She sensed that something unique was happening but she was too dazzled to comprehend it.

It was only later, when she cuddled against Gideon's warm, damp frame, that her intuition came up with an explanation. At the height of their physical connection their auras had flared but they had not clashed; instead they had harmonized in some inexplicable way. The brief moment of exhilarating *awareness* had been breathtaking.

There was no way to know if he had experienced the same sensation, or, if he had, whether it mattered to him. But she knew she would never forget it.

This was what her intuition had been trying to warn her about earlier, she realized. It explained the shivers and the anxiety. Sex with Gideon had been dangerous not because she might damage his energy field, but because it changed everything. For her.

It was just sex, she thought. *Don't let your imagination run wild.*

But it wasn't just sex.

Well, shit. Now what?

Gideon was right. She had developed a bad habit of catastrophizing.

CHAPTER THIRTY-SEVEN

THE VIOLENT POUNDING on the door of her apartment startled Irene just as she was about to pour herself a cup of coffee. She had been unable to get back to sleep after the disturbing call from Amelia, so she had abandoned the effort.

She had showered and dressed for the day, made a large pot of coffee, and sat down at the computer. It was going on five a.m. now. She had tried to get some work done but she could not stop thinking about Amelia's warning. *Falcon is the reason I'm calling. Your new boy-friend murdered three people tonight and I'm pretty sure he would have killed me and my assistant, too, if he'd had the opportunity.*

The drive from Lucent Springs took approximately two hours. If Amelia was right—if Falcon had been in the desert town earlier to-night and if he had left around the time she had called—he would be returning to San Diego about now.

Another series of demanding raps reverberated through the apartment.

Falcon. It had to be him.

She looked at the aquarium on the end of the kitchen island.

Daisy and Dahlia were cruising through the underwater forest of fake plants and miniature statues, on the lookout for their next meal.

"I may have made a serious mistake," Irene said.

The goldfish ignored her. Unfortunately, she could not ignore the door. If she didn't respond, the jerk in the neighboring apartment would call the manager.

"I'm coming," she said,

She left the coffee on the counter, went to the door, and peered through the peephole. Falcon was on the other side. He was wearing his leather jacket over a black T-shirt and jeans and she knew he probably had a shoulder holster and pistol under the jacket. The outfit went with his tough undercover cop attitude. But there was something different about him tonight.

It took her a couple of beats to figure out what had changed. When he wiped his forehead on the sleeve of the jacket, she realized he was sweating. There was a haunted look in his eyes. Falcon was scared. Terrified.

She undid the locks and opened the door.

"What's wrong?" she asked. "What happened?"

"Things got fucked up bad," Falcon rasped. "You have to help me."

CHAPTER THIRTY-EIGHT

THE FAINT CLICK of a key in a lock followed by a small draft of air brought Gideon out of a nightmare-free sleep, the third he had enjoyed since the messy ending of the Colony case. Make that since meeting Amelia. *Coincidence? I think not.*

He opened his eyes but he did not move. Something felt different. Yes, the intruder had just entered room ten via the parking lot door, but this was another sort of different.

It hit him with a disorienting rush. He was in the wrong bed.

He had promised himself that as soon as Amelia fell asleep he would move to the other bed. Instead, he had drifted into a heavy sleep—in her bed. Even more astonishing was the fact that Amelia was also asleep. She had not awakened in a screaming nightmare.

Fascinating. But he would ponder it later. First he had to deal with the uninvited guest in room ten.

Reluctantly he eased himself away from Amelia's soft curves and sat up with care, trying not to make any noise. There was a faint squeak from the bedsprings but the intruder did not pause. The shadows shifted on the floor when a figure moved past the partially open connecting door.

He reached for his cane and got to his feet, profoundly grateful that he had put on his briefs before getting back into bed with Amelia. He did not consider himself to be unduly modest, but the thought of confronting the intruder while nude was unsettling, especially since he was pretty sure he knew who was in the other room.

He crossed to the connecting door and pulled it open. The light that he had left on in the bathroom in room ten glinted on the large knife the intruder gripped in both hands.

"Good morning, Ms. Shipley," he said. "A little early to be up trying to kill me, isn't it?"

At the sound of his voice, Katy Shipley turned toward him. In the dim light her eyes had a vacant expression. She was no longer the friendly tourist trying to shake off a bad divorce. She looked like a woman who was under a spell.

"You murdered Merlin," she said. Her voice was flat, utterly devoid of emotion. "I am his bride. He chose me above all others. Now I must avenge him. Then I will follow him into death."

She moved forward, the knife poised to strike. Gideon went into his talent, trying for a pulse of energy, not a killing blow.

"Gideon, wait," Amelia said from the bed.

It was too late.

Katy stiffened as the fierce gale of nightmares swept over her. Without a word she crumpled to the floor.

CHAPTER THIRTY-NINE

THERE WAS NO need to put her into a nightmare," Amelia said, scrambling out of bed.

Gideon did not take his attention off the unconscious woman. "I've been trying to tell you, that's pretty much my job description."

"No, it's not," she snapped, irritated by both his attitude and her nightgown, which had become tangled around her legs. She paused to straighten out the garment and then hurried, barefoot, toward the connecting door. "The thing is, I'm pretty sure she was already in one."

Halfway to her destination she paused and turned to look at the three crystals on the nightstand. They glinted in the shadows. She had set them out, as usual, before going to sleep next to Gideon.

On impulse she went to the nightstand and grabbed one of the stones. She continued on to the doorway and watched Gideon lean down to pick up the knife. He took a moment to check Katy's pulse.

"She's okay, isn't she?" Amelia asked. "Her aura looks fairly normal except for one band of currents."

"Pulse is a little shaky but as far as I can tell she just fainted," he said, straightening. "I tried to go easy this time. Not sure it worked."

"Excellent! I didn't think you had hit her with the full force of your talent."

"Let's postpone this discussion. In case you hadn't noticed, I am standing here in my underwear and there's an unconscious woman on the floor."

Amelia pulled herself together. "Right. Priorities. You should put on your pants."

"I'll do that."

He stalked past her into the other room and scooped up his trousers.

She studied Katy. "I'm pretty sure I can wake her up, but I think you're the one who can neutralize the trance."

"You think I hypnotized her?" he asked, surprised.

"Maybe. In a way. But I'm almost positive that someone else put her into a deeper trance before you came along."

"You're sure that whatever it is you're seeing isn't my doing?"

"I can view the effects of your talent, too," she said. "But it's more like an REM sleep state. The damage I'm talking about is different. It will be a long time before it wears off, if ever."

Gideon sat down on the edge of the rumpled bed and pulled on his trousers. "Are you saying she is under the influence of a post-hypnotic suggestion?"

"Yes. You're the one who told me Merlin was a psychic-grade hypnotist and that he was delusional. Why wouldn't he try to use his bride as a weapon of vengeance?"

"Merlin is dead, Amelia."

"That doesn't mean he didn't implant a hypnotic command before he died. If I'm right, Katy is the innocent victim of a psychic madman. I think you can help her."

"I wouldn't put money on the 'innocent' part." Gideon stood and fastened his trousers, wincing in the process. His hand went briefly to his ribs. "How, exactly, do you suggest I go about undoing a hypnotic suggestion, assuming there is one?"

"One theory of hypnotic trances is that they are a version of the dreamstate. Like sleepwalking. You're the expert on dreams."

"Nightmares," he corrected grimly. "And I'm not an expert. I can trigger them, that's all."

"How did you recover my memories tonight?"

"As far as I can tell, you did that on your own."

"If I could have unlocked my memories on my own, I would have done so months ago. But tonight I was able to see them in the shadows when I sensed your energy field trying to manipulate mine." She opened her hand and looked at the crystal. "I think I somehow steered the currents of your talent in the direction I wanted them to go."

"You channeled my energy?" he asked in disbelief.

"Just certain currents. With the help of the crystal."

"How the hell—?"

"We're wasting time," she said. "I've got an idea. Give me your hand. I think physical contact will help me do this more efficiently."

"What, exactly, do you want me to do?"

"Go into your psychic senses, but target me, not Katy. Gently. I'm going to see if I can guide your energy to the frozen section of her aura."

"Why?"

"I might be able to use your talent like a psychic defibrillator and jolt the frozen currents back into a normal, stable rhythm."

"Have you ever done anything like that before?"

"No," she admitted.

"Do you realize how off-the-walls your plan sounds?"

"What have we got to lose? If we don't do anything, she'll probably wake up, but the hypnotic suggestion will still be in place. She'll keep trying to kill you."

"Not," Gideon said evenly, "if I make sure the nightmares are very, very bad the next time around."

"Oh, come on, you know you don't want to drive her mad or put her into a permanent coma."

"What makes you so sure of that?"

"You're one of the good guys. Think of Katy as another client."

"A nonpaying client? I've got enough of those."

"I believe 'pro bono' is the correct term. Hurry. We need to do this before the sun comes up." She paused a beat, struck by a thought. "I sound like some kind of vampire, don't I?"

"I wasn't going to say anything."

She ignored him, knelt beside Katy, and reached up for Gideon's hand. He sat down on the edge of the bed and wrapped his fingers around hers. She rested the hand holding the crystal against Katy's forehead.

"Now what?" Gideon said.

"Give me a minute to figure this out." She opened her other vision to full strength. "All right, do what you did earlier tonight when you released my memories."

"I still think this is a bad idea," Gideon said.

"Do it."

"Here goes."

She felt the first brush of his energy field. Fragments of her nightmares stirred, threatening to spill out of the shadows. She suppressed them and concentrated on Katy's aura, searching for the currents that were locked. Focusing.

Relying on her intuition, she fought to channel Gideon's powerful energy, manipulating the currents with her own talent and the aid of the crystal.

She knew the precise instant when the frozen currents snapped out of stasis and began to oscillate in a normal pattern—mostly because the blowback struck her senses like an exploding storm.

The jagged shards of nightmares, old and new, roared out of the darkness, sweeping her into a whirlpool of hallucinations. Frantically, she tried to suppress the violent images the way she had earlier. But this time they refused to slink back into the shadows. Gideon's talent threatened to overwhelm her.

"*Amelia.*"

Gideon's voice, cold and clear, acted like a beacon in the churning fog of dreams. She focused on it and the manacle-like grip he had on her hand. The combination guided her back to the surface.

When the room settled around her again she took a few deep breaths and willed her pulse to return to normal.

"Shit, I told you this was a bad idea," Gideon said.

When she opened her eyes she found him watching her with a mix of dread and guilt.

"I'm okay," she said quickly. "I just need a moment."

Relief flashed in his eyes. It was quickly followed by outrage.

"Damn it, Amelia."

"Please," she said, tugging her hand free. "Save the lecture for later." She looked at the woman on the floor. "Katy, wake up."

Katy's eyes fluttered. She opened them and looked at Amelia.

"What . . . what are you doing here?" Then she saw Gideon sitting on the bed. Comprehension infused with panic twisted her face. She sat up. "Oh, shit. I came here to kill you."

Amelia got to her feet. "I've got an idea. Why don't I make coffee for everyone? But first, let's move into the other room. I really don't like this one."

CHAPTER FORTY

S HE TOOK A moment to work through the logistics of making three cups of coffee with a single two-cup brewing machine and then unplugged the coffee machine in room ten. She carried it, along with the coffee pods and cups, through the connecting doorway and set the things down on the table in her room.

"Katy, take the chair," she instructed gently.

Katy looked dazed but she followed directions.

Amelia gave her a reassuring smile and then took a moment to pull on her light travel robe. Next she busied herself with the task of brewing coffee.

When she turned around she saw that Gideon had put on his shirt and was in the process of tossing a quilt over the rumpled sheets on the bed. For some reason it amused her to know that he found the intimate scene awkward in the presence of a third party. It was a side of him she had not seen until now. At least he was dressed, she thought. She was running around in a nightgown and robe.

"The whole time with The Colony feels like a bad dream," Katy said. She raised her hands and massaged her temples. "I mean, I know it was real. But I don't understand how I could have allowed myself to get swept up in a cult."

"The experts will tell you that no one ever joins a cult," Gideon said. "People think they're getting involved with a movement. That they are part of something larger than themselves. Sacrifices are required. Things go bad from there. In your case, you were the victim of a very skilled hypnotist."

Katy lowered her hands and folded them in her lap. "Merlin was a hypnotist?"

"That's right," Gideon said.

Katy shook her head. "Before any of this happened I would have told you that I couldn't be hypnotized. I didn't think I was the type."

"Most people think they can't be hypnotized, at least not against their will," Gideon said. "Luxford started out as a con man, but at some point he convinced himself he really was born to control a cult."

Katy shuddered. "And I was going to rule by his side, his chosen bride. He was twenty years older than me and not even good-looking in an older man sort of way. I must have been out of my mind."

"No," Amelia said. She set a cup of coffee on the table in front of Katy. "You were in a trance."

"I was convinced that I had a duty to avenge his death," Katy said. She looked at Gideon. "It's so weird. During the day I told myself to forget him and move on. But when night fell I could not resist the compulsion to stalk you. I had this stupid plan, you see. I would leave things on your doorstep. The invitation. The flowers. The veil. And then I would kill you. Afterward I was going to kill myself."

Gideon accepted a cup of coffee from Amelia and looked at Katy. "Where did the plan come from?"

"I don't know," Katy said. "I honestly have no memory of making any sort of plan. But somehow I knew what I was supposed to do."

Gideon watched her for a moment. "Let me guess. You visited Luxford in jail after he was arrested, didn't you?"

Katy frowned. "Yes. Once."

"That must have been when he planted the hypnotic suggestion and explained exactly what you were supposed to do," Amelia said.

"But I don't want to kill anyone. I just want to go home."

"How did you get the key to my room tonight?" Gideon asked.

"There was a spare in the motel office. I saw it hanging there this afternoon. Tonight when I felt the compulsion come over me I used a credit card to break in to the office and take the key."

"What about the knife?" Amelia asked. "Where did you get it?"

"I brought it with me from San Diego," Katy whispered, stricken. "I remember buying it one night in a shopping mall. The same night I bought the veil and the flowers and the invitation."

"How did you find Gideon here in Lucent Springs?" Amelia asked.

"That's easy," Gideon said. "She put a tracker on my car."

Amelia stared at him. So did Katy.

"Seriously?" Amelia said. "You knew there was a tracker on your car?"

"I discovered it after the wedding invitation landed on my doorstep," he said. "I left it in place. Figured my stalker would turn up in person sooner or later. I admit I didn't expect you to follow me to Lucent Springs, though, Katy."

Katy blinked. "Did you know who I was when I arrived here at the motel?"

"I wasn't positive," Gideon said. "Not until you made your move tonight. But, yeah, the timing made me suspicious. So did the self-help book."

Katy grimaced. *"When Life Gives You Lemons: Ten Steps to Moving On.* I hoped it would help me recover from the trauma of the cult. Are you going to call the police now?"

"Not unless you're having second thoughts about murdering me," Gideon said.

"No, I swear it," Katy said, clearly anguished.

"Gideon was just joking," Amelia said quickly.

"Not entirely," Gideon muttered.

She shot him a warning glare. He ignored it.

Katy started to cry. "I don't want to hurt anyone. I just want to get my life back."

"Of course," Amelia said bracingly. "And that starts with breakfast. Don't forget it's free here at the Cactus Garden Motel."

CHAPTER FORTY-ONE

THE INTERVIEW WITH the Lucent Springs police took place in Captain Richards's office. It did not last long.

"Richards sure wants to wrap this up in a hurry, doesn't he?" Amelia said as she and Gideon walked outside the small police station and headed for the SUV.

"Why not?" Gideon asked. "As far as he's concerned the scene at the hotel was a classic drug deal gone bad. Mayfield, you, and I had the bad luck to stumble into it."

"Very neat and tidy except that Falcon got away." Amelia opened the passenger door of the SUV and climbed inside. "What do you think he'll do?"

"I don't know," Gideon said. He settled behind the wheel. "If he was really involved in a traditional drug ring he would try to disappear."

"We do know drugs are a factor in this mess."

"But not the standard street shit." Gideon started the engine and drove out onto the road. "That makes predictions tricky, but we've got one lead."

"Irene. I'm really worried about her."

"For good reason. According to you she's been dating him for a while now. She probably knows more about him than she realizes. He'll be aware of that."

"Yes." She thought about that ominous statement and then tried to go to the bright side. "But wouldn't he steer clear of her if he's trying to disappear? If he killed her like he did those men at the hotel last night, that would open up a homicide investigation, and the cops always view the boyfriend as the first suspect. He has to know that."

"I agree. If he's smart he'll vanish. But Falcon has already screwed up his main objective—grabbing you—a couple of times. I don't think we can count on him being an exceptionally smart bad guy."

"I'll call her again."

"You've called her three times already. Last night and twice this morning. Each time she told you that she's okay and that she hasn't heard from Falcon."

"I know, but if she was being held against her will Falcon would force her to say that, wouldn't he? And she did sound tense, Gideon."

"You're catastrophizing again. There's nothing more we can do from Lucent Springs. We'll find out what's going on when we get back to San Diego."

"Huh."

"What?" Gideon asked. He sounded wary. Suspicious.

"It occurred to me that if Irene is okay you might be able to use your talent to help her pull up some memories of Falcon that would help us locate him. Memories she might not be consciously aware of."

Gideon's jaw tightened. "I don't think that's a good idea."

"That's what you said just before you helped me recover my own lost memories. You said it again before we dehypnotized Katy Shipley."

"I still don't know exactly what happened when you did whatever it is you did to recover Katy's memories."

"I told you, I channeled your energy through the crystal to unfreeze the hypnotic suggestion, that's all."

"You make it sound like we just did a small tune-up."

"It worked. Katy was fine afterward. You saw her."

"You were the one who scared the hell out of me."

"I'm okay, Gideon. There was a bit of a shock when it happened. Some kind of blowback. I wasn't expecting it. But I'm fine. I'm getting the hang of channeling your talent. It's a lot like focusing a camera. The crystal really helps. I just need practice."

"That's a dangerous theory."

"Maybe your Uncle Shelton will have some helpful advice. You said he's something of an expert on the paranormal."

"We are not going to get my uncle involved in this," Gideon said.

"Why not? He's a scientist."

"A *mad* scientist when it comes to the paranormal. I, and everyone else in the family, try not to encourage him."

"You're afraid he'll agree with me about the need for experimentation and practice, aren't you?"

"Oh, yeah."

"Well, we can talk about it later."

"No," Gideon said. "We won't."

Time to change the subject, Amelia decided. She glanced at the dashboard clock. "It's getting late. We need to get on the road."

"I want to take one last look at the hotel before we leave," Gideon said. "I doubt the local police did a thorough search last night. In the dark they easily could have missed something."

She thought about the fact that three men had been shot to death in the lobby of the Lucent Springs Hotel. She really hated death properties. But this wasn't a real estate shoot and she could not afford to be squeamish. There was too much at stake.

"Good idea," she said, going for something resembling professional enthusiasm.

He glanced at her. "You don't have to go inside the lobby."

"Yes," she said. "I do. It won't be so bad during the daytime."

It was bad.

Amelia stood at the entrance, trying to calm her rattled nerves, and watched Gideon move methodically around the lobby, searching the gloom-filled interior.

She did not need the bloodstains on the floor or her own memories to tell her where the three men had died. The residue of violent energy was strong enough to break through the suppressing effects of daylight.

Gideon shot her a concerned look. "Are you okay?"

She folded her arms very tightly around her middle. "Yep. Not my first death property."

"Death property?"

"I've run into this sort of thing before on real estate shoots."

"Go wait in the car."

"No," she said. "I have to learn to control this reaction. I've got an idea. I'll be right back."

She swung around and hurried outside to the SUV. Opening the rear door, she reached into her tote and took out the velvet pouch of crystals. She went back to the entrance and poured the three polished stones into her palm. They felt warm and calming.

Gideon paused in his search to watch her. "You think the crystals will help you deal with the energy in here?"

"Maybe," she said.

She closed her fingers around the stones and silently chanted the mantra her aunt had given her. *I am calm. I am serene. I am centered. I exhale the bad energy and inhale the good.*

After a moment the shivery sensation eased. She was still intensely aware of the dark vibe in the lobby, but she could keep it at a distance. At least temporarily. *Practice,* she thought. *I just need more practice.*

"They're working, Gideon," she said.

"Good," Gideon said. "That's great."

She knew he was trying to sound encouraging.

"Don't say it," she warned.

Gideon moved behind the blackened stone monument that had once been the front desk. "Say what?"

"That I'm experiencing the placebo effect."

"Hey, whatever works," he said.

"Exactly."

Gideon did not reply, because he was bending down behind the desk. When he straightened he had a slip of paper in one hand.

"What is it?" Amelia asked.

"A receipt from a gas station," Gideon said. "Not one here in Lucent Springs. The station is located in a community on the coast about twenty miles north of San Diego."

"What's the date? Maybe one of the shooters dropped it last night?"

"No," Gideon said. Satisfaction infused his voice. "It's dated seven months ago. Two days before you and your friends were grabbed here at the hotel."

CHAPTER FORTY-TWO

HALF AN HOUR later Gideon dropped his shaving kit into the duffel, zipped the bag closed, and gripped the handle. It was past time to get back to San Diego and talk to Irene, but he was feeling good about the gas station receipt. It was not a strong lead but it was one more data point. You never knew how the pieces fit together until they did.

He wrapped his fingers around the handle of his cane and took one last look around room ten. Experimentally he heightened his senses. He couldn't see any paranormal evidence of death, but Amelia was right. There was an unpleasant vibe in the space.

He went through the connecting doorway into Amelia's room. It was as if he had moved through a portal into another dimension, one where there were no bad vibes, just compelling memories. Everything was different in this room because it was Amelia's.

He contemplated the bed. The sex had been special. Life-changing, at least for him. And he had fallen asleep afterward. He never let himself fall asleep afterward. It always led to disaster.

But not this time. Amelia had evidently slept as well as he had, at least until Katy Shipley had tried to murder him. Details. The important thing was that he had slept next to Amelia and she had not been swept into a raging nightmare. Now, there was an experiment he looked forward to repeating. Often.

The bathroom door opened behind him.

"Gideon?" Amelia sounded concerned. "Everything okay?"

He turned to look at her. She was wearing her usual outfit—black jeans, a black pullover, and sneakers. Her hair was caught in a clip at the nape of her neck. She had a small toiletries bag in one hand. For a moment he could not look away. It took an effort of will to pull himself out of the small trance.

"Yes," he said, "everything is okay. Ready to go?"

"Yep." She dropped the bag into her rolling suitcase, zipped it shut, grabbed her camera bag, and went toward the door. "I noticed that Katy Shipley's car is gone. Looks like she packed up and headed back to San Diego."

"Yes. Amelia?"

"Hmm?"

"Do you recall having *any* bad dreams last night?"

"Nope." She stopped and turned to look at him. "I can't even remember them now. I slept better than I have in months. Right up until Katy tried to kill you. What about you?"

"I slept fine," he said. "But I don't understand why you didn't wake up in a screaming nightmare."

She raised her brows. "I told you, I don't have any issues with your energy field."

"That makes sense when you're awake, but not when you're asleep."

"How do you know?" She frowned. "You're really having a problem with this sleeping together thing, aren't you?"

"I like answers," he said. "I know I said I don't buy the woo-woo stuff about crystals, but I'm starting to wonder if maybe there's something to the claims. Those three rocks of yours were on the nightstand last night."

She narrowed her eyes. "Don't you dare blame our good night's sleep on my crystals."

"Are you upset?"

She raised her chin and gave him an overly bright smile. "Of course not. We should get on the road. Got a two-hour drive ahead of us, and that's assuming no serious traffic when we get to San Diego."

She was upset. Maybe annoyed. He wasn't certain which but he was damned sure the safest thing to do was pretend everything was normal and move on.

"Right," he said. He went toward the door. "The thing is, I didn't have any nightmares, either."

"Gideon, wait."

The sudden urgency in her voice stopped him cold. She no longer looked upset or annoyed. She looked anxious. Worried.

"What?" he said.

"I think you should take one of the crystals." She reached into her tote, took out the velvet pouch, and selected a stone. "This feels like the right one for you."

"I told you, I don't believe in the power of crystals."

"But now you're starting to wonder if there is something to those old theories. Well, here's your chance to run your own experiments the next time you get involved in a relationship."

He tightened his grip on the duffel. "I don't want to run experiments like that." *Not with anyone else*, he added silently.

She took a couple of steps forward and held out the stone she had chosen. "Think of it as a memento of this case."

He opened his mouth to tell her that his mementos consisted of nightmares that he exorcized with his paintings. But his intuition warned him that he really needed to change the subject. The fastest way to do that was to take the crystal.

"Thanks," he said, aware that he sounded grouchy, not grateful.

She pretended not to hear the less than gracious vibe in his voice and dropped the crystal into his hand. He closed his fingers around it. The stone was pleasantly warm. It felt good. He slipped it into the pocket of his trousers.

"It's just a souvenir," she said reassuringly.

"Right. A souvenir."

CHAPTER FORTY-THREE

THERE WAS TRAFFIC on the way back to the city. Of course there was traffic, Amelia thought. This was Southern California. The result was that it was midafternoon by the time Gideon pulled into the parking lot of her apartment complex.

By mutual, if unspoken, agreement she and Gideon had avoided the subject of their relationship. They had focused on what they had learned in Lucent Springs. That had given them plenty to speculate about, but underneath the surface conversation she was still asking herself why she had insisted that Gideon take the crystal.

No, it was not a souvenir. Souvenirs were throwaway things, like a beach towel with the name of a seaside hotel on it or a tiny umbrella from a fancy cocktail. The crystals were important to her. They were not cheap souvenirs.

She had been shocked and hurt when she discovered he was considering the possibility that her nightmare-free night had been caused by the crystals. He was grasping at straws—or, in this case, rocks. Maybe he was afraid to acknowledge that the two of them had forged a bond last night. That they were at the beginning of a promising relationship, not a casual hookup. Okay, maybe it was doomed to be a very *short* relationship, but it was not a casual affair. It was important, at least to her.

Or maybe he had simply lost interest. Had she misread him?

There were a lot of uncertainties involved, but the one thing she was absolutely sure of was that she did not want him crediting the crystals for whatever had gone right last night.

Yet she had given him one of the stones and told him to think of it as a souvenir. Why? Maybe, deep down, she simply wanted him to have something of hers to keep. A symbol of their possibly short-lived connection.

"Oh, good," she said as Gideon shut down the engine. "There's Irene's car. She's home."

Gideon glanced at the vehicle parked in a nearby slot. "Her car's here. That doesn't mean she is."

"You really are a negative thinker, aren't you?"

"Goes with the job. And my talent."

Amelia cracked open the door. "I'll check her apartment as soon as we get upstairs."

Irene appeared just as they reached the second-floor landing. Amelia breathed a sigh of relief. Irene's face was drawn tight with worry but otherwise she looked fine. She was definitely not a hostage.

"Irene." Amelia rushed up the last two steps, hauling the suitcase behind her. "You don't know how glad I am to see you."

"I heard you on the stairs," Irene said. "I'm glad you and your friend are back. I didn't know whether to panic or not. I'm so confused."

"About Falcon?" Amelia asked.

"Yes." Irene grimaced. "He showed up at my front door after you called last night. He said the mission had gone bad. He had to disappear."

"I've called you several times today," Amelia said. "Why didn't you tell me you'd seen him?"

"Because he said I shouldn't tell anyone. He said his life was at stake. He wanted some cash because he couldn't use his credit cards. He was scared, Amelia. Really scared. I've never seen him like that. Honestly, he was a nervous wreck. I'm surprised he was able to make the drive back from Lucent Springs without crashing. I wasn't going to tell you but now I'm really worried."

"Why now?" Gideon asked.

"He promised me that he would text or phone to let me know he was safe," Irene said. "I haven't heard from him. I don't know what to do."

Gideon reached the landing. "What, exactly, did he tell you about his mission?"

"Just that his cover had been blown and he was in terrible danger. He said the cartel boss had discovered that he was a cop and had put out a contract on him." She turned to Amelia. "See? You were wrong about him. He was telling me the truth."

"Maybe," Amelia said.

Gideon glanced down the stairs. Amelia followed his gaze and saw a tenant walking her dog on the garden sidewalk.

"The last thing we need is an audience," Gideon said quietly. "Let's go inside Amelia's apartment and talk about this in private."

CHAPTER FORTY-FOUR

AMELIA TOOK THREE bottles of sparkling water out of the refrigerator and carried them into the living room. She handed them out and then sat down beside Irene on the sofa.

Gideon had settled into the recliner. For a man who wasn't interested in a long-term relationship, he was certainly making himself at home, she thought.

"One thing we can tell you about the man you call Falcon," he said to Irene, "is that if he is an undercover agent, he did not stick around to introduce himself to local law enforcement in Lucent Springs."

"How do you know he was the one who returned to the scene of the shootings to finish off those three men?" Irene asked. "Maybe it was another member of the gang."

Amelia looked at Gideon. "I suppose there's a possibility that someone else was involved, someone we never saw."

"It's possible." Gideon did not bother to hide his skepticism. "But it doesn't feel like it. Falcon was running the show. He came back to make sure none of his people survived."

"That sounds so ruthless." Irene shook her head. "I mean, I knew he was dangerous, but it's so hard to believe he was conning me all along."

Amelia kept quiet. There was no simple way to explain to Irene that the man who called himself Falcon had used her as a cover so that he could stalk his real target two doors down the hall. That would mean inviting Irene into the rabbit hole of a conspiracy theory involving people with dangerous psychic powers and bizarre experiments. As far as Irene was concerned, anything to do with the paranormal came under the heading of "entertainment."

Irene looked at Gideon. "Do you think I might be in danger?"

"I doubt it," he said. "If Falcon wanted you dead he would have murdered you last night when he stopped by to ask for cash and tell you that he was leaving town."

Irene shuddered. Water splashed out of the green bottle. She grabbed a napkin and quickly blotted up the drops that had landed on her trousers.

Amelia glared at Gideon. "Really?"

He winced. "Sorry. I was thinking out loud."

"He's right," Irene said. She swallowed hard. "I hadn't thought of it that way. I've been thinking about calling the police all day, but what would I tell them? That I dated a drug dealer who claimed to be an undercover agent? They would probably conclude that I was involved in the drug trade, too. An arrest would ruin my career."

"What do you know about Falcon?" Gideon asked.

"Just what he told me," Irene said. "Now I don't know how much of that was fiction."

"Do you know his real name?" Gideon asked.

"No. He said it was safer if I knew him only as Falcon."

"What about an address?" Gideon said.

"He's renting a small house a few miles from here. I expect he's gone now."

"Have you ever been there?"

"Once or twice," Irene said. "It's very ordinary. Nothing special. Sort of run-down, to tell you the truth. We never spent the night there because he said it might draw the wrong attention. He preferred hotels. More anonymous, he said."

"If you'll give me the address I'll drive by and check to make sure he really did leave town," Gideon said.

"It's on my phone." Irene pulled up the address and read it to Gideon. When she was finished she looked up. "Are you going to notify the police?"

"Yes," Gideon said.

Irene looked resigned. "They'll want to talk to me, won't they?"

"Not if he's legit," Gideon said. "If he really is undercover, there will be fail-safes in place in the system designed to protect him."

Irene shivered and put down her mug. "I hope he was telling me the truth. Even if I never see him again, I prefer to think that he was one of the good guys. Or maybe I just don't want to think I was dumb enough to believe his story."

AT THE DOOR Irene paused and looked at Amelia. "I almost forgot— your ex-therapist came by looking for you."

"Yes, I know," Amelia said. "He called while I was in Lucent Springs and told me he had come here to see if I was okay."

Irene snorted. "I heard him on the stairs. He pounded on your door a few times and then gave up and left. I gotta tell you, I never knew a therapist who made house calls, especially not without an appointment. It's almost like he's stalking you."

Amelia winced. "I don't think that's the situation, but I agree, it's getting a little weird."

"See you later. Maybe do drinks? I could use a few."

"Sounds good," Amelia said.

Irene went down the outdoor walkway and disappeared into her apartment. Amelia closed the door, locked the three locks, and went around the corner into the living room. She looked at Gideon.

"Are you really going to call the police?" she asked.

"Maybe," Gideon said. "Depends on what I find at that address Irene gave me."

"So that's where we're going next? Falcon's rental?"

"It's where I'm going next. You are staying here."

"Why?"

"Because I don't know what I'll find there and I don't want to have to worry about keeping you safe while I'm finding it. If it turns out I need your night vision I'll come back here and get you."

"You're going to break in to Falcon's place, aren't you?" she said.

"Depends on how things look, but, yes, I'd like to get inside if possible."

"I could be your lookout."

Gideon sighed. "Amelia—"

"I know where you're coming from, but here's your problem: you said I shouldn't be left alone until we know for sure I'm no longer in need of a bodyguard."

"I'm not going to leave you alone. I'll get a babysitter to keep an eye on you."

"Who?"

"Uncle Shelton."

"You're going to leave me in the care of the mad scientist in the family?"

"Uncle Shelton has had what most people would call a checkered career. The result is that he has a variety of skill sets."

CHAPTER FORTY-FIVE

S HELTON SWEETWATER ARRIVED as twilight descended. Gideon opened the door.

"I see you dressed for the part," he said.

"This is SoCal," Shelton said, sauntering into the hall. "Naturally I dressed for the part. Brings back memories of my younger days. Good times."

With his sleek sunglasses and an ensemble that screamed Armani— tailored light gray sports jacket, trousers, and pullover—Shelton looked like Hollywood's version of a high-end assassin. The image was enhanced when he slipped out of the jacket and revealed the shoulder holster and pistol underneath.

It was, Amelia reflected, the way Gideon would look if he dressed for the role. Then she remembered how he had appeared in the shadows of the Lucent Springs Hotel when he had taken down three armed men with only his talent. He did not need the costume.

"Amelia, this is my uncle, Shelton Sweetwater," Gideon said. "You could say Shelton is the butterfly that flapped its wings several years ago and sent out the ripples that created the storm we find ourselves in now. Shelton, this is Amelia Rivers. Just to be clear, she and her podcast pals blame you for their current situation. Goodbye, you two. I'll be back as soon as possible."

He paused long enough to startle Amelia with a quick kiss and then he was gone, his cane delivering a muffled cadence as he went down the outside walkway to the stairs.

Amelia used the process of closing and locking the door to recover from the small shock of the goodbye kiss. She had not been expecting it, she realized. Gideon was focused on his mission, yet he hadn't even hesitated. Evidently he assumed that a kiss on the way out the door was now routine for the two of them. That was a positive sign, she thought.

So why was she feeling rattled?

Shelton chuckled behind her. "Always knew my nephew would fall hard when he finally went down. It's that way with Sweetwaters. Paranormal biophysics in action."

She pulled herself together and turned to face him—and got another start when she saw that Shelton had removed the ominous sunglasses. He watched her with the fierce eyes of an apex predator. They reminded her of Gideon's eyes. She would have liked to photograph Shelton, she realized. There was a lot of interesting energy going on in his vicinity.

"Excuse me?" she said. "Paranormal biophysics?"

"It's all about the resonating frequencies of the auras of the two individuals involved, you see."

"Don't read too much into this situation, Mr. Sweetwater," she said smoothly. "Gideon and I have a professional relationship, not a personal one."

"I get the feeling your definition of professional and personal relationships is a tad different than mine. Probably a generational thing. Do yourself a favor—try not to break his heart. His mother would be really annoyed."

"I doubt if his heart is in any danger," she said lightly. *Mine, on the other hand . . .* She pushed the thought away. "Can I offer you coffee or tea? Maybe a light snack? It's after five and there's no knowing how long Gideon will be gone."

"Coffee and a snack sounds good," Shelton said. "And please call me Shelton."

"Have a seat, Shelton." She waved him toward one of the bar-stools at the island. "Call me Amelia."

"Thanks."

Shelton settled himself and hooked one elegantly shod foot on the bottom rung of the stool. She whisked around the end of the island and opened the refrigerator.

"I understand you've had a checkered career," she said.

"Is that how Gideon described my job history?" Shelton chuckled. "He's in no position to criticize. He took his time figuring out what to do with his own talent."

Amelia selected a wedge of cheddar and closed the refrigerator. She looked at Shelton across the expanse of the island. "Did he try to become a professional artist before he took up a career as a private investigator?"

Shelton snorted. "He knows he'll never set the art world on fire. He doesn't care. For him, painting is a way of centering himself. I was talking about his real talent."

She set the cheese on a serving board and opened a drawer to find a knife. "You mean his ability to drop someone into a hallucinatory dreamstate."

"Well, well, well," Shelton said. "So he told you about his ability, did he? He doesn't tell many people, you know."

"He pretty much had to explain things to me." She went to work on the cheese. "I was accidentally caught by the blast of energy he used to take down one of the bad guys in Lucent Springs."

There was a short, charged silence from the other side of the island. She turned her head to look at Shelton. She knew from the way he watched her that he was more than surprised. The term *dumbfounded* came to mind.

"No shit?" he asked.

"No shit."

"You don't look too traumatized, if you don't mind my saying so."

"I wasn't traumatized."

"Amazing." Shelton paused. "It's a tough talent, you know."

"Believe it or not, I figured that out."

"Shows up occasionally on the Sweetwater family tree, but not often."

Amelia arranged slices of cheese on the tray and added some crackers. She set the small repast in front of Shelton and poured a cup of coffee. In her experience people tended to relax and get chatty over food.

He gazed appreciatively at the snacks. "Thanks."

"Gideon mentioned that the Sweetwaters have a long history of careers in law enforcement," she said, trying for an encouraging tone.

Shelton picked up a cracker and topped it with a slice of cheddar. "I'm not so sure I'd go as far as calling our line of work 'law enforcement.' But there is a long-standing family tradition of hunting bad guys. You could say it's in the Sweetwater DNA. With our kind of talents it's either hunt bad guys or—"

"Become one of them?"

"Right." Shelton munched some cheese and cracker. "Gideon had a hard time accepting his unique ability when he was growing up.

He worked in the family business for a few years while he was in college and for a while afterward, but he made it clear he wanted to go his own way."

"He didn't want to join Sweetwater Security?"

Shelton's brows bounced. "He told you about the firm, too, I see. And he's only known you for what? Four days? Talk about aura resonance. This gets more interesting by the minute."

"You were explaining his difficulty dealing with his talent."

"I warned him he was going to have to make peace with the skill set he got stuck with. Hell, we all tried to tell him. Every Sweetwater knows that you have to figure out how to use your talent. If you don't, it can drive you mad."

"Seriously?"

"Seriously. After he left Sweetwater Security he drifted for a time. He tried the financial world, and he was successful, but he didn't find it satisfying. Did some adventure travel, but that got old. Experimented with a few adrenaline-rush sports. Fast cars, that kind of thing. Then, one day out of the blue, he decided to set up his little private investigation business."

"It seems to be working for him."

"Yes, it does. His parents are relieved, I can tell you that much. Of course, now his mother is starting to fret because he doesn't seem to be interested in getting married."

"Marriage is important to the Sweetwaters?"

"Oh, yeah," Shelton said. "Sweetwaters have always been a tight-knit clan because of the talent and the family business. Don't get the wrong idea—Gideon's not against marriage. He just hasn't met the right woman yet." Shelton gave her a knowing look. "Or maybe he has. In which case he'll figure it out damn quick. That's another Sweetwater trait. They know when they find the right one."

She glanced at the gold ring on his finger. "I assume you did?"

"Yep. Angie and I celebrated our thirty-seventh wedding anniversary last week."

She decided she did not want to pursue the discussion about Gideon's interest or lack thereof in marriage, so she propped one hip against the island, drank some coffee, and changed the subject.

"You don't seem to be worried about Gideon going out alone to check on the house that Falcon rented," she said.

Shelton shrugged. "He's my nephew. Naturally, I'm concerned. But he's a Sweetwater. He can take care of himself. He's got to do what he was born to do."

She nodded. "Hunt bad guys."

"Well, yes, but the thing is, Sweetwaters tend to specialize."

"In what?"

"Our clients contact us when they need a specialist who can deal with the category five types."

She stilled. "Define 'category five.'"

"Didn't Gideon explain? You hire a Sweetwater when you need someone who can track down a bad guy who has a heavy dose of talent. Regular law enforcement isn't equipped to deal with that sort. There's a saying in our business. *It takes a psychic to catch a psychic.*"

CHAPTER FORTY-SIX

THE BLACK SUV in the detached garage was coated with a fresh layer of dust. A small tumbleweed was caught in the undercarriage. There was no question that the vehicle had recently spent some time in the desert. The keys were on the console.

Gideon climbed into the driver's seat and checked the GPS log. Last trip: Lucent Springs and back.

Sometimes it was the simple, old-fashioned approach to investigation that worked best.

Satisfied that he had the right address, he left the garage and walked around to the back of the house. The shabby rental sat on a large, weedy lot in a gritty, semirural neighborhood on the outskirts of the metropolitan area. No ocean view. No pool. No sign of regular maintenance. No nearby neighbors who might get curious. All in all, a suitable safe house for a drug-dealing thug or an undercover cop.

The kitchen door was unlocked. He was not surprised. There was no need for stealth. He had a pretty good idea of what he would find inside.

He followed the scent of death into the living room. The body was on the floor. The dead man had been shot twice, once in the chest and once in the head. There was no identification in the pockets of the black leather jacket and black trousers. The pistol was still in the shoulder holster.

Falcon—assuming it was Falcon—had been caught by surprise.

"Looks like you trusted the wrong person," Gideon said softly. "Easy mistake to make."

He pulled out his phone and took a picture of what was left of the face. Irene could confirm the identity of the body.

When he was finished he dropped the device into a pocket and did a quick walk-through of the house. He did not expect to find anything useful, and for the most part he was correct. The two small bedrooms and closets were empty except for a handful of men's clothes, all in black and all in a size that looked about right for the dead man.

At first glance the vintage California tract house bathroom appeared as unilluminating as the rest of the residence. He was about to leave when he noticed the closet door. He opened it, expecting to find shelves containing spare rolls of toilet paper or a few towels.

He found himself looking into a walk-in closet. There was an assortment of emergency gear on the shelves—military MRE rations, bottled water, battery-driven communications equipment, a first aid kit, and a couple of flashlights. There was an unlabeled box on one shelf.

This was California, he reminded himself. He could be looking at a prepper's safe room—a reinforced space built for use in the event of an earthquake, a home invasion, or the apocalypse.

Then again, he might be looking at a secure space constructed for the convenience of drug dealers and/or killers on the run. His Sweet-water intuition leaned heavily toward the latter. Either way, if his hunch was right there was a strong possibility of an emergency exit.

He moved through the narrow doorway to take a closer look. The box on the shelf held four fake IDs—good-quality fakes.

He was in the process of replacing the lid on the box when he heard a muffled, metallic click. His Sweetwater reflexes kicked in but the cane got in the way. His injured leg twisted, threatening to send him to the floor.

He recovered but not fast enough to make it back through the doorway before the heavy steel plate slammed shut.

Not a safe room, he realized. A trap.

CHAPTER FORTY-SEVEN

AMELIA WAS LEANING against the kitchen island, munching a cracker, when the ghostly fingers touched the back of her neck and sent a frisson of dread across her nerves. She flinched and caught her breath.

"Gideon," she whispered.

She did not realize she had spoken aloud until she saw that Shelton was watching her intently from the other side of the island. She was suddenly sure there was a little energy in his eyes.

"What about him?" he asked, his tone sharper than it had been a moment ago.

Amelia finished the cracker and dusted crumbs off her hands. "I don't know. I'm worried about him. More worried than I was a moment ago, if that's possible." She glanced at her watch. "He's been gone quite a while, don't you think?"

"I told you, Gideon can take care of himself."

She winced. "You're right. I'm a little overanxious. He and I have been through a lot together recently. Stress."

Shelton studied her for a long moment. "You're not his usual type. For a Sweetwater, that's a good sign."

She felt the heat rise in her face. "I'm just another client as far as he's concerned. An inconvenient one."

"No, there's more to it than that. I've known Gideon all his life. The energy between the two of you is unmistakable. You're not just another client, trust me. The question is, how do you feel about him?"

"We've only known each other for a few days," she shot back, exasperated and a little panicky. "You're reading way too much into our energy or whatever you're picking up. I think Gideon needs me, that's all."

"For a Sweetwater, that's plenty."

"What are you talking about?" Understanding struck. She waved one hand. "Oh, no, no, no. You're way off base. I didn't mean he needs me the way you mean. He needs my help for an entirely different reason. For now."

"My turn to ask you what you're talking about," Shelton said.

She forced herself to concentrate on the question and her evolving theory about Gideon's talent.

"We've only run a couple of experiments," she said, "so I don't have a lot of data, but on both occasions I was able to channel his energy with the aid of a crystal. It was all a matter of focus, you see. Evidently my talent gives me that ability. But I don't see why, with practice, he can't learn to do the same thing on his own, in which case he could cut out the middleman—or the middlewoman. Make that the middle person." She frowned. "I think the crystal might have to be tuned, though. I'll have to ask Aunt Cybil about that."

Great. Now she was rambling. She couldn't help it. She was distracted. Her nerves were getting zapped by short flashes of unease. The sensation that Gideon was in trouble was growing stronger.

Shelton peered at her, very intent now. "Do you think anyone with a strong psychic talent can learn to channel energy through a crystal?"

"I don't know." She paused, briefly distracted by the question. "The process seems fairly straightforward. It's a lot like focusing an old-school film camera."

"Huh. It's an interesting idea. I've spent some time studying crystals, but I've never been able to make them work the way you describe."

"Aunt Cybil says the key is tuning." Amelia picked up her coffee again. "But, to be fair, she says that about everything."

"Tell me about Aunt Cybil."

"My mother's sister, otherwise known as the family eccentric. She's a professional psychic who gives performances on cruise ships."

"I'd like to meet her. Probably takes a certain kind of talent to tune a crystal."

A sharp rap sounded on the front door. Amelia darted out from behind the island.

"That must be Gideon," she said.

Shelton got up and followed her. "Check first."

"Of course." Amelia peered through the peephole. "It's Irene." She opened the door. "What's wrong? Are you okay? Is it Falcon? Did he call you?"

"No." Irene glanced back along the walkway. "I just got off the phone with your weird therapist. He said he was afraid you were having a psychotic break or something and that I should buzz him in the front gate so that he could check on you."

"You didn't unlock the gate for him, did you?"

"No, but we both know how easy it would be for him to follow someone inside, Amelia. He may be on his way here right now. If you don't answer the door, he'll come to my place. I've got to tell you, the guy makes me nervous. He's obsessed with you. Do you think he's dangerous?"

"I doubt it," Amelia said, "but to be honest, I just don't know for sure. You'd better come inside. There's someone else here. He's got a gun."

"Oh, shit," Irene said. She looked past Amelia, her eyes widening. "I can see that."

Amelia turned to follow Irene's alarmed gaze. Shelton was standing casually behind her. His pistol was no longer in the shoulder holster. It was in his hand. The gun was not aimed at Irene—Shelton held it against his leg, pointed at the floor—but it did not look any less threatening.

"Amelia's right," he said. "You'd better come inside. Amelia, close and lock the door. We'll all have a cup of coffee and wait for Gideon. If Dr. Pike shows up I'll deal with him."

CHAPTER FORTY-EIGHT

With the gloomy daylight from the bathroom cut off, the concealed prison cell behind the closet door was abruptly drenched in midnight. Gideon heard a faint hissing. An uncharacteristic burst of optimism offered up the possibility that an emergency generator had automatically come on, pumping fresh oxygen into the space.

This kind of irrational speculation was what came of hanging around with Amelia. All that positive energy made a man lose his sense of perspective. Of course it wasn't fresh air flowing through the unseen duct. It was gas. The only question was whether it was intended to kill him or merely render him unconscious. Probably the latter, he decided. Whoever had trapped him would have questions. They would want answers before they killed him.

He tried to recall the survival and emergency items on the shelves around him. He did not remember seeing any masks.

He yanked off his button-down shirt, wrapped it around his nose and mouth, and secured it with a bulky knot.

Satisfied he had done all he could to protect himself, he checked his phone. He did not expect to get service. He was right.

Dropping the phone into a trouser pocket, he groped for and found one of the flashlights. He switched it on and was mildly amazed when a beam of light speared the darkness. Given the way his luck had been running today he had been prepared for dead batteries.

He listened intently for a moment but there was only silence from the bathroom. Evidently no one was anxious to open the cell door. Probably waiting for the gas to take effect. He began the possibly pointless search for a concealed exit.

He considered the layout of the house and concluded that if there was a concealed way out of the cell it would go down, not through one of the walls. Anyone trying to escape would want to get as far away as possible. There wouldn't be much point in walking into a bedroom or a hallway.

Working on that theory, he pushed the shelving out of the way and began methodically tapping the floor with his cane. He had covered about half the space when the visions began to appear.

"Shit," he whispered.

Now, at least, he could confirm the purpose of the gas: It wasn't supposed to kill him outright. It was designed to make him delusional. Someone wanted him kept alive long enough to be questioned while under the influence of a powerful hallucinogen.

He was able to suppress the effects at first, but the nightmares were coming at him in waves. Reality began to sink beneath the rising tide of disorienting visions.

Not real. Not real. Not real.

But the silent chant could not hold off the flood. The gas was suppressing his ability to control his psychic senses. He was drowning in a dreamscape that came straight out of his own private nightmares.

Was this what it was like for those he targeted with his talent? No wonder they retreated into unconsciousness. The waking mind could not handle the wild storms of dream energy. Was he on his way into a coma?

No, he decided, at least not yet. He would be questioned first.

He tried to move the cane more quickly around the floor but he was having trouble with his balance. He misjudged the position of the walking stick. It slid sideways. He grabbed at the metal shelving but only succeeded in toppling it against one wall.

He went down hard. Pain jolted through his injured leg. The flashlight fell from his hand and rolled across the floor, the beam of light twisting and turning until it came to rest on a wall.

The visions intensified. He knew then that if he did not gain control he would go mad. He groped for the cane, struggling to get back on his feet.

The disembodied voice came to him out of the darkness.

"Can you hear me, Gideon Sweetwater? You are hallucinating now. But you have the power to make the dreams stop. All you have to do is answer my questions."

CHAPTER FORTY-NINE

. . . It's obvious you have a powerful talent, Sweetwater. That makes the first question simple. Who enhanced you?"

The disembodied voice was the only steady vibe in the shifting sea of chaotic dreams, but he knew if he concentrated on it, it would lead him to his doom.

"Just answer the question," the voice urged. *"That's the way out of the hallucinations. If you don't answer the question you will soon be trapped in an endless nightmare. You will never wake up."*

If he gave the voice any answers he would die in this room. And if he died he would not be able to help Amelia.

Amelia. He had to get to her. She was in terrible danger. Shelton might not be able to keep her safe.

Pain shafted through his leg again when he struggled to get up off the floor but he managed to haul himself to his hands and knees.

Amelia.

He would cling to her name, not the fucking voice.

"You must answer me, Gideon Sweetwater. The dreams will stop if you tell me who enhanced you . . ."

"Amelia," Gideon whispered.

Saying the name aloud steadied him. He half crawled, half dragged himself to the corner and propped his back against the wall. He reached into the pocket of his trousers. His fingers closed around the crystal. It was warm. Comforting. Clarifying.

"Amelia," he said again. Steadier this time. Stronger. Focused.

"*Forget her,*" the voice said. "*It is too late to save her. You can only save yourself . . .*"

CHAPTER FIFTY

WHAT WITH ALL the excitement lately, I forgot to tell you that your therapist was not the only person who came around looking for you while you were in Lucent Springs," Irene said.

"What?" Amelia yanked her attention away from the too-quiet screen of her phone and looked at Irene. "Someone else showed up here looking for me? Who?"

"Relax," Irene said. "I don't think you need to worry about this other guy. He was very businesslike. Well dressed. Good haircut. Looked successful. He said he was a real estate agent. Wanted to talk to you about setting up a photo shoot for a residence that he just listed."

"How did he get in?" Amelia asked. "The entry system didn't notify me of any callers while I was in Lucent Springs."

"This place isn't exactly a fortress." Irene drank some coffee. "I heard him knock on your door so I went out to tell him that you were not home."

"Did he say anything else?" Shelton asked.

"Not much." Irene got up from the stool and went behind the counter to refill her cup. "Just that he'd heard Amelia had a reputation for photos that bring out the drama in a property."

Amelia grimaced. "Translation: he's got a fixer-upper."

"No, I don't think so," Irene said. "He mentioned it was waterfront property in La Jolla."

"Waterfront property in *La Jolla*?" Amelia repeated in disbelief. "And he came here looking for me? This could be my big break. I wonder who gave him my name?" In the next instant a thought struck her, sending her spirits into a nosedive. Another unnerving chill feathered her spine. "Wait. You said the agent was male? Businesslike? Successful-looking?"

"All of the above."

"How old?"

"Middle-aged, but very well preserved middle age, if you know what I mean." Irene glanced at Shelton's attire. "Good clothes."

Amelia slipped off the barstool. "Excuse me, I'll be right back. I've got a photo I want to show you."

Irene frowned. "You think you have a picture of this guy?"

"Maybe. It's a long shot, but I'll feel better if you take a look at the photo I've got and see if you recognize the man in it."

She went around the corner and down the hall and opened the door of her darkroom. She switched on the overhead light and crossed to the shelf where she kept the prints of the Night Island photos.

She shivered when she picked up the envelope. She stopped, not sure what to do next. Her intuition was screaming at her to run but it was not offering specific information.

The only thing she knew for certain was that something in the darkroom had changed.

She pulled the heavy blackout curtain closed and turned off the overhead fixture.

The energy prints seethed in the artificial night. They were fresh and they were everywhere—the floor, the computer, the envelope containing the Night Island photos. She recognized them.

She took a deep breath and reminded herself that she was not alone in the apartment.

She went back down the hall, past the laundry room, past the front door, and turned the corner into the kitchen–living room. She was too late.

Shelton was slumped, unconscious, on the dining counter. The coffee mug that Irene had refilled a short time ago was on its side. A small rivulet of spilled coffee ran to the edge of the counter and dripped to the floor.

She had a beat to realize that Irene was not in the kitchen or the living room. The laundry room door stood partially open. It had been closed earlier.

She turned to run for the front door.

There was no time. She sensed the presence behind her, felt the sting of the syringe needle in the back of her shoulder, had a few seconds to understand that Irene had been waiting for her inside the laundry room, and then the bottomless tide of night rose up to take her.

She fought the darkness, trying to focus on Irene, who was bending over her, easing her descent to the floor.

"The coffee," she whispered, her voice thickening rapidly. "You drugged it."

"I'm afraid so," Irene said. "It's very fast acting. Your bodyguard never knew what hit him."

"You searched my darkroom while I was gone."

"Now how did you figure that out? Never mind. After I found the photos from Night Island I knew for sure I had a problem and had to move quickly."

Amelia heard the front door open. A man spoke.

"Ready?" he asked.

"Yes," Irene said. "Take her downstairs and put her in the van. What's the situation with Gideon Sweetwater?"

"Under control. He showed up at the house, like you said. Found the safe room. The gas got him. Weaver is questioning him now. When he's done he'll make sure Sweetwater disappears. What do you want me to do with the one in the kitchen?"

"Don't worry about him. He'll be out for a while. When he recovers he won't have any memories of what happened."

"Are you sure you don't want me to finish him?"

"We don't have time to figure out how to get rid of the body," Irene snapped. "Now pick her up. Hurry. If anyone sees you say she's ill and we're taking her to the ER."

Amelia felt muscular arms sliding under her shoulder and knees, hoisting her up into the air. She could no longer fight off the dark. This was how it had been seven months ago when she and Talia and Pallas had been lured to Lucent Springs. Was she going to lose another night of her life? Maybe she would never wake up. Never see Gideon again.

That last thought acted like a shot of adrenaline, rousing her briefly. Gideon was in danger and there was nothing she could do to save him.

Gideon, I love you.

The short flash of energy dissipated. The last thing she heard was Irene's voice. It came to her from a long way away.

"Really sorry about this, Amelia. Under other circumstances I think we could have been friends."

CHAPTER FIFTY-ONE

WE KNOW THE *enhancement serum requires regular boosters,"* the voice said. *"How long will you last if you don't get your next dose on time? A few hours? Days, maybe? I can give you an injection of the drug. I've got an extra dose on me. All you have to do is answer my questions . . ."*

Gideon closed his eyes and kept his back planted against the reassuringly hard surface of the wall. He concentrated on the crystal he clutched in the palm of his hand.

He was sure he could feel Amelia's energy in the stone. Maybe it was the hallucinogenic gas or simply the damned placebo effect, but it was all he had so he leaned into it. He could have sworn the crystal distracted him from the voice and helped him steer a path through the visions. His Sweetwater intuition stirred beneath the smothering weight of the dreamscape. It told him that his only hope was to maintain his silence.

"Fuck this," the voice said. *"The boss will be pissed if you die before I get answers out of you. I don't have time to wait for you to feel like talking. We'll do this the old-fashioned way. The unpleasant way."*

The metal barrier slid open. Gideon tightened his grip on the crystal and opened his eyes. A figure loomed in the doorway, silhouetted against the gloom of the bathroom. His face was partially concealed behind a respirator mask. He had a pistol in one hand.

"On your feet, Sweetwater. I need answers."

A rush of ice-cold rage slammed through Gideon.

"I need information, too," he said.

Intuitively, as if it was the most natural thing in the world, he channeled the full force of his psychic senses through the crystal.

The stone responded to his energy the way a finely tuned race car did when the driver stomped on the accelerator. He suddenly had more focus, more control, and more raw power than he had ever had.

Instead of hitting the target like a grenade, the psychic blast struck with the devastating impact of a sniper's bullet. The man in the mask convulsed violently, reflexively pulling the trigger of the pistol as he fell.

The bullet tore into the wall beside Gideon. The roar of the weapon was somewhat muffled by the acoustic paneling but the sound was nevertheless loud enough to leave Gideon's ears ringing.

For a moment he did not move. After a few seconds he became aware that he was still clutching the crystal.

Carefully he slipped the stone back into the pocket of his trousers. *Note to self:* If he was going to use crystals in the future he would have to develop a new level of control. The learning curve thing.

The atmosphere in the cell was clearing rapidly. The hissing had stopped. Opening the door probably turned off the gas.

He staggered to his feet, braced one hand against the wall, and leaned down to retrieve his shirt and cane. He had to get to Amelia.

When he was fairly certain he wouldn't lose his balance he crouched beside the unconscious man, collected the pistol, and checked for a pulse. The guy was alive but it didn't look like he would wake up anytime soon, if he woke up at all. There was no ID.

Gideon headed for the kitchen door.

He exited the house and limped toward his SUV. There were no sirens in the distance. No sign of the vehicle his captor had used, either. It was probably concealed somewhere nearby. He did not have time to search for it.

When he reached the SUV he paused to take out his phone and call Amelia. He was thrown directly into voicemail. He did not bother to leave a message. There was no point. He tried Shelton next but he didn't expect an answer. He was right.

Whoever was behind the project to kidnap Amelia had succeeded in grabbing her. He told himself they would not kill her, at least not right away. He refused to think about the possibility that Shelton was already dead.

He desperately needed a starting point. Irene was looking increasingly relevant. He tried her phone. When the call went straight to voicemail he was pretty sure he was right. Irene was not an innocent bystander.

He was about to switch on the engine but he hesitated, studying the garage where Falcon's dust-covered vehicle was parked. He thought about the gas station receipt he had found at the Lucent Springs Hotel.

A frisson of something that felt a lot like certainty but was probably nothing more than hope whispered across his senses. He had missed something important when he had searched Falcon's vehicle. He needed to take another look.

CHAPTER FIFTY-TWO

S HELTON WAS DEEPLY asleep but alive. His pulse was steady and strong.

Relief briefly flooded Gideon's senses. He left his uncle snoring on the dining counter and found some paper and a pen in the darkroom. He scrawled a quick note and positioned it where Shelton would see it when he woke up.

He took a quick look around, registering the toppled coffee cup near Shelton's hand and the missing pistol. Then he went back outside and looked over the edge of the walkway barrier. Irene's car was still in its parking spot. He continued down the hall to her door and knocked. He was not surprised when there was no answer.

He forced the lock and went inside. The soft hum of an aquarium tank broke the silence. Two goldfish watched him search the apartment but they lost interest when it became obvious he wasn't going to feed them.

There was no sign of any tech—no laptop, no phone—but Irene's car keys were on the console near the door.

He picked up the keys and left. It would be next to impossible to carry an unconscious woman out of the apartment complex without someone noticing. It didn't take long to find an eyewitness.

The resident in the apartment between Amelia's and Irene's answered the door with a can of beer in one hand.

"Yeah, I saw 'em carry her out of here and put her in a van," he said. "Rivers looked totally out of it. Her friend said she was sick. They were taking her to the nearest emergency room. Between you and me, I figured Rivers had OD'd. She was getting a little weird, know what I mean?"

"How many people are we talking about?" Gideon asked.

"Irene What's-her-name from next door and the dude who drove the van. So, two."

"What can you tell me about the man who carried Ms. Rivers to the van?"

"Looked like a gym rat. Steroid city. Never saw him before in my life. What is this all about?"

"I think Ms. Morgan and the man who drove the van kidnapped Ms. Rivers."

"Holy shit."

"Exactly."

CHAPTER FIFTY-THREE

S HE CAME AWAKE on the remnants of a classic anxiety dream in which she was desperately trying to find Gideon and simultaneously warn Talia and Pallas that Irene Morgan was dangerous. Oh, and there was a killer named Falcon somewhere in the picture. But she was lost in a thick fog.

For a moment she instinctively held herself very still, her eyes closed, and struggled to suppress the splash of panic that threatened to override her senses. She forced herself to concentrate in an effort to separate real memories from the misty landscape of the dream.

One by one the images fell into place—the energy prints in the darkroom, Shelton unconscious on the dining counter, Irene emerging from the laundry room with a syringe.

The last dreamscape clip was infuriating enough to make her open her eyes. She found herself looking up at a perfectly normal ceiling. She was on a bed. The bed was still neatly made and she was still wearing the jeans, tee, and sneakers she'd had on earlier.

Gideon.

She refused to think about the possibility that he might be dead.

She would know if he was gone, she thought. She clung to that conviction.

She bolted to a sitting position—and fell back onto the quilt when she was overcome with a wave of stomach-churning dizziness. She took a couple of deep breaths and tried again, moving more cautiously this time. The room wavered and shifted a bit but settled down after a moment.

She swung her legs over the side of the bed but she did not try to get to her feet. Her first reaction was relief. She was not on a hospital gurney and there was no one wearing a surgical mask bending over her. When she remembered to check her watch she saw that it was almost midnight. So, she had lost a few hours but not a whole night. She groaned, remembering the last moments in her apartment.

"I never saw you coming, Irene. So much for friendship."

And so much for her stupid talent. She had viewed Irene's aura and her prints often enough during the past few months. Why had she never detected the threat? Apparently she still had a lot to learn when it came to reading energy fields. Stupid learning curve.

The lamp beside the bed was on. In the soft light she could see that the room was furnished like an expensive guest suite in someone's private home. Shades covered floor-to-ceiling windows. There was an adjoining bath.

First things first.

She used the facilities and then crossed the room to press the switch on the wall. The shades rose, revealing a wide deck overlooking a moonlit cove and the night-darkened ocean beyond.

One of the windows proved to be a glass-paned door that opened onto the deck. She tried it immediately but it was electronically locked from the outside.

The suite was nicely furnished and it had a multimillion-dollar view, but it was built to serve as a prison.

She went back across the room and tried the main door. She was not surprised to discover that it, too, was secured from the other side.

She moved to the bedside table and turned off the lamp. There were energy prints scattered around the room. Over time people had come and gone in the space, leaving a light ankle-deep fog. She saw Irene's prints, too. The seething currents in the splashes of energy laid down by her ex-friend indicated a high level of tension, but they appeared stable. Maybe that's how it was with sociopaths?

There was a second set of new prints near the door. They were anything but stable.

The unnerving tracks were fever-hot and radiated an unwhole-some energy that her intuition told her was verging on dangerously chaotic. She was sure that whoever had left the prints was barely holding it together.

A muffled click followed by a short buzz made her flinch. She turned quickly and watched the main door open. Irene walked a few steps into the room.

"I take it pizza-wine-and-movie night has been canceled this week," Amelia said.

"I know you've got questions," Irene said. "But so do we. That's why you're here."

"Did you murder Shelton?"

"No. He's sound asleep. When he wakes up he won't remember anything."

"Where's Gideon?"

"You might not believe this, but I have no idea. He seems to have disappeared."

"You're lying."

Irene sighed. "It's the truth. The last we heard, he showed up at the safe house and was being interrogated. Then we lost contact with the agent in charge. Unfortunately we're a little short-staffed these days, thanks to you and Sweetwater."

"What do you want with me?" Amelia said.

"I'll explain everything but first there is someone I want you to meet."

"Your pal Falcon?"

"No. Falcon is dead."

Amelia went cold. "Seriously?"

"Yes," Irene said.

A man appeared in the doorway before Irene could answer.

"Hello, Amelia. A pleasure to meet you again. My name is Cutler Steen. I realize you don't remember me—"

"I remember you," Amelia said. "You're the creepy guy in the Night Island photograph, the whack-job responsible for kidnapping my friends and me and shooting us full of some weird drug. How many innocent people have you murdered in the course of your crazy experiments?"

"So you do remember me." Cutler looked intrigued now. "That is extremely interesting. The drug you and your friends were given is supposed to induce permanent amnesia. I wonder if your core psychic senses combined with the enhancement serum has allowed you to overcome the memory loss."

Amelia ignored him and turned back to Irene. "How did you get involved with this creep?"

"I had no choice in the matter," Irene said. "He's my father."

CHAPTER FIFTY-FOUR

T HE ENHANCEMENT SERUM was developed by a small, private off-shore research facility," Cutler began.

"The Aurora Islands Pharmaceutical Laboratory," Amelia said.

Cutler looked shocked, or maybe horrified. "How in fucking hell did you discover that?"

"The podcast has its sources." Amelia switched her attention to Irene. "I'm guessing that when you took those trips to the islands during the past few months you did not end up in Hawaii."

The three of them were in the great room of the big house. She was perched on the edge of a large leather chair. Irene sat on the matching leather sofa across from her.

Cutler Steen prowled the room. Everything about his body language indicated a barely controlled agitation. He looked like a man who might explode at any moment. From time to time Irene cast him an uneasy, covert glance.

Curious family dynamic, Amelia thought.

A muscular man with a shaved head hovered in a doorway. Not a butler, Amelia decided.

"No," Irene said. "I did not visit Hawaii on those trips. I went . . . home to see my father and the rest of my family."

The slight pause before the word *home* was another interesting factoid, Amelia decided. One thing was clear. Gideon was alive. She was certain of it. He would be searching for her, and he was very, very good at that kind of thing. She had one job now. She needed to buy time.

"Your home is on an island?" she asked.

"My father is the head of a large global business," Irene said smoothly. "There are tax and logistical advantages to the island location."

"Got it," Amelia said. "The Steen family business is running drugs on an international scale."

"I am not in the fucking drug business," Cutler snarled from the far side of the room.

"Gosh, I wonder where I got that idea," Amelia said. "Probably because my friends and I were drugged and kidnapped and then forced to become test subjects for some extremely dangerous drugs. Yep, that was why I jumped to such a ridiculous conclusion. Silly me."

Cutler looked as if he wanted to throttle her but he succeeded in gaining control of himself. "You have no idea who you are dealing with or the stakes involved in this situation."

"Maybe you could explain both to me," Amelia said. She looked at Irene. "But first I've got a couple of questions for you. What makes you sure that Falcon is dead?"

"I'm the one who shot him," Irene said calmly.

"Oh." Amelia took a beat. "Okay, I did not see that coming."

"When he showed up at my door that night he was in a panic," Irene continued. "He kept saying Sweetwater had tried to drop him straight into hell and that the only thing that had saved him was one of his men who got in the way. Claimed he'd barely escaped and that he was on the run. He had to get out of the country. He wanted my help."

"You knew who and what he was all along. Why did you kill him?"

"He said he wanted me to escape with him. But I was sure he planned to use me as a hostage."

Amelia stilled. "I don't understand. How would that have worked?"

"He thought that as long as he controlled me he would have access to the drug. My father is the only one who can supply it, you see. He deals directly with the Aurora Islands people. He has never read me or my brother and sister into the details of the arrangement that he has with the source. To make a short story shorter, I agreed to run off with Falcon. I went back to his place with him. He wanted to collect the fake IDs stored at the safe house. When I got the chance, I shot him."

Cutler paused his pacing long enough to grunt. "Falcon was becoming unstable. He couldn't handle the drug."

And maybe you can't handle it, either, Amelia thought, but she did not say that aloud. The possibility that the drug was making Cutler unstable was terrifying. Did it mean she and her friends were doomed, too?

A sudden thought occurred. She looked at Irene, who was pouring coffee for herself with a steady hand. "You're not on the enhancement drug, are you?"

"No," Irene said. "My father thought it would be unwise to experiment on ourselves until we had enough data from the drug trials to make an informed decision. He changed his mind a couple of months ago, however, and began injecting himself with the serum."

She spoke in a cool, nonjudgmental voice, as if she was simply offering a reasonable answer to a reasonable question. But the unstable
vibe in the atmosphere flared. Amelia did not have to look at Steen
to know that Irene's casual words infuriated him. There was probably nothing more annoying than having your offspring point out
your poor decisions.

"The drug fucking *works*," Cutler growled.

"If it doesn't make you insane or kill you outright," Irene added.
"We knew going in that not everyone could tolerate the serum. The
goal of the trials was to develop a profile of the ideal candidate, quantify
the risks, calculate the proper dosage, and establish the maintenance
schedule, if one was necessary."

Amelia looked at Cutler. "If the idea was to be careful and me-
thodical, why did you jump the gun?"

"Because thanks to you and your friends we were able to build a
profile of the ideal candidate and *I fit the fucking profile*," Cutler shot
back.

"Which is?" Amelia asked, her breath very tight in her chest.

Cutler took a deep breath, visibly pulling himself together, and
resumed his pacing. "The basic requirement for success appears to
be that the subject possesses a degree of natural paranormal ability,
a core talent."

"But you had no practical way to test for that particular quality
until you found the list of names from the old research study," Amelia said.

"The list changed everything," Cutler said. "Up until that point
all we had was a string of failures. But when the directors of the
pharma company gave us the list of people like you, people who had
been tested and found to have a genuine paranormal talent, we
turned a corner. We knew we were on the right track."

Amelia narrowed her eyes. "People died in those tests."

"It's true we lost a few subjects due to their inability to tolerate the drug. Having some degree of latent talent is not enough to guarantee success. But you and your friends not only survived—you appeared to be stable. That was a big step forward. Unfortunately, though, it looked like you hadn't developed any measurable new paranormal ability. That was . . . discouraging."

"My father considered you and your podcast friends to be failures," Irene said.

Cutler stopped and slammed a clenched fist into the nearest wall. "Because paranormal talent is so damned difficult to observe or measure, especially from a distance."

"My friends and I grew up with at least some awareness of our psychic vibes," Amelia said. "We learned early on that it was best to keep quiet about it. We all doubled down on that approach after you ran your experiments on us because we didn't want people to think we were completely delusional."

Cutler shot her a fierce look. "I didn't realize that until recently. In the meantime we did have some clear successes."

"You managed to produce a couple of psychic assassins," Amelia said. "My friends ran into one on Night Island. Congratulations. You must be so proud. Definitely the kind of scientific advance that will improve the quality of life for human beings around the world. Yep, I can see a Nobel Prize on the horizon for you."

"Shut your fucking mouth, you stupid bitch," Cutler roared.

The atmosphere in the great room was electric. It was easy to believe lightning would strike at any second. For a moment Amelia was afraid she'd gone too far.

But Irene stepped in to manage the situation. It was obvious she'd had some practice with the task. The relationship between father and daughter was clearly fraught.

"I'm sure you're curious about the origins of the enhancement serum," Irene said, pretending not to notice that Cutler looked like he badly wanted to murder someone.

Cutler fixed Amelia with a lethal expression. "How did you find out about Aurora Islands Pharmaceuticals?"

"Among other things that Dr. Fulbrook left behind in his room at the Cactus Garden Motel was a portion of a box with the label of the company on it. Oh, and he also left a helpful note."

Cutler stared. "How did you discover that Fulbrook stayed in that motel?"

"I hired a private investigator, remember?" Amelia said. "I admit I had my doubts at first, but it turns out Mr. Sweetwater is very good at his job."

Cutler flushed a violent shade of purple. "Sweetwater will be dead before the night is over."

Amelia checked the time. "It's been a few hours since he walked into your trap. He's still alive. I'd know if he wasn't. I'm psychic, re-member?"

"You stupid bitch."

"You don't know what's happening at Falcon's house, do you? You've lost contact with whoever you sent to take out Gideon. No wonder you're on the brink of a panic attack."

This time she knew she had gone too far. Cutler moved toward her, rage heating his eyes.

"Dad, please," Irene said quietly. "We need information. Let me finish questioning her."

Cutler turned away without a word and resumed his restless

pacing. Amelia drew a shaky breath. *Note to self: Try not to poke the bear again.*

"Interestingly, the drug is not the result of a new scientific breakthrough," Irene continued as if there had been no interruption. "From what we've been able to learn, it's based on a formula that was developed in the course of some clandestine research conducted by the U.S. government back in the latter half of the twentieth century."

"The Bluestone Project," Amelia said.

"How much do you know about Bluestone?" Cutler demanded.

"Very little," Amelia said. "Just that it was a top secret program designed to conduct research into the paranormal. The U.S. government was really into the psychic thing at the time. So were the Russians."

Irene gave her an approving smile. "I'm impressed. The *Lost Night Files* crew has uncovered some very closely held secrets."

"We haven't had much choice," Amelia said. "You and your father stole a night of our lives. We want answers."

"So do I," Cutler grated.

"You're the one who orchestrated this mess," Amelia said. "That makes you the guy with the answers. What do you think I know that you don't?"

Cutler took a few steps closer to her, stopping a short distance away. His eyes glittered with a feverish light.

"I want to know why you and your friends are still alive," he said. "Why are you still sane? You should be dead or locked up in an institution by now."

Amelia watched him warily. "Because?"

"You survived the first round of trials, but you haven't had the fucking boosters."

"Right. The boosters. Well, we can't say for sure, but we have a couple of theories."

Cutler took another step closer, hands bunched. "Tell me about your theories."

"One is that our core paranormal senses were strong enough to handle the new sensory input, so we've been able to adapt. It wasn't easy, you understand, but we managed."

"That theory doesn't explain anything." Cutler resumed the restless pacing. "I've got a strong core talent. I tolerated the initial dose of the drug. I tolerated a second injection. The serum worked. But after that I realized I needed a booster. And then another. The same is true for the members of my security team who survived the first and second doses of the serum. We all require boosters. Why don't you and the others?"

Irene was sitting very still now. She watched the scene taking place in the great room as if it were a high-wire act, one being performed without a net. The security people were staying out of sight.

"Let me get this straight," Amelia said, feeling her way. "You're asking me to diagnose your problem?"

Cutler froze. "Can you?"

"Maybe," she said. "I'm still getting the hang of reading auras but I might be able to analyze yours."

Cutler's mouth thinned with disappointment and disgust. "That's all you can do with your talent? View auras?"

"Well, I can see energy prints, too, of course. That's how I recognized Falcon when he and his men ambushed Gideon and me at the old hotel. Do you want me to take a look at your aura?"

"Yeah, sure, go ahead," Cutler said. It was clear he did not expect much.

"We'll have to go outside onto the deck," Amelia said.

Cutler glared. "Why?"

"My talent works best in darkness." She looked around. "I suppose we could turn off all the lights in here. Your choice."

She could tell Cutler was torn, but he was a desperate man. He made his decision.

"All right," he said. "We'll go out onto the deck." He glanced at the guard hovering at the entrance to the great room. "Twitchell, stay here. Keep an eye on us."

"Yes, sir," Twitchell said.

Amelia noticed that the guard looked anxious and desperate, too. He was on the drug, she realized.

Irene got to her feet. "I'm coming with you. This should be interesting." She looked at her father. "How will you know if Amelia tells you the truth about what she sees in your aura?"

Cutler did not take his feverish eyes off Amelia.

"I'll know," he said.

Amelia remembered something Irene had once said about her father. *He always thought he was the smartest one in the room. And he was. Right up until he wasn't.*

At the time Irene had used the past tense, as if her father was dead. That bit of sleight of hand had been a cover to conceal the truth. Cutler Steen was very much alive. But it looked like the rest of Irene's analysis was right.

You're buying time. Just keep talking.

"It would be best if you dimmed the lights in here a little so that they don't shine too far out onto the deck," she said. "The darker it is, the more accurately I can read the currents of your energy field."

Cutler shrugged and looked at the guard. "Twitchell, dim these lights, but don't turn them off altogether."

"Yes, sir." Twitchell reached out and pressed a wall switch.

The great room lights lowered to what, in other circumstances, would have been deemed a romantic level.

"That's enough," Amelia said.

Cutler opened the glass doors and led the way across the large deck. Amelia followed him out into the moonlit night. So did Irene.

Cutler stopped at the far side of the deck, gripped the railing with one hand, and turned to watch Amelia.

She took a breath and heightened her senses.

Cutler's energy prints seethed on the wooden boards of the deck and on the railing. She was not surprised to see that his aura blazed in the shadows, powerful but dangerously erratic. Several bandwidths appeared to be in the process of growing weak. Failing.

She cleared her throat. "Please keep in mind that I'm still getting the hang of this aura reading business—"

"What in fucking hell do you see?" Cutler said through his teeth.

She decided to go with the truth. There did not seem to be any point in lying. "You are being slowly poisoned, Mr. Steen."

CHAPTER FIFTY-FIVE

KNEW IT," Cutler Steen said, his voice soft and savage. "Those fucking directors. They'll regret playing games with me. They'll give me the real formula before they die."

Irene stared at him. "What are you talking about?"

Cutler turned to face her. "Isn't it obvious? The Aurora Islands lab people think they no longer need me to continue the drug trials. They know they can't get close enough to take me out personally. Anyone they sent to do the job would be dead before they got anywhere near me. So they decided to poison the version of the drug they provided to me and my men. They thought they could get rid of all of us without taking any risks."

"Why would they do that?" Irene said. "They need the trials. They can't continue to develop the serum unless they have a reliable way of testing it."

"They found someone else they think they can use," Cutler raged. "A cartel boss or one of my competitors. Hell, the leaders of most countries would jump at the opportunity to get their hands on the drug."

"We don't know for certain that you're being slowly poisoned," Irene said. "Amelia told you she's new at aura reading."

"That's right," Amelia said. "There's a real possibility that I don't know what I'm doing here."

Cutler rounded on her. "I knew something was wrong. They said I needed the boosters to keep going. But it didn't make sense because you and the others were alive and apparently stable. At first I assumed the drug simply hadn't worked on you but now I know the reverse is true."

Amelia looked at Irene. "You figured this out months ago, didn't you? That's why you rented an apartment in the building where I live. That's why you made sure we got to know each other. You wanted to observe me."

"I know you won't believe me but I really did enjoy your company," Irene said.

"Bullshit."

"Shut up, both of you," Cutler said. He focused on Amelia. "How long have I got?"

She caught her breath. "I can't answer that question. I have no idea. The drug is weakening you but I don't know if it will kill you outright. You may just lose whatever new talent it gave you."

"No, it's doing something to me. I can feel it." Cutler's voice rose. "I need answers."

"So do I," Amelia said. "What are you going to do now? Kill me?"

Irene spoke up quickly. "Of course not, Amelia. It would be stupid to do that. You're too valuable. You and your friends are proof that the serum not only works, it can be successfully tolerated by individuals who meet a certain profile."

Irene was looking at her but Amelia got the sense that she was speaking to Cutler, trying to convince him of her logic.

"I have to track down that lab," Cutler said. "Get my hands on the formula and take control of the manufacturing and distribution. I need time."

"Don't we all," Amelia said. "I'll make you a deal, Mr. Steen."

"You are in no position to make any kind of bargain," he said.

"Well, actually, that's not true. You see, I diagnosed what's wrong with you but I didn't tell you that I might be able to fix the unstable currents in your aura, or at least keep them from weakening even more."

Cutler went still. "You're lying." But there was frantic hope in his eyes.

"Where are you going with this, Amelia?" Irene asked quietly.

"I'm not lying," Amelia said. "I admit I can't guarantee success. I've only been able to run one experiment, and the circumstances were quite different. But my intuition tells me that I can not only perceive auras, I can manipulate them to some extent, provided I have the right tool."

"What tool?" Cutler demanded.

"An old-fashioned film camera would work, I think, one with a prism and a mirror."

Cutler grunted. "Where the hell do you suggest I get one of those at this hour of the night?"

"I can also work with a crystal," Amelia said.

Irene frowned. "We don't have any crystals in this house unless you count the glassware. Will that work?"

"I think it would depend on the quality of the glassware," Amelia said. "But I've got a better idea. Your father has a very good crystal."

Cutler shook his head, bewildered. "What are you talking about?"

"Your watch." She glanced at the expensive timepiece on his wrist. "The face is covered with a crystal."

Cutler and Irene both looked at the watch as if they had never seen it before.

"You're right." Cutler touched the watch. "It's a sapphire crystal."

"The type doesn't matter," Amelia said. She was winging it now but she didn't have much to lose. "The quality is the important thing."

The glass door onto the balcony opened abruptly. Twitchell appeared.

"Boss, sorry to interrupt, but there's some kind of disturbance going on at the front gate," he said.

Cutler scowled. "What are you talking about?"

"Vehicles started arriving a few minutes ago. Brinks and I have been watching on the monitors. At first we thought it was a political rally or a protest. Figured they had the wrong house. We advised them to move along. Then they started shouting. It's getting louder. Listen."

Chanting could be heard in the distance.

"Free Amelia. We're in this together until we get answers."

"Free Amelia. We're in this together until we get answers."

An exultant thrill flashed through Amelia. "Those are *Lost Night Files* fans."

"Do you want us to call the cops, Mr. Steen?" Twitchell asked.

"Are you fucking crazy?" Cutler raged. "No, I don't want the cops here. Go down to the gate. Take Brinks with you. Show those idiots the guns and remind them this is private property."

"If we start flashing the weapons around someone will call the cops," Twitchell warned. "They'll be here in sixty seconds."

"It's just a bunch of dumb podcast fans," Cutler said. "I pay you to deal with situations like this. If you want another dose of the drug, you will get things under control at the gate now."

"Yes, sir."

Twitchell disappeared, leaving Amelia alone with Irene and Cutler.

"I wonder how they found me?" Amelia said.

"That," Cutler seethed, "is a very good question." He jerked the pistol out of the holster and looked at Irene. "I think I know the answer."

"No." Irene stared at him, eyes widening. "Please, I swear, I never told anyone that Amelia was here."

Cutler raised the pistol. "It's a sad day when a man discovers that he can't even trust his own offspring."

"Why would I bring the podcast people here tonight?" Irene said. "I'm the one who arranged to grab Amelia when Falcon and the others failed, remember? If it hadn't been for me you still wouldn't have her. And now she's telling you she can save your life and maybe your talent, too."

Amelia kicked up her senses again and studied Irene's energy field. There was no mistaking the panic in the currents. Irene was terrified of her father. She was convinced Steen would murder her without any hesitation. The realization that your parent could kill you in cold blood took the definition of complicated family dynamics to a whole other level.

"Your daughter is telling you the truth, Mr. Steen," Amelia said firmly.

Cutler shot her an assessing look. "Does your aura reading ability enable you to know if someone is lying?"

"Not always, obviously," she said. She watched Irene, who was motionless. "If I were infallible I would have realized long before now that Irene was playing me from the start."

"Amelia, it wasn't like that," Irene whispered.

"Yes, it was," Amelia said. She turned back to Cutler. "I have no reason to back up Irene's story. I'm certain she's telling you the truth now. Trust me, she did not summon the podcast fans tonight."

"What makes you sure of that?" Cutler said.

"Think about it. It's not like you could call or text a certain number and organize a flash mob. Only a member of the *Lost Night Files* crew would know how to contact the fans and get them to turn out at a specific address on such short notice. Your daughter's only connection to the podcast is me, and I certainly did not summon them here. How could I? I didn't even know this place existed until tonight."

Cutler hesitated and then reluctantly lowered the pistol. The chanting grew louder. Someone had brought a bullhorn.

"Twitchell and Brinks should be at the front gate by now," Cutler said. "What's going on? Why haven't they taken control?"

Irene looked at Amelia. She did not say anything but her gratitude was not hard to read. She truly had feared for her life. *And I was upset because my parents got a divorce*, Amelia thought. Perspective was everything.

She started to turn back to Cutler but Gideon spoke from the deep shadows on the far side of the deck.

"Twitchell and Brinks are not in any condition to take charge of the gate, Steen," he said.

"*Gideon*." Relief and panic flashed through Amelia. "Steen has a gun. Irene probably has one, too. Everyone around here is armed to the teeth."

Cutler moved much faster than she expected, closing the short distance between them. He wrapped an arm around her throat and dragged her hard against his chest, making a human shield of her. She was intensely aware that the front of his shirt was soaked with a sick sweat.

She was also aware that in her current position, pinned against Cutler, she could touch the watch on his wrist.

"You must be Sweetwater," Cutler said.

"Yes, he is," Irene said. She was still tense but the panicky vibe was gone. She was back in control. "What's going on out at the front gate?"

"I told the *Lost Night Files* producer that I needed a distraction," Gideon said. "She was very helpful."

"Phoebe," Amelia whispered.

"She put out the word to fans in the local area," Gideon said. "Evidently they are a very loyal bunch. Amelia, are you okay?"

"Yes," she said. Her voice was annoyingly thin. *Control. It's all about control.*

"Come one step closer and I'll put a bullet through her head," Cutler warned.

Gideon did not move. "I understand. Amelia?"

"I've got this," she said, her voice steadying.

"You're sure?"

"Pretty much."

"There's always plan B," Gideon reminded her.

"How in fucking hell did you find this house?" Cutler's voice rose. "It's hidden under a dozen layers of shells and trusts. There's no way you could locate it, not in a few hours."

"Sometimes the simple approach works best," Gideon said.

"What are you talking about?" Cutler raged.

"You forgot about GPS," Gideon said. "Or, rather, Falcon forgot about it. So did Irene. Maybe it just never occurred to them it could be a problem."

Irene drew a sharp breath. "I don't—" Her voice trailed off as understanding sank deep.

"What do you mean?" Cutler shouted.

"I found the address of this house on Falcon's GPS log," Gideon said. "That made me curious. Then there was the receipt from the gas station a couple miles down the road. When this location turned up on the log in Irene's car I knew there had to be something interesting here."

"... *Free Amelia. We're in this together until we get answers ...*"

"I've had enough," Cutler grated. "Amelia and I are leaving. If you try to stop me, Sweetwater, I swear I'll kill her. I've got nothing left to lose."

"You can't get away without going through that crowd," Gideon said, "not with a hostage. You might have a chance if you leave Amelia behind."

"Do you really think I'm dumb enough not to have an exit strategy?" Cutler said.

"You were always the smartest man in the room," Irene whispered, her voice fierce with barely restrained fury.

Cutler ignored her to move across the deck, hauling Amelia with him. He stopped and brought the heel of his low boot down hard on a section of the wooden planking. A large, square trapdoor sprang open, revealing a well of dense shadow. Briny air carrying the scents of the ocean wafted upward.

Amelia saw a flight of narrow steps leading down. Two distinct sets of energy prints burned on the wooden treads. She recognized both.

She raised one hand to touch the face of Cutler's watch. But at that instant he released her throat and wrapped his fingers around her upper arm instead. He pushed her toward the steps.

"You go first," he ordered. "If Sweetwater tries anything, you'll die first. Clear?"

"Yes," she said. Her voice steadied. She had made her decision. She was about to run a dangerous experiment on Cutler Steen. Talk about karmic-style justice.

She did not have her camera to help her focus and she could no longer reach the crystal in his watch. But she did not need control for what she was about to do. Her intuition told her that physical contact was enough. Cutler still had a bruising grip on her arm.

"Amelia?" Gideon said once more.

"Stay tuned," she said. She was both exhilarated and terrified by the prospect of what she was going to try to do.

She went into her talent in a way that, until now, she had never attempted, never realized was even possible. It was like pulling the trigger of a gun. A part of her was shocked; horrified. But her survival instinct took over. *Trust your intuition.*

True, her intuition was not one hundred percent reliable—see stupid friendship with Irene Morgan—but nothing in life was risk-free.

She launched the full force of her talent at Steen, enveloping him in a violent, senses-dazzling tsunami of energy. She heard a scream. Not her, she decided. Cutler Steen. His aura sparked and flashed and burned with paranormal lightning.

He yanked her out of his way and flung himself down the dimly lit steps. He would have plummeted to his death if not for the narrow confines of the stairwell. His hands skidded along the walls, slowing his descent.

He vanished around a sharp turn. The screaming stopped but the sound of his scrambling footsteps reverberated up from the depths.

Gideon's cane thudded on the deck as he rushed toward the tunnel. "He's getting away."

Amelia realized he was intent on pursuing Steen down the steps.

She remembered the second set of energy prints on the treads and reached out to grab his arm.

"*No*," she said. "Don't go after him. Please. Stop."

Gideon hesitated, his eyes heating with battle-ready tension. "I can handle him."

"I know. That's not it. I just don't think you should go down there."

"Are you sure of that?"

"Almost positive."

"Almost?" The rumble of a powerful boat engine vibrated up the stairwell. "Lost him. Why the hell did you stop me?"

"The thing is, I noticed two sets of prints on the stairs. One set belongs to Steen."

But Gideon wasn't paying attention. He moved to the deck railing and looked down into the quiet cove. Amelia joined him. Together they watched a high-powered cruiser roar away from a concealed dock and fly across the cove, heading for the bay and the ocean beyond.

The explosion came a few seconds later, shattering the moonlit tranquility of the cove. The cruiser disappeared in a volcanic blast of fire that lit up the night. An instant later the vessel was consumed in the flames.

"Okay," Amelia said, taking a deep breath. "I didn't know *that* would happen, but I had a feeling something very bad was going to take place down there at the bottom of the stairs."

"Good call," Gideon said. He turned. "She's gone. No surprise."

Amelia swung around. She and Gideon were alone on the deck.

"Of course she's gone," Amelia said. "Her work here is done."

"She's the one who sabotaged Steen's boat?"

"Yes."

"How did you know?"

"I didn't," Amelia said. "Not for certain. But she hated her father and she was afraid of him."

". . . *Free Amelia. We're in this together until we get answers . . . We're in this together until we get answers . . .*"

"We had better make an appearance at the front gate," she said. "I want to let those people know they not only helped rescue me, they were instrumental in bringing another cold case to a close. This is going to make a fantastic podcast episode for *The Lost Night Files*. Phoebe will be thrilled."

"Before we go out there, I've got a question," Gideon said. "You saw the threat in Irene's energy prints on the dock stairs."

"Yes."

"That can't have been the first time you saw her prints, and you must have viewed her aura from time to time. Any idea why you didn't perceive the threat to yourself?"

"I've been wondering about that. Maybe my energy reading skills are not reliable, or maybe I'm still on the learning curve, still trying to figure out how to decipher them. But I think there's another explanation."

"What?"

"Maybe she never had any intention of hurting me. Like her father, she wanted answers, but her goal back at the start was to observe me. She wasn't so sure I was a failure. As time went on we became friends."

"With friends like that . . ."

"I know. But the thing is, in her own way, she was trying to protect me. She killed Falcon."

"And somewhere along the line she figured out how to use you to get rid of Cutler."

"I think so, yes. Don't get me wrong. In hindsight, I do see that she wasn't great BFF material."

"The woman executed that thug, Falcon, in cold blood, and if you're right, she arranged the explosion that killed her father. Trust me, Irene is very dangerous."

Amelia thought about the violent currents of energy she had used to destroy Steen's psychic senses. "So am I, Gideon."

"I know." He wrapped an arm around her and brought her close for a fierce embrace. "That's one of the many things I love about you."

She froze. *"What?"*

He released her and started toward the glass doors of the living room. "Let's go call off the *Lost Night Files* fans before they come through the gate with pitchforks."

CHAPTER FIFTY-SIX

I CAN'T BELIEVE the authorities are blaming me and the *Lost Night Files* crew for everything that happened," Amelia fumed. "Talk about unfair. Talk about poor police work."

She swept through the doorway of her apartment, stalked around the kitchen island, and plunked the colorful sack containing two orders of breakfast sandwiches and two coffees on the counter.

Gideon closed and locked the door and made his way to the island. He angled himself onto a stool and hung his cane on the edge of the counter.

"To be fair, the cops didn't exactly blame you and the others," he said in what she suspected was intended to be a soothing tone.

She took the two extra-large-sized coffee cups out of the sack and yanked off the lids. "Yes. They. Did."

She and Gideon had finished the interview with the police a little over an hour ago. An investigation into the explosion on Steen's cruiser was underway but Phoebe had warned everyone they wouldn't find much. She had already searched for him on the dark web. For all intents and purposes, Steen was a ghost—currently in the literal sense, if you believed in that sort of thing—and also online. It was as if he had never existed. The same was true of Irene Morgan.

Amelia knew that she and Gideon were sleep-deprived, but they were far too wired to even try to get some rest. Also, there wasn't much point, she thought. The rest of the *Lost Night Files* team was on the way to San Diego by air and car. They would be arriving at various times throughout the day and they planned to come straight to her apartment for a debriefing.

"The authorities simply made it clear they didn't want to hear about your conspiracy theories," Gideon said, "and let's be honest. There was no need to go down that road."

She glared and pushed one of the coffees across the counter. "They aren't conspiracy theories. They are the true facts of the case. We both know that. And by the way, thanks for not backing me up when I tried to explain things to the cops."

"It was for your own good."

"Nobody likes to hear those words," she warned.

"You know as well as I do that law enforcement doesn't take crimes involving the paranormal seriously."

She groaned. "Yeah, I know."

"The cops were happy to go with my version of events, and that was all we needed to wrap up the case. In my own defense, I would like to point out that I did back you up. I just left out the paranormal elements."

She drank some coffee while she thought about that. His version of events was that *The Lost Night Files* had inadvertently stumbled into an investigation that had drawn the attention of a violent drug-smuggling ring. The kingpin had decided to make the entire podcast crew disappear, starting with her.

She had to admit it was the truth, as far as it went. The discovery of a large stash of illegal narcotics hidden in a locker at the concealed boat dock had cemented Gideon's story.

"Admit it," he urged. "There was no need for an explanation involving bizarre serums that enhance the paranormal senses. The cops were satisfied with the fact that a serious amount of old-school street dope was involved."

"I'll bet Irene Morgan or Irene Steen, or whatever her real name is, hid the drugs the cops found at that boat dock. Got to hand it to her, she planned and executed a very complex scheme to get rid of her father."

"*Executed* being the operative word," Gideon said.

"Yes." Amelia shivered at the memory of the spectacular explosion. "If you had followed him down those steps. Jumped into the boat—"

"I didn't follow him down those steps, thanks to you. And even in a worst-case scenario, I doubt if I would have jumped into the boat, not with this leg."

"He had a gun. You would have been a sitting duck in that stairwell."

"Any resemblance between me and a duck is strictly in your imagination."

"You're not taking this seriously, are you?"

"I don't have time to listen to your catastrophizing, because I'm too busy with my own. How do you think I felt when I realized Irene had managed to grab you?"

"Fair point." Amelia unwrapped the breakfast sandwiches and set them on plates. "I'm sorry your uncle got drugged."

"Not as sorry as he is. Shelton feels like an idiot. And he's fine, so you don't need to worry about him."

Amelia put Gideon's plate in front of him and carried her own around the end of the island. She sat down on one of the stools. "Do you think those two guards at Steen's house and the one you took down at Falcon's rental will talk?"

"Maybe," Gideon said around a mouthful of sandwich. "But I doubt if they'll be able to give the authorities any useful information. You saw the two at the cove house. They woke up but they were hallucinating. They may not survive, not if you're right about their auras looking bad."

"They were using the same contaminated version of the drug that Cutler Steen was using."

"Pretty sure the directors of the Aurora Islands Pharmaceuticals operation wanted Steen dead."

"Because Steen made them nervous?" Amelia asked.

"He was a ruthless man. They had been working with him for over a year. They knew what he was capable of. They probably remembered that old advice about dining with the devil."

"Bring a very long spoon." Amelia drank some coffee.

"I doubt if they objected to Steen's methods—they went into business with him because of those methods. But at some point they must have started to worry, not just about his intentions toward them, but because he was attracting some unwanted attention."

Amelia smiled, grimly satisfied. "Because the *Lost Night Files* podcast was getting traction. Closing in on the whole operation."

"Yep."

She stopped smiling. "Well, the case may look neat and tidy to the authorities, but they are going to miss the larger picture. Someone out there has created a dangerous drug that has the ability to enhance the paranormal senses. Oh, and by the way, there can be some unfortunate side effects. A lot of people will either go insane or die."

Gideon sighed. "Amelia—"

She ignored the interruption. "Several of the so-called test subjects died in the course of Steen's experiments, Gideon."

"I know."

"But no one is going to look for the person or persons who launched those illegal drug trials. What's more, those individuals still have the formula for the serum. It's not fair. It's not justice."

"Get used to it," Gideon said. "The ending may not be perfect as far as you're concerned, but in my experience this is as good as it gets in the psychic investigation business. You and your friends have been producing *The Lost Night Files* long enough to know that."

"Okay, but I still say that if the authorities had taken us seriously after we were kidnapped the first time in Lucent Springs—if they had done their job—none of this would have happened."

"You're starting from a false premise," Gideon said. He finished his sandwich. "The authorities would never have taken your lost night story seriously, because they do not accept the reality of the paranormal."

"You're right." She brightened. "The authorities failed us but the fans of the podcast certainly came through when we needed them."

Gideon smiled. "Yes, they did."

Her phone rang just as she was about to take another bite of her sandwich. Assuming it was a call from one of the *Lost Night Files* team, she glanced at the screen. *Bridget Hampstead*. She put down the uneaten portion of the breakfast sandwich and stabbed accept.

"Bridget? Did the McCall listing finally sell?"

"Yes, it did," Bridget said, buoyant to the point of giddy, as she always was when she closed a deal. "A very nice young couple. They are getting help with the down payment from their parents. Thanks to your photos, the buyers were able to visualize the potential of the house. He works in construction, so he's not afraid to tackle a fixer-upper. She's a schoolteacher with an artistic eye. The house is perfect for them."

"I hope so. Congratulations. Glad it finally sold. How soon do you think you'll be able to pay me for the photos?"

"Just as soon as I get my commission," Bridget said smoothly. "The sale closes in sixty days."

"*Sixty days.*"

"That's fast for a deal like this one. I've got more good news. We're on a roll. I picked up a new listing yesterday. Another starter home. This one definitely needs your special touch—"

"Sounds interesting," Amelia said. "I'm a little busy at the moment but I'll check my calendar and see if I can squeeze in another real estate shoot."

"I was hoping you could hop on it right away. I'd really like to start marketing the place. The inventory of starter homes is low right now. That means this one will move quickly."

"You mean like the McCall house? The one that took three months to sell and for which I won't get paid for another two months? Right. I'll get back to you." Amelia ended the call, picked up what was left of her sandwich, and took a savage bite.

"Let me guess," Gideon said. "One of your check-is-in-the-mail real estate clients?"

"Yep." She swallowed and reached for her coffee. The intuitive sense of knowing whispered through her. "'Get used to it.'"

"What?"

She gave herself a moment to let the feeling of certainty settle in before she continued.

"That's what you said a few minutes ago when I was whining about not getting justice. You said 'get used to it' because that was as good as it gets in the psychic investigation biz."

"So?"

"So I'm going to get used to it."

Gideon put down his coffee and watched her with a wary expression. "You're going to get used to waiting on the check-is-in-the-mail clients?"

"Nope. Back at the start you told me there was a learning curve involved when it came to figuring out how to control my talent. You were right."

"Okay. So? Where are you going with this?"

"Luckily I'm a fast learner. And what I've learned is that using my abilities to help other people get justice, or maybe just the answers they need, is what I want to do with my life."

"Uh, this is probably not a good time to make a major career decision," Gideon said. "It's been a stressful few days."

"Wrong. This is the perfect time. Don't you see? I've finally figured out why I've been so obsessed with photography all these years even though I'm not that great at it. I knew intuitively that there was something about the process that helped me focus my other vision. But I kept trying to make it work in the wrong lane."

"You're losing me here," Gideon said.

"I've been using photography in the wrong way," she explained. "I never found my lane. I am, however, very good at reading auras and energy prints and I'm getting better by the day."

"Do you, uh, have some idea of how you can make a career out of energy reading?"

"Yep." She chuckled. "Don't worry, I'm not going into the psychic demonstration business. Aunt Cybil discouraged me from doing that. She said it wasn't the most satisfying way to use my talent because most people see psychics as entertainers. The truth is, she's in that line because of the free cruise travel and the romance."

"The romance of the sea?"

"Well, that, too, but she means the men. You'd be amazed how many are attracted to psychics."

Gideon watched her with a mix of fascination and dread. "Is that right?"

"Not that you could prove it by me. My dating life for the past seven months has been a rolling disaster. Aunt Cybil says my problem is that I haven't added the element of glamour or mystique. I'm sure she's right, but in my own defense, I have been a little busy lately. But now I've got a plan."

"How nice for you. I'm so thoroughly confused I might have a nervous breakdown. What, exactly, are you going to do?"

"Isn't it obvious? It's clear to me that I was born to be a psychic private investigator. You know, like you."

Gideon's expression metamorphosed from fascination and dread to full-on deer in the headlights.

"I don't think you understand what you're getting into," he said carefully.

"Of course I do. I've been watching you work for the past few days, remember? Also, you could say I've been training to do this since we started the podcast. For the first time in my life I have a clear-cut goal. It feels great. I'll bet this is how you felt when you finally opened your own agency."

"Amelia, I've been working investigations for a while now, and I'm here to tell you, hanging out a sign that says *Psychic Detective* is a great way to attract a lot of weird clients."

"I know. The podcast attracts more than its share, believe me."

"This business can also get dangerous." He gestured toward the cane.

"Gee. Who knew? Gideon, in the past few days I've been shot at, drugged, kidnapped, and used as a hostage by an unstable psychic who almost murdered his own daughter."

Gideon's jaw clenched. "Don't remind me. All right, point taken. But I strongly suggest that you wait to make such a big decision. Give yourself some time to get past the trauma of the last few days."

"Blah, blah, blah. Don't worry, I know what I'm doing. I have a strategy."

"That's what worries me."

She ignored him. "You'll be my first client, of course. Eventually I'll be able to make the connections necessary to grow my business."

"Let me get this straight. You expect me to hire you as a consultant?"

"Admit it, Gideon, you need me."

Without warning his eyes heated.

"Yes," he said. "I do need you."

She caught her breath. "For my psychic talents?"

"I need you because I can't envision my life without you in it. Or maybe it would be more accurate to say I don't want to think about my life without you in it."

"You're sure? I mean, we've only known each other a few days."

He smiled an unexpectedly wistful smile. "I fell in love with you the day you hired me."

She frowned. "How could you know so quickly?"

"Because I felt like I'd been hit by a freight train."

"That's how you knew you were in love?"

"Well, sure. That's usually how it is with the Sweetwaters."

Her pulse kicked up. "I was afraid I'd made a serious mistake by hiring you."

"You're not much of a romantic, are you?"

"But I realized right away that my feelings were very complicated. Hard to sort out. I wasn't sure what was going on. Your uncle explained the biophysics of the situation. Something about aura resonance."

"Well, shit. You discussed us—our relationship—with my uncle? You and I haven't even talked about it. Not until now. I can't believe this."

"Calm down. He was very understanding. Helpful. Supportive."

"Thank you, Uncle Shelton," Gideon muttered.

"You're missing the point here. I love you, Gideon."

"What?"

She smiled, savoring the quiet, thrilling joy of certainty. "There is no question about it. I think I knew it that first day but, like I said, the situation was complicated."

Gideon's eyes were molten silver now. "Amelia—"

The doorbell chimed.

Startled, Amelia jumped off the stool. "I wonder who that could be?"

Gideon was already on his feet, suddenly all business. "I'll get it."

Amelia followed him into the front hall and managed to get to the door ahead of him. "It's okay. That's Egan, the gardener." She opened the door.

The gardener had a small white envelope in one gloved hand.

"Hi, Egan," Amelia said. "What's up?"

"Morning," Egan said. "I found this in the gardening shed. It has your name on it. The mail carrier must have dropped it."

"Thanks."

Bewildered, she took the envelope. Her name was, indeed, printed on the front in block letters. She was pretty sure she recognized the handwriting. She ripped open the envelope and discovered a note and a business card.

Dear Amelia:

I will miss our pizza-wine-and-movie nights. I realize I almost got you killed, but I want you to know I truly did value our friendship. In my family we don't do friends. It was nice to have a real one for a while.

I know you will take good care of Daisy and Dahlia.

Remember, don't overfeed them. And help yourself to my wine collection before the apartment manager realizes I'm not coming back.

Sincerely,

Irene

P.S. Don't forget to follow up on the real estate agent who wants to hire you to do the shoot on his waterfront listing in La Jolla. That was for real, I promise. His card is enclosed. Remember: Attitude is everything.

P.P.S. You were right about Falcon.

CHAPTER FIFTY-SEVEN

D O YOU THINK Cutler Steen's daughter poisoned him?" Pallas
asked.

"No," Amelia said. "But I think she figured out very quickly
that someone was adulterating the version of the drug that Steen and
Falcon and the rest of the security team were taking. She apparently
decided not to warn her father. But she couldn't be certain the serum
would do the job so she planted the explosives on the boat as a
backup."

It was almost five o'clock in the afternoon and the entire podcast
team plus Gideon and Shelton were gathered in her apartment. She
had poured some expensive wine from Irene's curated stash for everyone and was now on the kitchen side of the island, prepping the hors
d'oeuvre trays that had just been delivered.

Talia March and Luke Rand were seated on the sofa. They had
hired a charter pilot to fly them back to Seattle from the San Juan
Islands. In the city they had picked up Phoebe Hatch and boarded a
flight to San Diego. Phoebe was in a chair near the balcony door,
phone in hand. She was glued to the screen.

Pallas Llewellyn and Ambrose Drake occupied the chairs that faced the sofa.

Shelton had somehow managed to commandeer the recliner. That left Gideon with a barstool. He was angled on it, one foot braced on the floor. His cane was hooked over the edge of the dining counter.

The explosion in the cove and the arrests of some men suspected of transporting and distributing illegal drugs had barely made a ripple in the mainstream media. Just another drug bust. But Phoebe was tracking the online activity and reporting in every few minutes. Evidently the *Lost Night Files* podcast fans were celebrating their triumph on social media and word about the closing of the case was drawing considerable attention.

Pallas looked at Amelia. "Irene decided to monitor you because she thought you might be a success story?"

"Yes." Amelia took some plates down out of a cupboard. "Until recently Cutler Steen had written off all of us as failed experiments. Yes, we had survived, but we weren't exhibiting any indication of psychic talents."

Shelton spoke up from the recliner. "Like I told the government people when I was compiling that list back in the day, it's damn hard to measure or prove paranormal talent, especially if the test subject doesn't see any reason to cooperate in the process."

"Eventually, though, Steen concluded that Irene might be right about Amelia's talent," Gideon said. "If nothing else, he wanted to know why she and the rest of you weren't deteriorating the way he and Falcon and the others were. I think he targeted Amelia for kidnapping because she was still on her own. She lived alone and there was no close family in the area. It should have been an easy grab-and-go job, but things got complicated."

Luke raised his brows. "Because Amelia realized she was being stalked and decided to hire a professional investigator, one who had some serious talent."

Amelia looked at Gideon and smiled proudly. "Thanks to Shelton's list, I got a first-class investigator."

"That damned list," Shelton groaned. "I never expected to see it resurface, not after all this time."

Phoebe yelped in excitement and waved her phone. "Listen to this. We added a thousand new subscribers today and more are joining by the minute. With numbers like these we're going to have sponsors begging us to take their cash."

There was a short silence. Everyone looked at Phoebe.

Amelia knew they were all wondering the same thing. "And what are we going to do with that cash, assuming it does roll in?"

Phoebe stared at her, appalled. "What do you mean?"

Pallas took a breath. "She means we have to make a decision about the future of the podcast. *The Lost Night Files* has solved the mystery and closed the case it was created to close. Cutler Steen is dead. He won't be running any more drug trials. Our only connection to him is Irene, and she has vanished."

"What about the Aurora Islands Pharmaceutical Laboratory?" Talia asked.

"We can't quit now," Phoebe declared, passion infusing the words. "There are still so many questions to be answered. Who was making the enhancement formula? How many people on that list got one or more doses of the drug? Is the government somehow involved?"

"She's right," Shelton announced from the recliner. "Lots of questions left to answer." He sounded pleased.

"Phoebe and Shelton have a point," Ambrose said. "This is decision time for the podcast."

"Are we talking about keeping it going?" Amelia asked. "Because that would fit perfectly with my own career objectives."

"*Yes,*" Phoebe said.

Ambrose smiled. "I'm in. Hell, I'm a writer. I can always use the plot material."

Pallas picked up her wineglass. "I agree. We can't quit now. We're just getting started."

"There must be more people like us out there," Phoebe said. "People who need investigators who specialize in cases involving the paranormal."

Talia pushed her glasses higher on her nose. She looked intrigued. "If we're serious about this, we have to start turning a real profit."

"Whoa," Gideon said. "You all need to slow down and give this some careful thought. I've been doing this investigation work for a while, and I can tell you, it's not as simple and straightforward as you seem to believe—"

A series of sharp raps sounded on the door. Amelia and everyone else in the room except Gideon went still.

Gideon, cane gripped in his left hand, was on his feet, heading for the front door.

Shelton eased the recliner to the upright position and stood.

"Hang on." Amelia whipped out from behind the island and hurried toward the door. "Let's not overreact here. It might be the real estate agent who tried to contact me while I was in Lucent Springs, the one with the waterfront listing. I could really use a high-end client."

She reached the door a step ahead of Gideon and went up on her toes to get a good look through the peephole. She groaned when she saw a familiar face.

"Relax, everyone," she said. "It's Dr. Pike, my ex-therapist."

The others were all on their feet now. No one looked relaxed.

Another short, sharp series of raps sounded on the door.

"Amelia? Are you in there? It's Dr. Pike. Please answer the door. I've been worried about you."

"I'm fine, Dr. Pike," she said. She started to unlock the first of the three locks.

"I'll open the door," Gideon said, easing her aside. "I've got a few questions for Pike."

"Oh, for goodness' sake," Amelia muttered. "He's harmless."

"That's what you thought about your neighbor Irene." Gideon raised his voice. "Stand back, Pike. Hands where I can see them. I'm going to open the door. One wrong move and you will not be a happy camper."

"Amelia," Pike yelped. "I'm on my phone. I'm calling nine-one-one."

"I'm all right, Dr. Pike," she shouted. "Honest. Gideon, stop fooling around. You're embarrassing me. Open the door."

She was mildly surprised when he did just that.

Pike stumbled backward, clutching his phone. He stared at Gideon and then he saw Shelton, Luke, and Ambrose looming in the front hall. Panic flashed in his eyes but he did not run.

"Amelia?" he said.

"Come in, Dr. Pike. It's time you met my friends. Would you like a glass of wine?"

"You heard her," Gideon said. "Come in. I want to talk to you."

Pike moved nervously into the hall. Gideon shut the door before he could change his mind.

Amelia herded the crowd back into the living room. "Sit down, everyone. Dr. Pike, let me introduce you." She went around the room. When she was finished she smiled. "This is my therapist, Dr. Norris Pike. He was trying to help me deal with a little phobia I developed a few weeks ago."

Shelton spoke up sharply. "Pike? Dr. Norris Pike? Editor of the *Pike Journal of Parapsychology?*"

Pike widened his eyes. "You know my work, sir?"

Shelton chuckled and held out his hand. "Longtime subscriber and occasional contributor. You have been gracious enough to publish a few of my papers. I write under the name S. W. Sweet."

"What a pleasure to meet you." Pike seized Shelton's hand and shook it with great force. "I have admired your work for years. Your theories on the para-physics of aura resonance are brilliant. This is a wonderful surprise." He looked around. "Can I assume we are among like-minded friends?"

Shelton chuckled. "We are."

"I had a feeling that might be the case after a couple of sessions with Amelia," Pike continued. "But I didn't want to alarm her. I knew she was already afraid she might be delusional. And at that point I couldn't be certain she wasn't. I intended to ease her into the possibility that she had developed some genuine psychic ability. The next thing I know she disappears into the desert for a couple of days with a man she never mentioned in therapy. Given her phobia, that just didn't make sense. I was convinced she was in terrible danger but I knew the police wouldn't pay any attention to me."

"Excuse me." Tired of being discussed as if she wasn't in the room, Amelia clapped her hands to get everyone's attention. She looked at Shelton and Pike. "It's a lovely day. Why don't you two take some chips and wine out onto the balcony and chat? Sounds like you have a lot to talk about."

Ten minutes later Shelton and Pike had been banished to the balcony with their snacks and wine and were engaged in animated conversation.

Phoebe looked up from her phone. "Another wave of subscribers is rolling in. *Paying* subscribers. We've hit critical mass, people."

Talia took charge, as she was inclined to do. "Pallas, Amelia, *The Lost Night Files* is our creation. We need to make the decision. Do we move forward or do we shut down the project?"

"Wait, wait, wait." Phoebe bounced to her feet and waved the phone. "Before you decide, you need to know that we just got our first sponsor. An outfit called the Foundation. What's more, the operation is offering to give us some actual grant money."

"What's the Foundation?" Gideon asked.

"Some kind of private research firm, apparently," Phoebe said, reading off her phone. "The director is a guy named Victor Arganbright."

Luke grimaced. "It's legit. Headquarters are in Las Vegas. They've got ties back to the old Bluestone Project. But I should warn you there may be a few catches. The Foundation has cash but it also has links to a small government entity, the Agency for the Investigation of Atypical Phenomena."

It was Gideon's turn to wince. "Government connections can get . . . complicated."

"Just ask someone who writes thrillers," Ambrose said. "Someone like me, for example. Do you have any idea how many clandestine intelligence and investigation agencies and businesses are funded by government money? And none of them know what the others are doing."

The balcony door opened. Shelton and Pike walked back into the room. Both men were flushed with enthusiasm.

Shelton held up an empty chip bowl. "Can we get another round?"

"Yes, of course." Amelia went back behind the island. "We're celebrating because we just got our first sponsor and it's offering grant money."

"Congratulations," Pike said.

Shelton squinted a little. "Who or what is the sponsor?"

"It's called the Foundation," Phoebe said. "Ever heard of it?"

Shelton stared at her, astonished. "Well, I'll be damned," he said in reverent tones. "I thought that operation was just a legend."

Pike whistled softly. "So did I."

"It's real," Luke said. "For better or worse."

"That settles it as far as I'm concerned," Amelia said. "With that kind of backing, we can make the podcast work. I vote we keep it going."

"So do I," Talia said.

Pallas nodded. "I vote yes, too."

Amelia raised her wineglass. "We're in this together."

"Until we get answers," Talia said.

"Until we get answers," Pallas concluded.

"*The Lost Night Files* will ride again," Phoebe said.

Luke looked at Gideon and Ambrose. "Why do I have the feeling that life is going to remain interesting?"

Ambrose grunted. "You must be psychic."

Talia looked at Shelton and Pike. "We could use a couple of researchers with some scientific expertise in the paranormal."

"Absolutely," Pallas said.

"Definitely," Amelia added.

Shelton brightened. "I'm in."

Pike was intrigued. "So am I."

Gideon cleared his throat. Everyone looked at him.

"You're talking about getting involved with a mysterious sponsor that maintains clandestine government connections," he said. "You're going to be dealing with complicated contracts. There will be a lot of cash that will have to be protected and invested. You'll need to consider the financial side of things. Taxes. Payouts to the principals. Expenses. You will have to come up with a solid business plan."

Amelia gave him a glowing smile. "Luckily we have you on the team."

"I had a feeling I was doomed to become the bookkeeper," Gideon said.

Shelton chuckled. "I told you that business degree would come in handy someday."

CHAPTER FIFTY-EIGHT

Meanwhile, on an unnamed island somewhere in the South Pacific . . .

ADRIANA IRENE STEEN left the Irene Morgan identity behind when she boarded the private jet that would take her home to the island. Cutler would have been proud, she thought. His painstaking efforts to conceal himself and his empire had proven successful, even after his death. When the authorities tried to investigate the victim of the explosion in the cove they hit a very solid wall. There were no links to the island or to Adriana and her half siblings, Celina and Benedict.

The three of them gathered at the island mansion for a private memorial service. Champagne and caviar were served on the veranda. It was, after all, a celebration. There had been a few glitches along the way, but in the end they had achieved their goal. Cutler Steen had been permanently removed and his offspring had inherited the empire.

"I was sure the old man had started using the serum," Benedict said. "It was obvious he wasn't tolerating it well, but it didn't occur to me he was being poisoned."

"The question is, why did the directors of the lab decide to get rid of him?" Celina asked. "They needed those drug trials and it's not as if there are a lot of organizations that can run expensive off-the-books experiments like that."

"I think we can assume that the people running the Aurora Islands operation decided they could no longer trust Cutler," Adriana said. "They were right to be worried. We know he was obsessed with locating the lab and getting control of the formula. It would have been a very hostile takeover. Whoever is responsible for producing the drug would not have survived. They must have known that."

"The only thing we can be sure of is that Aurora Islands is a very small outfit," Benedict said. "They knew they didn't have the resources required to take the risk of trying to get rid of someone like Cutler."

"So the lab directors got him addicted to a version of the drug that required boosters and slowly poisoned him," Adriana said. "Very, very clever."

"In hindsight we could have skipped the fireworks at the end," Benedict said. "The poisoned serum probably would have done the job for us."

Celina leaned back in her lounger. "Maybe, but we couldn't be certain. He was deteriorating. Taking risks. Making mistakes. We all saw that. If the authorities had arrested him he probably would have taken down the three of us. We had to be sure."

Adriana tightened her grip on her champagne flute. "I can tell you that there was something very satisfying about the explosion."

"Yes," Benedict said. "Payback for arranging the murders of each of our mothers."

"We were his first round of experiments," Adriana said. "He wanted to find out if his talent could be passed on to his offspring. But that's all we ever were to him. Experiments."

Benedict smiled a sharklike smile and raised his glass. "*Successful* experiments. The old man should have remembered the lesson of Frankenstein. In the end, the creature always turns on you."

"To us," Celina said. "Cutler's Steen's creatures."

"To us," Adriana said. She sipped some champagne and lowered the glass. "Now we need to talk about the future. We've got a global company to run."

"The old man was old-school," Benedict said. "It's time to move on. The arms dealing business is too competitive, too dangerous, and too dirty. The future is in information gathering and analysis."

"Here's to the future," Celina said, raising her glass, "*our* future."

"Our future," Adriana said. She swallowed some of the champagne and lowered the glass. "I have to tell you that it was rather pleasant pretending to live a normal life for a while."

"What are you calling normal?" Benedict said.

"Living in an apartment without bodyguards hovering in the shadows. Having a friend down the hall, someone to share a bottle of wine and a pizza and a streaming movie with."

"You're talking about Amelia Rivers, aren't you?" Celina said.

Adriana nodded. "She saved my life there at the end."

Celina's eyes widened. "What do you mean?"

"Cutler concluded I had betrayed him. He had a gun and he was unstable. I'm sure he would have pulled the trigger. But Amelia convinced him that I hadn't turned on him. Fortunately for me, he believed her."

"Look at it this way, you never intended for her to get kidnapped and killed," Benedict said. "In a way you were trying to protect her from Falcon and the others."

"I hope she realizes that," Adriana said. "Because I told her the truth when I said that in another life we could have been friends."

CHAPTER FIFTY-NINE

And on another unnamed island in the South Pacific . . .

"THAT DOES IT." Gwendolyn Swan sat back from the computer and scrutinized her online handiwork. "The last traces of our communications with Cutler Steen are gone. There's no way the Foundation can connect his operation to us. We're good."

"I told you it was a mistake to use Steen," Eloisa said.

"No, you did not." Gwendolyn got to her feet and stretched. She had spent hours scouring the dark web to make sure every hint of Aurora Islands Pharmaceutical Laboratory had been erased. Fortunately, the extremely expensive vanishing program appeared to have worked as promised. "I distinctly remember you complaining because Steen's drug trials were progressing too slowly."

"He was paid to test the latest version of the formula—not to create psychic assassins." Eloisa grimaced. "At least we got some answers."

"Face it, all we really learned was that some people can tolerate the new version without a dose of paranormal radiation to activate it."

"No, we learned much more than that," Eloisa said. "We discovered that the formula can release previously latent or semilatent core talents. That's a huge step forward."

"And in the process we managed to do what we most definitely did not want to do," Gwendolyn said. "We not only attracted the attention of the Foundation, we caught the eye of the Sweetwaters."

"Don't worry, we're safe." Eloisa surveyed her small laboratory with an air of satisfaction. The room gleamed and sparkled with state-of-the-art equipment. "And we now know that Aurora Winston was on the right track all those years ago when she speculated that the right dose, given to individuals with the right paranormal profile, can greatly increase the sensitivity of the paranormal senses."

"True." Gwendolyn opened the door of the lab and walked out onto the veranda. The balmy island atmosphere settled over her. She savored the view of the diamond-bright ocean, the sandy beach, and the lush tropical foliage. "I don't know about you, but I need a drink. The past few days have been exhausting."

"Good idea," Eloisa said. She switched off the lab lights and followed her sister outside.

Gwendolyn stopped when a thought struck her. "It occurs to me that in one sense our experiments are still running."

Eloisa raised her brows. "What do you mean?"

"It will be interesting to see if the offspring of the test subjects inherit their parents' paranormal senses."

"They will get some version," Eloisa said. "No doubt about it. The formula works at the DNA level."

CHAPTER SIXTY

I T ADDS A calming, meditative element to the room, don't you think?" Amelia asked.

Gideon contemplated the aquarium. "I'm not so sure about that. The hum of the air pump is annoying."

"We'll get used to it."

It was late. The others had left after the pizza delivery dinner. The podcast crew was booked into a nearby hotel. By now they were probably continuing the celebration in the lobby bar. Shelton and Dr. Pike had taken their leave after making arrangements to continue their intense discussion the following day in Shelton's personal library.

She and Gideon were alone, kicked back on the sofa, stocking-clad feet propped on the coffee table. The long stretch of sleep deprivation was finally catching up with them.

"The noise of the pump probably won't be a problem in the bedroom," Gideon said.

"Exactly. You know, it might help if I got a bigger tank with a more expensive pump."

"Goldfish keep growing, Amelia. The bigger the tank, the bigger they get."

"I didn't know that."

"Let's change the subject."

"What do you want to talk about?"

He wrapped an arm around her shoulders and pulled her close. "Us."

She snuggled into his heat and strength and yawned. "What about us?"

"I love you. I know it's probably too soon for you to commit but I really need to know if you think that you might be able to one of these days."

"It's not too soon. I love you, Gideon. I started falling in love with you before we even met. When you called me back to set up the appointment to discuss my case, I really, really, really liked the sound of your voice."

"Yeah?"

"Probably just another example of Shelton's theories of aura resonance in action."

"Do not drag my uncle into this, not now. I'm trying to be romantic."

"And you are doing a marvelous job of it." She turned in his arms and raised her lips for the kiss that sealed the private vows.

Aunt Cybil was right. *Trust your intuition. Some things you know are true.*

CHAPTER SIXTY-ONE

THE *LOST NIGHT FILES* PODCAST
Episode 8: "Answers in the Ruins"
Podcast transcript:

AMELIA: We started this podcast with the goal of finding out what really happened to the three of us over the course of a night that we lost to amnesia. It was a night that involved kidnapping and illegal experiments designed to enhance psychic talents. We barely escaped with our lives only to discover that the authorities did not believe us.

PALLAS: We wanted answers and we set out to get them. We knew we were on our own. But thanks to you, the members of our audience, we were able to move forward with our investigation. Along the way we solved crimes involving mysterious disappearances and murders.

TALIA: The trail led to a criminal organization controlled by a man we know only as Cutler Steen. Tonight we can tell you that Steen is dead. His scheme to conduct illegal drug experiments on unsuspecting people has been destroyed.

PALLAS: You, our audience, played a vital role in saving the life of one of our own. In doing so, you helped us close this cold case. Thank you from the bottom of our hearts. You helped us journey through a long night and find the dawn.

TALIA: We will need your help in the future, because one of the things our investigation has revealed is that Steen and his evil enterprise were not the only psychic criminals out there who move among us, undetected, taking advantage of their paranormal talents to deceive, manipulate, and commit murder.

AMELIA: Stay with us, because, while this case has been closed, we are just getting started. Welcome to *The Lost Night Files*. We're in this together until we get answers.

A NOTE FROM JAYNE

I F YOU READ this far, you are now in the JayneVerse. Thank you and welcome! I hope you will stick around and do some more exploring. If you've stopped to ask for directions, here are a few suggestions to help you navigate:

This book, *Shattering Dawn*, is, as I'm sure you know, the third book in the Lost Night Files trilogy. Curious about the other two books? Check out *Sleep No More* and *The Night Island*.

Interested in discovering some of the secrets of the mysterious Foundation and the Swan sisters? I direct you to the Fogg Lake trilogy: *The Vanishing*, *All the Colors of Night*, and *Lightning in a Mirror*.

Curious to find out what is happening to the Sweetwaters in the future on Harmony? Check out *Sweetwater & the Witch* (under my Jayne Castle name).

As always, I invite you to visit my home on the web, www.jayne annkrentz.com, and my Facebook and Instagram pages.

Waving from Seattle,

Jayne